RECKLESS PURSUIT

MILLBROOK SERIES

WILLA BROOKS

CHAPTER ONE

ABIGAIL MARTIN

THE GRAYING bricks of Millbrook's town hall gleamed in the soft rays of the setting sun. I had lived here my entire life, and the sunsets of Dutchess County never got old. Every evening, as I drove home from the library, I marveled at the natural beauty, especially during summertime evenings.

Why did people flock to New York City, the most famous part of our state, when we had this? The last time I ventured there, I suffered from sensory overload and claustrophobia. Give me the cozy comfort and familiarity of a small town. I'll take it any day.

The double doors creaked open, revealing a sea of worried faces. This was the same room where I had helped run a bake sale back in grade school, when renovations in the gym forced us to improvise. Now, it simmered with tension and anxiety.

A percolator on the side table bubbled away, filling the room with the rich aroma of fresh coffee, but it wasn't enough to accommodate a crowd of this size. Folks would have to head on over to the coffee shop called Sugar & Brew for their java fix.

Sadie Lin, the florist who never attended these meetings, occupied my chair near the front. She fidgeted with the zipper of her jacket while staring absently ahead. Her presence alone signaled how desperate folks were growing because she never left her shop, even during blizzards when our village shut down.

Nearly every chair had been filled because we all had one thing on our minds: the rash of break-ins plaguing our town.

A hand waved me down, then patted the vacant seat next to her and removed her bag from the spot. The gray-haired man beside her, cracked a rare smile.

I shuffled to the empty seat, trying to avoid falling onto anyone's lap while making my way to Aunt Peg and Uncle Wyatt. "Thanks for holding space, you guys. It's been a madhouse at the library since Deb left for maternity," I explained.

Aunt Peg sported a '70s pixie cut, dyed carrot-red, which matched her natural color.

My own ruby-shaded tresses also came from a bottle, but no one would mistake them for natural tones.

Uncle Wyatt, with his arms crossed, leaned over Aunt Peg to speak to me. "Things that hectic at the library, Mops?"

Mops had been Uncle Wyatt's pet name for me since I was a three-nager because of my unruly mop of auburn hair. Although they were godparents and not blood relation, I'd known them for eons and regarded them as kin. Oddly enough, Aunt Peg and I shared more than just our rounded figures, but also blue eyes; hers were the cornflower variety, while mine veered toward blue-gray.

"Yeah," I responded, while patting my ruby bouffant, ensuring it was still intact. "Folks are taking to the new selection. Thank goodness I managed to siphon off enough peanuts from our budget to buy it."

Uncle Wyatt, known as Sheriff Stone to the good folks of Millbrook, pressed his lips together.

I scrunched my nose at the slip. Griping about the lack of funding had become my favorite pastime. It probably drove them nuts, so I tried to keep my complaining down to a minimum, but old habits died hard.

Aunt Peg rifled through her sturdy tote bag, pulled out a

cosmetics catalog, and handed it to me. "Oh, honey, before I forget, the new book came out."

She peddled cosmetics to earn her "mad money," as she called it. It explained why travel-size lotion bottles and nail polish littered my bathroom counter, none of which I needed. I was just trying to contribute to her side hustle.

As I leafed through the pages of beach offerings, murmurs from the townsfolk died down.

Mayor Dalton's voice filled the room. "Ladies and gentlemen, thank you for joining us. Since we have a full house tonight, I'll get right down to business."

"Business, being the robberies," someone upfront said.

Another said, "Why aren't we looking at who it could be? It's probably Levi Cross. How is this even debatable? He's back in town. Spoke to him a few days ago, and he said he'll be staying a while. He'll probably be riding that damn motorcycle all hours of the night, waking us up. Just you wait."

My ears perked up at the mention of Levi's name, and I abandoned my catalog perusal like a spicy meatball. Levi attended my high school, except he was a few grades higher, so we didn't cross paths much. If I remember correctly, he skipped out of gym class. He never struck me as the athletic type, anyway. Nope. He and his buddy, Oliver Beecham, were too cool for school, preferring a life of petty crime to education.

But in this case, Levi was a hundred-percent innocent. Nothing concrete to put my finger on. It just didn't feel like his style, based on the rumors I'd heard.

An idea flashed in my mind, and I leaned towards Uncle Wyatt. "What if you enlisted Levi Cross in cracking the case? You know, since he's back in town. He's got the experience to catch the burglars."

Uncle Wyatt's bushy gray brows plummeted so fast, you'd have sworn I'd kicked his dog. "Heck, no!" he exploded. Heads turned in our direction, making my cheeks burn. "That man is a criminal, Abby," he continued. "Had enough of him and his crackpot uncle."

Lordy be, this old chestnut again. Levi's Uncle Al lived on the outskirts of town near the border of Union Vale. He wasn't that bad. Although, Wyatt might have been right about Al being a crackpot, with him living alone in a Winnebago, and all. Loneliness and paranoia had that effect.

Aunt Peg rubbed her husband's arm to hush him up. "Come on, darling. Abby has a point. We're in dire need of help, and Levi might be our ticket. Besides, enough time has passed since that boat incident. Give him a chance to make amends. You have to admit that Al never gave you an ounce of trouble. We were all young once. Remember that time when we stole—"

Uncle Wyatt coughed and waved his hands, interrupting her.

Aunt Peg scoffed at him, and I raised the catalog to hide my chuckle at his antics.

After he simmered down, Uncle Wyatt scratched his gray beard stubble for a moment and released a huff. "Tell ya what. Abby, you go talk to him and see what he says. You're about the same age and went to school together. Besides, I've been loaded down with paperwork lately."

My eyes must've bulged out of my head like a cartoon character spotting a boulder drop.

For real. Didn't see that coming!

"Ah, we barely knew each other," I explained, squirming in my seat, betraying my unease. "We might've shared a few classes in high school. There's a good chance he doesn't even know I exist. You should go. You two knew each other."

You want the truth? Levi Cross intimidated the heck out of me. I remembered this handsome, brooding kid back in the day. He never said much, but when he did, it cut like a knife through butter. No rumors of him bullying, but danger radiated from him. Both magnetizing and terrifying at the same time. And I can vouch he invoked the same feelings for the rest of the female student body. A tantalizing forbidden fruit we all wanted to bite into, but feared the consequences.

Uncle Wyatt's face remained rock-stiff, brooking no room for arguments. "If we're gonna do this, you talk to him, or we don't ask at all."

I kept my growl of frustration low enough to go undetected... *I think.*

There was no fooling him, the joys of having a seasoned lawman in your family. Although, I'd managed to keep my relationship drama off his radar by not mentioning it at all. Unable to broach this impasse, I twisted my ruby lips and turned away, focusing on the room at large.

Someone seated in front of us said, "That break-in next door really messed with me. I stay up at night, listening to every creak and groan."

I contorted my expression into a grimace and immersed myself in the glossy pages as I tried to tune out the fear that permeated her voice.

Glen Wozniak, the amiable owner of the crowded deli on Main Street, turned to Uncle Wyatt. "Are our businesses safe? Our homes? Give us something because all it looks like is you showing up, jotting in your notepad, and leaving."

My uncle raised his hands in a placating gesture. "I know y'all need answers, and I don't blame you. But if I share everything we know right now, it might hurt our chances of catching the perp. Rest assured, the boys and I are working hard, and we're doing everything we could to keep you safe."

The weight of guilt crushed me, and I bit my lip. These people required more assistance than the police could handle. I had to squash my fear and talk to Levi. Wimping out wasn't an option.

I released a breath, leaned over to Uncle Wyatt, and willed out the words. "Alright, I'll go tomorrow morning and see what he says." After all, somebody needed to make the first move.

What's the worst that can happen? He turned me down? I can live with that.

CHAPTER TWO

ABBY

IN THE SPIRIT of honoring my offer at the meeting last night, I parked my Camry in front of Clara Cross's charming, colonial-style home, nestled just outside our village center. The sultry air made a bead of sweat form on my upper lip. I tapped it dry while heading up the cracked pavement. Nothing like talking to a hot guy while sporting a glistening 'stache to boost a lady's confidence.

Maybe I was jumping the gun here. What if the years hadn't been kind to him?

Suppose his beer belly tested the fibers of his shirt.

I needed to rein in my hormones before they hijacked my brain. But still, no lady needed a 'stache.

Anyway, after his parents passed away in a tragic car accident, he signed over the house to his Aunt Clara. Clara lives in Bali, so Levi returns once a year to do minor repairs before taking off again.

Personally, that arrangement never made a lick of sense to me. What rationale is there in holding on to a house where no one lives in? Wouldn't it be more sensible to sell it and let another family enjoy it? Different strokes for different folks, I suppose.

The house stood like a work of art, flaunting its rectangular shape and symmetrical facade. With white clapboard siding and black shutters framing it, the exterior exuded classic charm.

I've always loved this place, despite its unkempt garden. If I had lived here, my mission in life would have been to transform the garden into a blooming paradise. Plus, I'd paint the door with a splash of turquoise, instead of its bland brown, which matched nothing around—save the patch of dirt.

Whispering under my breath, I recited, "Hi, I'm Abby Martin. I came to let you know that Sheriff Stone said there's a job at the station available for you...if you're interested."

Too wordy.

I'd already forgotten half of that. Winging it might have been the better option.

Steeling my spine, I blew out a breath and rapped on the door.

A slim, sexy woman wearing a black halter dress swung open the door. Her eyes locked on mine for a split second before they sparkled with desire, just as she gave me her back.

Levi, a vision wrapped in blue terry cloth, filled the doorway. His wet, brown hair glittered in the morning sun. Six-pack on full show.

My breath hitched in my throat. Geez Louise, what did I nearly walk into?

"Thanks for having me over," she purred. "I enjoyed myself. Maybe we could do this again?"

Why did it feel like she was staking her claim? But that couldn't be right because I posed no threat. Her slender, long-legged figure was the polar opposite of mine. I tried my best to cover with my rockabilly style, but, well, you know. I nearly raised my hand to pat my hair in place but caught myself and lowered it. No need for that. Neither of them would care about my flyaways. Instead, I smoothed my green dress and slid up the sleeves of my black cardigan.

Levi's lips curled into a slow, seductive smile that didn't quite reach his eyes, and he didn't answer her obvious setup.

Okay. Odd.

Maybe he liked to play it coy, or maybe that was a standard guy thing. Whatever the reason, it didn't bode well for Ms. Legs.

Undeterred, she stretched up, kissed Levi for longer than necessary, making a point. The words "get a room" popped up in my mind as they made out in front of me, but I shoved it aside because this was his property, and that would have been rude.

Then she strutted past me with smudged red lipstick, a smirk, and a triumphant model's gait.

I blinked like a strobe light while I collected myself from... um, whatever just happened.

These two were dripping with sex appeal, while most folks were still dripping excess grease from their bacon. They were liable to give a woman the vapors, I'll tell you that.

And Levi. My God. A sculpted face with a pronounced jawline. A head taller than I remembered in high school. Lean with broad, muscular shoulders and a narrow waist. Sleeve tattoos blacked out his skin, but the one that caught my attention was the word "Rachel," inked boldly across his chest.

Ms. Legs had a name.

Rachel.

Ugh.

Suddenly, my hands shook, and I felt an intense need to bolt. So, I rooted myself to the cracked pavement, and took a deep breath in a last-ditch attempt to calm down before making my pitch.

"Good morning, Levi," I said. "I'm Abby Cross."

Levi arched his brow, folded his arms, and braced against the doorframe. An amused smirk tugged at the corner of his mouth.

My heart skipped a beat watching him. Why did he have to be next-level attractive? Wait, a minute. What did I—?

My forehead creased as I reviewed my words.

Oh, dear Lord, no!

I blushed to the degree of molten lava.

My heart rate notched up. "Sorry for the blunder. I meant," I blew out another breath, making my voice shaky. "Hi, Levi, I'm Abby Martin, and I came here to ask if you'd be interested in working at the sheriff's station."

Levi's head jerked back, and his chocolate eyes widened, clearly not expecting my proposition. He inclined his head and addressed me for the first time. "With Sheriff Stone?" He snorted. "Not a chance in hell. We'd kill each other on the first day."

Seriously, I was dying to learn the story behind their animosity, but I forced it to the back of my mind and concentrated on convincing him why working with Uncle Wyatt would be beneficial.

I changed tack, my voice growing peppier than a cartoon chipmunk's. "This is your chance to mend fences with Sheriff Stone and the town. Help us catch this burglar, and folks might see you in a different light."

Levi's face, chiseled like a sculpture, twisted into a mask of anger, sending me into a panic. His tone dripped with scorn. "I don't need to prove anything to anyone. Frankly, I don't give a damn how folks see me, either."

How did this go off the rails so fast? He seemed alright in high school, despite his reputation. Certainly not this obnoxious.

I clung to that thought and said, "But you could help people, and helping people is important. You could make a real difference. Folks around here are nervous, and they'd be much obliged if you lent a hand."

Levi's lips curved into a bitter smile, reminding me of my ex, Monroe. My heart wilted, denied the sexy smiles that women like Rachel received. Instead, I survived on the affectionate ones from family and friends or the intimidating ones from my ex.

He reinforced that sentiment with his next words. "Since we're handing out unsolicited advice, here's one for you: don't rush into things before you know what you're getting yourself into. That kind of recklessness will get you into trouble."

A normal person would have left, but not me. I stood there like a stunned baboon, trying to make heads or tails out of his comment.

My mouth worked, doing its utmost to discern his meaning, but nothing came to mind, so I asked a genius question. "Ah...huh?"

Levi straightened and delivered a savage blow. "Let me reiterate, since listening isn't your strong suit. I don't care about folks around here, and I sure as hell won't be working with Stone. Now, we done here, or are there more words of wisdom you need to spout?"

I stepped back, subconsciously putting space between us. "Well, um, no."

He moved into his house and slammed the door in my face, blowing my hair back.

What just—

What just happened?

I clenched my jaw and balled my fists, furious enough to punch his stupid door. Instead, I shouted, "A simple 'no thanks' would have sufficed!"

CHAPTER THREE

LEVI CROSS

GLORIA ABBOT, the secretary of Sterling Construction, stared me down. Her eyes exuded the warmth of two chips of ice, and her hair gleamed a crone's gray.

Even my smooth greeting, complimenting her pearl necklace, ricocheted like bullets from Iron Man. That might have pushed her over the edge, considering my history.

But I couldn't throw in the towel just yet. It was too early in the job hunt to cast my employment hopes aside.

I'd burned enough bridges in this town that no one would cut me any slack, no matter how many smiles I flashed.

One of the cool things about New York City was its crowdedness. You never met the same person twice, which kept me in their good graces because no one knew me well enough to form judgments. If I hadn't botched my last assignment, I wouldn't have been here, enduring this ridiculousness.

The things I did for a paycheck.

Stirring up commotion was my only shot at breaching Sterling's inner sanctum. It needed to be loud enough to draw him out.

Crossing my arms with a determined expression, I raised my voice sufficiently for Sterling to hear. "So you're telling me that there are no slots open in his schedule? Not even a teeny-weeny one?" I flashed a pleading grin.

Gloria's face rivaled Captain America's uncrackable shield. "You'll have to make an appointment like everyone else, Mr. Cross," she replied.

I peeked at the door.

No dice.

Not even movement from inside. Time to step things up.

My voice had escalated. "What if this is an emergency? You're tellin' me there's no room in his schedule for emergencies?!"

Sterling yanked open the door and thrust his graying head out. His eyes narrowed to slits. "Why the hell are you carrying on out here like you're in the middle of Times Square? I can't hear myself think."

Jackpot!

I tamed my triumphant grin into a polite smile. "Just wanted a few minutes of your time, boss."

Sterling sized me up, his eyes darting from my head to my toes, as if I were a questionable piece of merchandise.

That sobered me instantly, but I tried not to let it mess with my head because landing this job was key to laying low. Believe me, I hated working for these types as much as I hated Brussels sprouts—which is saying something, because I stole those too to put food on my family's table.

His expression softened. "Alright, fine. Come in, but don't get too cozy. I only got a couple of minutes to spare this morning."

I expelled a slow breath and savored my insides unclenching as I trailed after Sterling.

The white walls in his office and blue curtains were the only swaps, but Sterling's mahogany desk remained the same, dwarfing the cramped space. I wouldn't put it past him to wield this intimidation tactic during his one-on-ones. From my dad's stories of Sterling, he enjoyed using power plays to gain the upper hand. Plausible when you own a construction company, and your employees are brawnier than you.

I sank into the emerald leather chair, my gaze locked on the gray-haired man across from me. His stern, square-jawed face made him look prone to outbursts, setting my nerves on edge.

"Alright, kid," he began, cutting through the pleasantries faster than a samurai sword. "What do you want from me?"

Refusing to be intimidated, I flashed a jackal's grin. "I'm here to inquire about a job, sir."

As I spoke, Sterling furrowed his brow, his beady eyes roving my face. "You look familiar. Have we met before?"

My smile faltered as I braced myself for his reaction. "Yep, yours truly. Levi Cross, sir."

Sterling's eyes opened wide. "You again? Don't tell me you've returned to steal my stapler," he quipped, chuckling to himself.

Steal his stapler?

Seriously?

"Nah, sir," I said through a laugh. "I've upgraded to bigger and better heists since then."

When Sterling's complexion paled, I backtracked, "I kid, sir. I've turned over a new leaf."

Mostly.

I continued, "I'm solely interested in exploring job opportunities—"

"Sorry, Cross, can't help you there," he said, shooting me down before I finished my sentence.

My heart nosedived in my chest. Landing this gig would have injected my anemic bank account with the iron it needed.

The bell in Graham's Garage announced my arrival. Memories of Craig came flooding back, and I marveled at his establishment, seriously impressed by how far he'd come. Posters of cars and trucks hung on the walls alongside a few framed photos of Craig in hospital scrubs holding a newborn.

We'd been buddies back in high school, but while I had chased skirts and cut my classes, Craig tinkered with car engines to fine-tune his rides.

It came as no surprise when I heard he'd opened his own auto mechanic shop.

Craig materialized from the back and made his way over to me, wiping his greasy hands on a stained rag before shoving it into his back pocket. Far stockier than I remembered, but his short blond hair was just the same. What surprised me were the bags under his eyes, as though he hadn't slept in a few days. He looked exhausted and wired at the same time. Wonder what was up with that.

I inhaled, taking in the smell of grease with it. Scrunching my nose, I rallied my courage for what I was about to ask. "Hey, Craig. Long time no see. Any chance you've got a spot open?"

Craig pinched his lips together, his expression conveying regret. "Sorry, man. Wish I could help you out, but we're all set for now," he said with zero recognition in his eyes—for which my stung pride breathed a sigh of relief.

A boulder-sized ball of anxiety had lodged itself in the pit of my stomach. Cold-calling had proved to be a long shot, and I knew it, but damn, rejection hurt. Bitterness tinged my smile, and my voice sounded dejected. "Alright then, thanks for letting me know."

Craig dipped his chin, and I pivoted, leaving the shop. The blazing daylight made me squint, so I fished my shades out of my front pocket and slipped them on to shield myself from the summer glare.

The garage door closed behind me, busting off a chunk of my dignity with it. I strode down the street, flanked by the quaint little shops that canvassed the village. Normally, I soaked up the sun any chance I got. Like any red-blooded New Yorker who despised winter with a passion and needed the sun to warm their frigid bones, summer was my jam, my happy place.

But today, it behaved like the unrelenting glare of a cop's flashlight, halting my getaway. Even the cinnamon rolls from Luigi's Bakery, which usually set off a drool-fest, failed to lure me in. Nope, not today. My gut wasn't having it. It was too busy churning with disappointment and growing anxiety over my unemployment to give a damn about pastries or sunshine for that matter.

As I ambled along, I happened upon a phone store, its pristine display cases brimming with the latest models, mocking me from behind the glass. My own phone languished on life support, in dire need of an upgrade, but I couldn't afford to shell out cash for that luxury right now. If my state of unemployment keeps up, I'll have no choice but to return to the city and risk a jail sentence if the investigators decide I was Rick's accomplice.

Right then, a flash of memory zapped into my mind. Back in the day, my dad had lost his job at Sterling Construction, and we'd struggled to make ends meet. And when I say struggled, I mean really *struggled*.

Fresh produce? Forget about it. Canned foods became our reality. After a while, it got old.

Around that time, I embarked on a life-altering trip to Union Vale, where I resorted to snagging food from the outside stalls. The thrill, man, the thrill intoxicated me and lured me down into the rabbit hole of illicit activities.

Even after my dad secured a job at a local mechanic's shop, I couldn't kick the habit. That high, after I pulled off a successful heist, became an addiction I failed to shake.

Just then, movement caught my eye, and that obnoxious woman who came by earlier crossed the road and headed toward Sugar & Brew. Her fire engine hair bounced with each step, as did her ample breasts under her green cardigan, reminding me of a pin-up from a bygone era.

Her name was lost in the cobwebs of my memory. What was

it again? A better question: was the sheriff aware that one of the locals offered jobs on his behalf?

This hick town, man, had lost its damn mind.

"Cross?" A voice came from behind, clenching my insides in a primal reaction from a life I thought I'd left behind. Years passed, but some things never faded.

I spun. Sure enough, the voice fit the sight... more or less. The bags under his eyes looked like two deflated balloons, and the way his belt disappeared under his gut suggested he enjoyed a few beers too many. Sheriff Stone in his middle-aged glory.

I answered with a curt, "Yeah?" Keeping cards close to my chest was my specialty around law enforcement.

Stone tipped his brown hat back, revealing those steely eyes, trained to spot a lie from fifty paces. "Come down to the station for a chat, would you?"

Oh, hell no!

"I didn't do anything. I wasn't involved in anything, and you can't accuse me of—"

Stone held up his hands. "Easy, Thomas Crown. You're not in the hot seat. I just want your two cents. That's all."

"Let me think about it first. No promises, though."

CHAPTER FOUR

LEVI

AS I STEPPED into the police station, the walls' new paint job jumped out. The place had received a modern upgrade with a scattering of desks. For a second, I wondered if I had the right building.

Sheriff Stone stood near the front, talking to a ginger deputy who looked like he should have been tearing it up on the basketball court instead of tearing the seams of his ill-fitting deputy's uniform.

Stone sipped from a mug while his other hand rested on his hip. Still can't wrap my head around how much he had changed. This man is a far cry from the guy who polished his gun when I came over to take out his daughter. Geez, that felt like ten minutes ago. In my absence, time tempered him into a seasoned veteran, worn down by the trials of the job.

I approached the old man, my limbs stiff, and my stomach gurgling.

Stone's shaggy brows pulled together, his sharp eyes sizing me up over the rim of his mug.

"Sheriff Stone? Walking in here without handcuffs feels strange." I flashed a mega-watt grin, yet his face didn't budge from its grim line.

My smile slowly receded.

Tough room.

Clearly, levity was lost on him, so I shifted gears and cut straight to business.

"Thought you should know that a woman showed up at my door this morning and said you were offering me a job. A redhead. Curvy, beau—ah, blue eyes...ring any bells?"

The cloudy expression cleared from Stone's face, and his brows lifted. "You're interested? Received a text from Abby this morning, saying you turned it down. That's why I approached."

Abby. *Of course.* The pushy redhead, who introduced herself as Abby Cross. The locals around here were seriously nutty, swear to God.

Maybe he didn't crack a grin because she whined about our earlier interaction. It all clicked into place now.

For confirmation, I asked, "She told you that? That's it?"

Stone sipped his mug, and his eyes darted around my face. "Was there more? Did something else happen?"

Damn. Impressive, really. This man had the instincts of a bloodhound, sniffing out a play before you even made it. Hard to believe he didn't catch the burglars already.

The deputy standing next to Stone, whose name tag read "Barns," stood with his thumbs hooked under his armpits, and his feet shoulder-width apart, watching our exchange like a ping-pong spectator.

I rested one hand casually on my hip and glanced down momentarily to gather my thoughts. "Her offer came out of nowhere, and it caught me off guard. And honestly, I took her for one of the gossip hens needling me for information. I had no reason to trust her. I didn't even know her, so I dropped in to check it out."

As my words hung in the air, guilt dug its fangs into my chest at how I treated her.

Stone continued to stare me down as though we were in the

interrogation room. Then he let up with a huff. "Right. Let me show you where you'll be working if you accept the job."

Barns' face twisted as if he'd been force-fed sour milk. "Sir, you're offering him a job? To work with us? Here? He's not qualified."

His pissy tone raised my hackles.

Seriously? Was bro really that paranoid about his job that he'd block my search for one? Low, if you asked me.

Stone responded, "All hands on deck. Come with me, son."

When Stone led me into the library, I reeled back at seeing Abby working behind the check-out desk.

Freakin' great. I was on a roll today!

She handed over a stack of books to a patron and wished them a cheerful *happy reading.*

But when our eyes locked, her smile deflated like a popped balloon, and her expression grew cautious, much like it had earlier this morning.

Why did her skin look so clear? It reminded me of freshly fallen snow. Pure. Heavenly.

That wasn't even the weirdest part. That medal belonged to Stone's warm grin when he stopped by the desk. It made me do a double-take because its appearance rivaled the rarity of watching Bigfoot traipsing through a garden full of lilies.

"Cross," he said, "You've already met my niece Abby Martin, our librarian."

Say what now? His niece? Did I hear that right?

My jaw dropped as if I had been tased, while I scrambled to process this new info.

Abby's knockout eyes shot away from mine. With a timid nod, she mumbled, "Hello."

Her terse reply radiated in my chest like acid reflux. I creased my brow and rubbed my fist against the ghost ache. She'd been smiling and happy moments ago. Now this.

Stone's eyes darted between us. He definitely suspected something had happened but didn't voice it. Instead, he cleared his throat. "You'll be working the Microfiche machine. I'd normally ask one of my deputies to do this, but we're short-staffed at the moment. Comb through newspapers to find anything on the break-ins. If you see a particular pattern, let me know. Clear?"

His words washed over me like the muffled drone of Charlie Brown's teacher, 'cause my thoughts were consumed by the librarian. I couldn't stop wronging women in the Sheriff's family, starting with his daughter. Well, I hadn't wronged her. We just didn't click when I took her out. Anyhow, working here would be a terrible idea.

Stone repeated himself, louder this time. "We clear?"

I shook my head, stunned out of my reverie. "Crystal, sir," I clipped.

Stone backed away. "Alright," he rumbled. "I'll leave you to it." Then he took off, finally leaving me alone with his niece.

Soft jazz floated down from the overhead speakers, something I hadn't noticed earlier. Abby dug jazz? Her vintage get-up led me to believe she might enjoy the big band era. I wanted to ask about her musical preferences, but that would have been off-topic.

I inhaled, gearing up for our talk.

Abby stared at the screen like her life depended on it. Her strongest tell was her cheeks, which nearly matched the shade of her lipstick.

I'd give anything to run the back of my hand across her face to soothe her.

Strange thought.

What the hell was wrong with me? I'd never acted this way over a woman before. My behavior this morning was messing with my conscience in a big way.

I strolled closer to her and gentled my voice. "Abby. Look at me, please."

Her eyes flickered to mine for a split second, and I glimpsed hurt and humiliation before she diverted them back to her monitor.

The pang in my chest festered like a wound reopening.

I moved closer to her and caught a faint whiff of something sweet. I inhaled deeply, drawing it into my lungs. It smelled like roses mostly, mixed with something exotic. Don't ask me why, but it calmed my anxiety.

"Abby," my voice, rasping with sincerity. "Sweetheart, look at me. And keep your eyes on me this time, okay?"

She exhaled and followed my directions, but her warm eyes from this morning turned cold and hard like shards.

I winced as they cut me to the core, but I deserved it.

"Abby." I tried again, my voice hoarse with emotion. "Slamming the door in your face and shutting you out this morning was wrong. I hurt you, and I'm very sorry. You were right. 'No thanks' would have sufficed."

Abby's mascara-coated lashes fluttered over her saucer eyes, and her full lips parted. She murmured, "You heard that?"

I leaned in, my voice lowered to a rough whisper. "I'm so sorry for how I treated you. I wronged you, and I regret it deeply. I was just—"

"Put off by my buttinsky tactics?" she finished. "You know, I'd been replaying what happened to make sense of why you'd reacted that way. Believe me, I didn't mean to come off so high and mighty. I'm very sorry about that."

A grin broke out across my face. Who was this woman, and why was she so genuine? Refreshing after dealing with the kind of people I had dealt with over the years. One thing's for sure, we needed a do-over.

I extended my open hand to her. When she took it, I locked my fingers around hers and brushed my thumb along her silky-smooth skin. Those mesmerizing eyes of hers nearly made me forget to tease her.

Completely criminal.

"Hi, I'm Levi Cross," I said. "Pleasure meeting you, Abby Cross."

Abby burst out in a peal of laughter, filling the space with warmth absent a second ago. "I'm never going to live that down, am I?"

An elderly woman with her white hair in a bun, clutching a canvas tote bag, sidled up to the counter. She held her heart, and her cloudy brown eyes wrinkled in amusement. "Oh, Abigail, how lovely to see your smile return after that long face you wore this morning."

Damn. I brought her down.

God, why did I have to be so stupid?!

My guilt had a field day, sucker-punching me in the gut this time. I huffed in self-disgust.

Abby's smile faded as though she was eavesdropping on my thoughts, and she glanced over at me.

Her pearly white teeth bit her red lips, and I swear, a zing zipped through me, making me squeeze her hand in response.

Abby's pretty eyes widened before she yanked her hand out of my grasp, severing our contact, and focusing on the old lady. "Need help with anything, Jane?"

Jane, oblivious to us, answered, "Yes, I need a book on securing your home to prevent intruders."

Abby nodded and rose from her seat. "Yes. We have the perfect how-to book. You're just in luck. It was returned a few days ago." She walked out from behind the desk. "That one has been constantly checked out." Abby led the woman to the back.

Moments after she disappeared, a beefy dude with light brown hair that reached down to his shoulders strode up to the desk. His tattered blue jeans and faded gray shirt had seen too many wash cycles. Overall, he didn't strike me as the book-reading type.

He glanced at the vacant chair before surveying the library. "Abby working today?"

Could this be her man? With his amber eyes and matching hair, I could see why she might be into him. He seemed self-assured, and there was kindness in his eyes. Kind of like a Golden Retriever.

I stood up to my full height, realizing that I edged him out by a head. I slipped my hands into the pockets of my black jeans, displaying my tattoo sleeves. "You just missed her," I replied casually. "She went in the back to help out a lady."

The guy's eyes went weary, almost calculating, like he was trying to read my intentions. Then he eased up and said, "Hey, Doug Kaminsky. Abby's friend."

Friend?

How *friendly* were they?

"Levi Cross. Nice to meet you." I let my name sink in for a moment, hoping my reputation did the talking.

Doug's eyes widened in recognition, and his whole demeanor shifted to excitement, making me raise my brows. "Hold up. You're the Levi Cross?"

The?

You'd think I was Dillinger risen from the dead the way these folks acted. Yet, I couldn't be the only pro in town, or they wouldn't be in their current jam.

Abby returned with a book in hand, moved behind the desk, where she made quick work of checking it out for the old lady. She smiled at Kaminsky. "Doug, I see you've met Levi." Then she addressed me. "Doug here is a staff writer for the Tribune and comes around to find leads for stories. He's also dating one of my best friends."

A surge of relief rippled through my veins at their platonic status. I winked at her and delighted in the pink stain spreading across her porcelain cheeks. Her skin displayed her emotions with clarity, like an open book.

I could get used to this.

But I shouldn't. I didn't plan on sticking around for too long. *Wince.*

She diverted her pretty eyes and rested her hands against her neck.

I answered, "We just met, sweetheart."

That nickname was supposed to be my secret weapon, a playful little shift in gears to catch her attention. But Abby acted like it bounced right off her. She didn't so much as flinch. I had expected at least a spark, a flutter of lashes, anything, not a masterclass in indifference. Most women would have been putty in my hands by now. Stung a little.

Abby said, "So, Doug, how are you holding up? Last time I saw you was at your grandma's funeral."

My brows pulled together as a pang of guilt walloped me again. Damn. I was on a roll today. Now, I feel bad for my posturing earlier. I folded my arms and simmered down.

"Alright," he answered. "Trying to be there for mom. Gonna pick up Delilah later and head over to Grandma's for a house cleaning before she puts it up for sale." He blew out a breath. "Anyway, came to ask if you got any leads for me."

Abby responded, "Not anything you haven't heard. I can barely keep our home security books on the shelves. You could run down to Pickwick's and ask them about the books people are buying. That might be a story. Oh, and Uncle Wyatt hired Levi here to help with the investigation."

Doug's eyes lit up like Christmas morning, so I pumped the brakes before he got too excited.

"Thinking about it. I haven't decided yet."

CHAPTER FIVE

LEVI

I PUSHED OPEN the door to O'Malley's Pub. The stale beer smell hit me like an old, long-lost pal. Squinting from the lighting and cigarette smoke, I made my way to the bar, shoulders hunched, fists jammed into my pockets.

That *Times* article, man. You want to hear the crazy part? Weeks of scrolling, dead ends everywhere, drove me up the damn wall. Then, just this evening, I stumbled across the article, and that "collusion with others" part triggered me to hit the bottle.

After scooting onto the barstool, Ben, the bartender, held up a bottle of Budweiser.

I nodded my thanks, and he plopped it down in front of me. Points to him for remembering. Something should be said about small-town bars.

Taking a long pull, I dragged my phone from my pocket and scrolled through the article again, praying I'd misread it.

It is not yet clear what information Marsden obtained. It is also not clear whether he acted alone or in collusion with others.

Nope. Read it right.

The barstool next to me creaked as a pair of mile-long legs

emerged from a crimson dress. The hem of the dress danced just above her knees, revealing a hint of a tattoo—which I knew for a fact was a dragon.

I glanced over at the familiar dark-haired woman from the other night, Lydia. One of her sharp eyebrows quirked up in a challenge.

My chest constricted, and my breath caught. Double crap. Drama.

"Sup, Lydia," I finally managed, hoping it came off casual. "How's it hanging?"

I winced at my sandpapery throat, so I downed another gulp of beer to wet it.

Lydia flashed her pearly whites, clearly enjoying my discomfort. "Oh, you know, same old, same old. Enjoying a Mai Tai while dodging wandering hands, the usual Wednesday night. Anyway, what brings you here again? After your brush-off when I left your house the other morning, I seriously thought you'd pull a Houdini."

I swirled the beer bottle. Was it a smart move to unload about an impending federal investigation to a past hookup? No chance in hell! I cleared my throat and spilled my second biggest problem. "Job openings around here are like stumbling on a secret passage into Fort Knox. Virtually impossible."

Lydia leaned in, her voice dropping to a conspiratorial whisper. "So, here's the scoop. Stagecoach Inn is about to have an opening in the kitchen. One of our cooks, Clyde, is this close to walking out." She held up her thumb and index finger, a hair's breadth apart. "Our head chef is Satan incarnate, and Clyde can't stand him. I'd give it a week, tops. The big question is, can you cook?"

"Wow, Stagecoach Inn. My friend's mom used to work there as a maid back in the day. But getting back to your question, I'm more of a 'set it and forget it' type. Nothing pro quality, anyway, and definitely not skilled enough to withstand a cussing out from a kitchen prima donna. Stone might haul me off to jail by the end of my first shift."

A robust laughter erupted from Lydia as she threw her head back. Conversations paused as heads turned, drawn to her. Unfazed by the sudden spotlight, she lowered her head slowly, a sly smile still playing on her lips. Propping her head on her hand, she drawled, "He's a regular Julius Caesar ordering around his subjects. Think Gordon Ramsay after a case of the Mondays. Handsome as hell, though, but its not like any of us have a shot." She rolled her hazel eyes, shook her head, and sipped her cocktail.

Raising the bottle to my lips, I said before sipping. "So, in other words, he's a basket full of sunshine."

I could envision the volatile chef she was describing, losing his mind over parsley a millimeter out of place. I'll tell you one thing: applying at Stagecoach went from maybe to hard pass. Although, I might reconsider if they needed a dishwasher or a burger patty defroster.

I settled back, eyeing Lydia. Conversation flowed effortlessly between us. My sole issue? Lydia was a dead ringer for my ex, Rachel. But I couldn't hold that against her. I could even admit the resemblance was the driving force behind the hookup.

This no-strings attached lifestyle was getting old. Maybe it's time to actually let someone in and see what happens before I end up a crazy old man like my Uncle Al, who lives in a Winnebago on the outskirts of town.

My phone buzzed in my pocket. I dug it out and Abby's name appeared on the screen. I lifted the phone to my ear. "Hey, Abs."

"Levi, thank goodness you answered. I need your help with security," Abby's voice sounded hyped up on the other end.

I sat straighter. "Abs? Did something happen?"

Lydia gave me a questioning look. I got up and headed outside.

"No, nothing happened," she answered immediately, untangling my insides. "Your unique skills might help in safeguarding my house. I just thought it was sensible, considering all the craziness going on around here lately and with my ex acting up. Sorry for scaring you."

Her ex? I'll pretend I didn't hear that. Who needed another complication in the form of some over-inflated jock named Chad?

"My—ah—unique skills?" I teased. "I'm not Iron Man, girly, but thank you for the compliment."

Abby made cute little gasps over the phone as she floundered for words. "Well, let's just say I have faith in your... ability to set up security. I'll pay for everything, don't worry."

A job. Maybe I could spin this security thing into a full-time gig.

How nutty was it that Abby counted on me to install surveillance in her home? About the same as Little Red Riding Hood asking the wolf to be her bodyguard. Except, no chance in this lifetime I'd ever hurt Abs. I gun for corporations, not innocent people.

"You trying to bribe me with a job, Gumshoe?" I teased, waiting for her reaction. The smile never left my face.

"Gumshoe?! I'm a gumshoe now? Let me guess. You found out about my love for true crime. Who blabbed? Oh, right. Doug might've while you were at the library."

Abs read true crime? Plot twist. "Gumshoe" totally slipped out – way safer than calling her Jessica Rabbit, especially since being around her made me feel as smooth as Roger.

My grin damn near hurt my cheeks. "Seems fitting. You're not just any librarian. You're going to help solve this mystery, if I take the job." I paused for a moment, letting the words sink in, because I still wasn't a hundred percent sold on the idea.

Abby fell quiet for a second. Then she shot back with unexpected sass. "The only mystery to me is why you didn't accept my offer. I've been racking my brain, trying to figure out what more I could say to entice you, but I've come up with diddly-squat."

Diddly squat?

I burst out laughing. Seriously, who says that nowadays? But what she was asking sobered me, causing my smile to retract all the way. How could I have told her the pay was too low to cover my bills without hurting her feelings? It seemed letting her down had been my M.O. since we met, and I was getting sick and tired of doing it.

I cringed. "I appreciate the offer, Abby. I really do, but you know how it is. Besides, I'm not sure if I'm the right person for this job. My expertise comes in dismantling security systems, not installing them."

"Nonsense!" Abby persisted. "You're perfect for this. You're smart, you're resourceful, and if you can figure out how to get in, you can keep others out. Come on, what do you say, Iron Man?"

I chuckled, digging her infectious optimism. Helping her out wasn't a bad idea either. If it gave her peace of mind, then who did that harm?

My gaze drifted out to the deserted country road.

The pay might not have been enough to cover my mounting debts. The lease for my apartment in the city wouldn't expire for another few months, so that was still a worry until then. I hadn't paid the storage locker dues where I housed my tools for breaking and entering, which meant the company would confiscate it. It saved me the hassle of dumping evidence.

But then again, this gig wasn't about fattening my wallet, not really. Abby needed protection from Chad. Plus, a tiny voice whispered, maybe, just maybe, this was my shot at redemption for slamming the door in her face. My lame apology, this morning, didn't cut it. For me anyway.

"If you need security, I'm your man," I said, letting my last words linger for a second. "I'll drop by to see what needs to be done."

Abby practically shouted, "Thanks, Levi. This means a lot!"

A deep sense of purpose welled up from inside. "I'll always have time for you, Gumshoe. Glad to be of service," I replied, using her nickname because I couldn't help myself.

We ended the call and I pocketed my phone while some people walked past me into the bar where Lydia waited.

CHAPTER SIX

ABBY

THANKS TO THE BULK EMPORIUM, my pantry overflowed with delectable treats to appease our small group, comprised of my two best friends, Lexy and Delilah, along with Aunt Peg. My motto was: if they were willing to forgo their home dinners for a lively literary discussion, providing a decent spread was the least I could do. This probably explained why my home became their preferred meeting spot.

Of course, the plush seating and an array of colorful toss pillows didn't hurt. Neither did the scatter of flickering lanterns. What can I say? I relish cozy environments.

After doing a head count on the tray brimming with hearty sandwiches, I carried them to the living room. The ladies would be here in a few minutes for our monthly book club meeting.

That left enough time to clear the clutter of true crime books off the table before they arrived, because the gals found them macabre. The doorbell's ring disrupted my preparation, and I froze for a beat.

Oof, they were earlier than expected. I was certain I had a few more minutes to haul out the extra seating.

Startled, I hurried to the door, my heels thudding on the dark hardwood along the way. When I opened it, Levi stood there, holding an enormous shopping bag.

My jaw fell slack as my mind scrambled to rustle up the right words. "Hi. Ah, I don't mean to be rude, but I wasn't expecting you."

Levi's chocolate-brown eyes dimmed, and his chiseled jaw dropped a smidge, causing me to scrunch my face for hurting his feelings.

I shook my head and stepped aside, allowing him to enter.

As Levi strode past, his cologne left a lingering mist, more potent than when we last met. "Sorry for dropping by unannounced," he said. "I was itching to get started on prep work. You got time for me?"

I can't say what it was, but his last words ignited a spark in my veins, much to my annoyance, because he had a girlfriend.

Closing my eyes for a brief second, I hoped my voice was infused with the sincerity I felt. "Really, thanks for coming. It's just that the girls will be here soon for our book club meeting. If you don't mind listening to us yacking away about books, feel free to stay as long as you like." Gesturing to the table, I said, "I hope you don't mind, but I've made some sandwiches. They're over there. Please, help yourself."

Levi's sculpted face gave way to a grin, and I could have sworn his eyes dipped to my lips for a split second.

Yep.

Definitely wishful thinking on my part. After all, he had Rachel's smudged-up lips. Why would he want my perfectly lined ones?

Ugh.

I shooed away that thought like the fruit fly it was.

Levi reached into the bag and pulled out a large box of surveillance equipment.

"Since I'm here, babe, I'll get to work. Don't worry, I won't be too long. I'll just set this up and get out of your hair."

I didn't see him much after I helped him find the ladder in the garage. He stayed outside, working around the house afterward. It left nanoseconds to scramble around, as per usual, right before these get-togethers.

Five minutes later, Lexy, Delilah, and Aunt Peg settled in my living room.

I announced, "Oh, just a quick heads up! Don't freak out if you hear some hammering and drilling outside. Levi's installing security cameras. With all the weird stuff happening lately, I figured it wouldn't hurt to beef up the house's defenses with a few pairs of extra eyes."

I studied Lexy's expression because she and Levi had history, and not the kind you might assume.

She stared at the sandwiches, her long black hair pulled back in a ponytail. Her normally animated, friendly face was devoid of emotion.

A pang of pity pierced my chest at her expression, but I didn't show it. Instead, I motioned to the food. "Have at it, ladies."

We caught up on the goings-on in our lives before diving into book talk to prevent going off-topic.

Lexy began, "We're prepping for Booktopia in a few months at the Inn! Autographed copies, yay!" Her face fell. "Ugh, that's if Peabody doesn't invent some last-minute crisis that requires all hands on deck." She waved away the dismal thought. "Nope, nope. Good vibes only. Gloria asked me to cover her shift while she takes her grandkid to the auto show in the city. I'll see if she's willing to swap shifts with me during the fair."

My lips quirked up in response to her zest for life, which lit up her gray eyes as she spoke.

Ms. Alexa Ray Edwards, a seasoned flea market aficionado with a heart for haggling and a sixth sense for retail value, balanced life as a maid at the Stagecoach Inn.

Lex and I were like night and day. She was always up for going places and trying new things. Me? I was more of a homebody, content to cozy up with a good snuff lit and a steaming mug of French vanilla. We didn't become friends until she answered my book club ad, and her adventurous spirit gradually coaxed me out of my comfort zone.

Back in our high school days, the dynamic trio consisted of her, Levi, and Oliver Beecham.

One time, during a bar meetup, she confessed that she never got over Oli. He disappeared without a word right after graduation. It was creepy, really. Lexy scoured social media for this man, but she came up empty-handed every time, and it wasn't like anyone could get a hold of Levi to ask about Oliver either. He just vanished into thin air.

Honestly, with all the sketchy people those two dealt with, I wouldn't be surprised if Oliver ended up six feet under. Mean to think, I know, but mess around with fire, you know the rest. Anyway, that seemed to be the case here.

Delilah McEntyre, or Deedee as we called her, sat next to me on the couch. Long auburn locks cascaded down her delicate frame like a molten waterfall. Even as she mowed down her sandwich, an act that would make most of us mortals look like Fred Flintstone enjoying his brontoburger, she still pulled it off with the refined grace of a movie starlet. Picture an edgier Disney princess, and you've got Deedee.

I dwarfed her like Shrek.

Despite all of that, her generosity and friendliness made it impossible for me to be a hater. Her drawing skills landed her a job as a cartoonist at the Tribune, where she met Doug. The lovebirds had been dating for a few years. I wouldn't be surprised if she came in here one day and announced that Doug popped the question, but Doug was slow as molasses when it came to relationships.

Deedee said, "You won't believe what Doug and I found while we were helping his mom clean out his grandma's attic. Pictures. When he asked his mom about them, she broke down in tears."

Our voices overlapped with "Oh no" and "Sorry, this is so hard on Sue."

Aunt Peg wrinkled her nose. "Pictures? What kind of pictures, dear?"

"Ones of Sue holding a baby boy that Doug had never seen before," Deedee answered. "Black hair, striking blue eyes. We think he died before Doug was born because Sue never mentioned him."

Aunt Peg's eyes widened. "Oh dear, I should check in on her."

Delilah's nose scrunched, and her tone held a slight edge. "Believe me, this has been a real blow to Doug too. He's having a tough time processing why Sue never mentioned the baby, but he can't ask because she's too fragile right now."

I placed a hand on Deedee's back, offering support. "Sorry, Deeds. Let me know if there's anything I can do."

She flashed a closed-mouth smile and patted my hand.

Lexy's eyes softened with sympathy. "That goes for me too, babe. Speaking of 'holding up,' how's the Sheriff doing, Peg? I heard they gave him a hard time at the last town hall meeting."

Aunt Peg pressed her lips together and brushed a stray lock of red hair out of her eyes. "Wyatt has been putting in so much overtime, he practically lives at the station, but he hasn't made headway. I've been trying to convince him to go fishing, you know, to clear his mind, but that man is as mule-headed as they come."

She didn't offer more about the case, not that I blamed her. Aunt Peg attended these meetings to get out of the house. Uncle Wyatt wasn't much of a talker, and when he wasn't working, he unwound by relaxing in front of the TV or went fishing on weekends. Poor Aunt Peg had to bear that alone. She needed a connection to the outside world, so she relied on our book club and her cosmetic sales. We included her as much as we could with non-club related outings, even though our age gap probably made her feel out of place.

A demanding knock made us jump, a knock we were familiar with, and we let out a collective groan.

I rose from my seat, dragging my wooden feet toward the door with the enthusiasm of walking to the guillotine.

The jerk hammered again.

I steeled myself and opened the door to Monroe, my ex, a squat, balding man. His buzzard-like eyes sized me up hungrily. "Really, Abby?" he spat. "So you're not going to pick up when I call? That's rude!"

A barrage of obscenities rushed to the tip of my tongue like a raging river, and I wanted to drench him in it. Instead, I took the high road and schooled my words. "That's because we're done, and I have nothing to say."

Levi emerged from the side of the house, his footsteps crunching on the gravel walkway. He zeroed in on Monroe but asked me, "Abby, what's going on?"

"So, this is the schmo you traded me in for?!" My squat ex's face dripped with disbelief, as if the mere idea of me choosing Levi over him was downright ridiculous.

If I wasn't so pissed, I'd laugh. Monroe continued. "Another bad decision, huh? I've told you before, your judgment could use some serious work. Don't be surprised if he trades up for someone who takes better care of herself."

The condescension.

It took all my restraint not to clock him in the eye. How dare he?! The nerve! The freaking nerve!

Levi shifted his weight forward, hardening his body language into a predatory pose. Menace filled the air, diminishing my ex's antics to child's play. Monroe may have thrown tantrums, but Levi's energy was something else altogether. It brought his thug nature to the surface.

The urge to shrink into the safety of my house and slam the door hit hard, but I couldn't give in to that. This was my home, damn it!

Monroe swallowed hard, his Adam's apple bobbing.

Levi stepped into the gap that separated me from my ex and ordered, "Abby, go inside."

I edged back a few steps. Ah, remember all that crazy talk earlier about standing my ground? Kidding! My inner Boudica must have been on a sugar high, rambling nonsense.

Slamming the door, I raced to the front window and jockeyed for a place alongside the ladies who crowded it.

The taller man loomed in front of my ex, his broad back blocking him from view. All I could see was the top of Monroe's head and a sliver of a cheek, which puffed out in what I *think* was supposed to be a sneer. But those wide, panicked eyes told a story of their own.

Levi's voice boomed like a drill sergeant addressing a new recruit. He pointed to the road and said, "Haul your sorry ass off this property! Your welcome wagon days are done!"

Monroe's facade disintegrated, leaving behind a pair of puppy-dog eyes that once had the power to melt me like warm chocolate.

"I care about Abby," he pleaded.

Oh, for crying out loud! That sly dog was fully aware that I had my eyes on him, so now we're in for a show where he's pretending to be the king of good intentions. Give me a break!

Levi rested his hand on his hip, occupying more space. "This ain't your stomping ground anymore. Cross this line again, and I'll personally see that every cop in town gets the memo about you messing with my girl."

His girl?

The ladies all looked at me, their eyes wide with surprise, but I dismissed Levi's comment with a shrug. He was just saying that to needle Monroe.

But the way he said it, like it was a statement of fact.

Bubbles flooded my stomach, and a goofy grin spread across my face. Monroe didn't have the cojones to throw down with Levi, so it was hilarious watching him try to play tough.

Then, something happened. Monroe leaned forward, his eyes

narrowing into slits, calculating and cold. That cruel sneer twisting his lips spoke louder than any threat. It said, "I've got the upper hand, and you're about to find out how."

Delight curdled in my stomach as my heart stumbled. My breath hitched, and I bit down on my bottom lip. The words "oh shoot" came to mind.

"So, you planning on dialing her uncle, the sheriff?" Monroe taunted. "He's got no love for lawbreakers. You forget that? Whose corner do you think he's gonna stand in?"

Aunt Peg huffed, offended by Monroe's taunt.

Anxiety erupted in the pit of my stomach, and my sweaty palms fogged up the glass. This creep had been feeding me the line of "who's going to believe you" since the moment he showed his true colors, and like a sucker, I'd bought into his bull. I mean, seriously? When I thought about it now, it made no sense. Who would take Monroe's word over mine? It wasn't like he was a model citizen, either.

Levi declared, "You had your shot, and you blew it. Time to hit the road and leave her be." His tone left no room for argument.

Monroe's tough-guy act crumbled to bits, like our library budget. His eyes darted to mine for a split second, then he hunched over, pivoted, and marched down my driveway toward his car. Moments later, the car's headlights blinked to life, illuminating the dim street. His tires screeched as he peeled out of the parking spot, leaving a smoke cloud in his wake.

My gaze remained fixed on my ex's departing car as it shrank into the distance, until it eventually turned the corner.

Gosh, what did I ever see in that obnoxious man?

A fiery blush scorched my cheeks, and I couldn't believe I had thought so low of myself to put up with him. The fear of being alone had led me to compromise my integrity, and dealing with the fallout just plain sucked.

Feeling downright embarrassed for allowing that no-goodnik

to wreak havoc in my life, I hugged myself, trying to chase away my goosebumps as I made my way back to the door.

Levi didn't come back inside. Instead, he returned to finish up his work.

Aunt Peg followed me and wrapped me in a warm hug, then pulled back. "Well, now. That was sweet. Wyatt will be happy when he hears that Levi came to your rescue. But I'm afraid that this is too much excitement I can handle in one night. I'll head off now."

Lexy followed Aunt Peg's lead and headed to the door. "You know what, me too. Maybe we should reschedule. Thanks for having us over, Abs." She shook her head. "Seeing that moron get his comeuppance was freaking awesome. Finally!"

I'd bet that her leaving had more to do with avoiding Levi and the memories his presence dredged up for her than with the excitement, because she lived for that stuff.

"Tell me about it," I grinned. "Take care, hon."

I waved at her and received a half-hearted one as she rushed out of the door.

Poor girl. I hope she didn't become a stranger because she was trying to dodge Levi.

Not long after, Doug showed up to pick up Deedee.

Levi poked his head inside the door and spoke in a drier than normal tone. "Babe, done here. I'll bring the ladder back into the garage and then I'm out." He stopped in his tracks and took in Delilah, his expression softening, as though absorbing the majesty of a master's painting.

In an instant, venom surged through my veins, cruelly reminding me that I was no Delilah, and certainly not Rachel. Instinctively, I wrapped my arms around myself, seeking comfort in any form of security.

How ridiculous? I shouldn't have felt this way, not after what I witnessed the other morning between Levi and Ms. Legs.

My reaction didn't make a lick of sense. Even as Doug and

Delilah stood close enough that it left no doubt what they meant to each other, jealousy beat me down.

My phone rang on the corner table, and I sent up a prayer heavenward for the interruption as I hurried for it. Jane's name flashed on the screen. Surprised, I answered.

"Abby, please come over," she begged. "They broke into my house!"

CHAPTER SEVEN

ABBY

I HOPPED out of Levi's car, eager to escape the stifling silence that had hung between us during the drive. It was even more oppressive than Monroe's tirades, and I couldn't take it another minute. I would have driven here myself, but I had dropped off my Camry at the shop for a brake repair earlier that afternoon.

Prodding Levi about the reason behind his mood wasn't the smartest move, so I left him alone to simmer down. I figured it had something to do with being forced to deal with my relationship drama. Luckily, Doug and Delilah were en route, so they did much of the talking.

The gang followed me past a police cruiser parked outside Jane Fritz's colonial home. Jane's ghostly face appeared in the doorway. She clutched the doorknob like a lifeline, her knuckles white as bone. This woman's zest for life led her to borrow books with diverse recipes to experiment with. Now? Gosh, so sad.

Her eyes, puffy and rimmed with red, spoke of hours spent crying.

I felt a pang in my chest watching her struggle to keep it

together. "Hey, Jane," I said softly, concerned that my normal decibels might upset her. "We got here as soon as we could."

Deputy Casey Barnes' basketball-player size filled Jane's living room. He scanned us with his sharp, steel-blue eyes. They came to rest on Levi, and his lips turned down in a frown.

Casey and I shared an unsavory past. Long story short, we went out on a group date when we were twelve, and he ditched me for Seela Gains, the prettiest girl in our group. From then on, I stink-eyed him, fully aware that his boyish, good-looks were a mere smokescreen.

"Come in," Jane whispered, her voice cracking. "Thanks for coming. I don't know what else to do!"

The smooth doorframe caught my eye, and something felt off, but I couldn't put my finger on it. We thanked the older woman as we sidled past, our footsteps crunching on the broken glass as we moved farther into the room.

Goodness, it looked like a tornado had touched down.

Chairs overturned, glass shattered, and the walls were stripped of their adornments. The break-in left its mark on the pristine floral wallpaper, with nail marks and scratches. A framed portrait of Jane's late husband, Edgar, hung crookedly, its glass cracked. The vintage wooden sideboard doors swung open, displaying its emptiness.

Her sofa, the sole item of furniture that stood upright, with its cushions haphazardly arranged, was soiled by shoe prints.

Those scumbags! How could anyone be so heartless? Didn't they understand that they were hurting real people? Good, innocent people. My nose stung, bringing tears to my eyes. This was so much worse than I had ever imagined.

Jane settled on her couch. Her ensemble reflected her classic and timeless style: a simple, slightly rumpled floral-printed blouse. Her hand rested lightly on her lap. She still wore her glistening wedding band.

Despite her stooped posture, Jane exuded an air of quiet

resilience. She leaned forward, offering a weak smile to our group.

Deedee and I planted ourselves at her side, while the guys stationed themselves by the door. Levi's hand balled into a fist on his hip, his jaw clenching tightly as he scanned the room. Doug followed suit, his expression grim.

I placed a hand on Jane's shoulder. "How are you holding up?"

"We're here for whatever you need," Delilah said, while looking around. "Let us take care of the mess so you can focus on getting back on your feet."

"Hands off!" Casey warned. "It'll screw up the investigation. Now, Jane, tell me exactly what you remember."

Doug's amber eyes drilled a hole in the back of Casey's head, and he mouthed the words, "WTF." Clearly, he had caught on to the weirdness of Casey's reaction. And knowing Doug, he would probably do some digging as soon as he got home.

"I came back from Bingo and found it this way. I called the police, then you." She squeezed my hand.

I wrapped my arm around her delicate shoulders. "You did the right thing."

Seriously, at this rate, my cozy furniture days are numbered. I should rent a storage locker and live in a shoebox for a while, because nowhere is safe anymore.

Levi's jaw pulsed as he studied the locks on the door, while his gaze ping-ponged between them and me.

My chest constricted at his hostility. He didn't need to vocalize his feelings for me to know what bothered him. I longed to cross the room and explain myself, to apologize for dragging him into this mess with my ex.

Casey asked Jane a few more questions, and then, once he had finished with his investigation, he told her to notify her insurance company.

Uncle Wyatt materialized in the entryway, addressing Levi. "What's your take, son?"

Casey's lips curled into a snarl before he concealed it.

Let it be said: that man should never play poker.

Levi stood up. "From what I could tell, it seems like a professional cat burglar, one who can make keys. They don't need to break in, per se." He swiveled towards Jane. "Bolts are a way to secure your door when you're home. An alarm system will be better while you're out."

Casey muttered loud enough to be heard. "Advice from criminals. *Fantastic.*"

Delilah and I shot daggers at Mr. Wonderful.

Unfazed, Casey stood with his thumbs tucked in his belt, channeling a bad-guy version of Poncherello.

Levi dodging that job made perfect sense now. Who in their right mind would sign up for a daily dose of smack-talk?

Uncle Wyatt, oblivious to the vibe between these two, nodded at Levi. "We could use your expertise at the station."

Casey rolled his eyes and grumbled, "Just great."

Jane expelled a breath. "I don't know what I'd do without all of you. Thank you all for coming. I'm so glad for your advice, Mr. Cross. What an exceptional young man you've grown into. Marley and Tod would've been proud."

A play of emotions flashed across Levi's face at the mention of his late parents. He kept his reply short, saying, "Thank you, ma'am."

CHAPTER EIGHT

ABBY

I FOUND solace in returning checked-in books to the shelves while a jazzy melody played from the speakers. The soft light glinted off the spines of the organized tomes, soothing my rattled nerves. After all the craziness of last night, I needed this early morning ritual to focus on.

Witnessing firsthand how those crooks turned Jane's life upside down made me lose sleep. They'd eventually get to my house. That storage locker idea might be something to look into.

Levi's silence as he dropped me off last night didn't help matters either. But he won't be in town for long anyway, so I'm probably getting worked up for nothing.

Suddenly, the door swung open, shattering my concentration. I froze, my fingers clinging to the book.

Levi walked up to the aisle and leaned his back against the shelf, his arms crossed. He wore the outfit from the night before, and his dark tattoos peeked out from under the sleeves of his shirt. He hadn't run a brush through his tousled hair, and his brown eyes were intense but downcast.

My heart, my stupid heart, a frantic bird in my chest, thrilled at the sight of him.

"Levi," I began, "Figured you'd be out job hunting. What brings you here?"

Was that the smartest thing to say? No idea. I found myself at a loss on how to deal with him. I'd never encountered a man like Levi before. He was too much, too intense, and too sexy for my own good.

Levi didn't answer immediately. Instead, he kept his eyes locked on me. His unwavering stare made my fingers grow clammy as I shuffled a book around after placing it in the wrong spot. I pressed my lips together and continued organizing the books. If he was going to stand there like a creeper, then fine. I had work to do.

Finally, he broke his long-standing silence. "Didn't have time to ask after everything went down the other night, babe. Answer my questions first."

My mind snagged on "babe." Yet his tone didn't betray the slightest hint of flirtation. He could've interchanged it with "chick," "lady," or "woman," and it would've all meant the same.

I asked, "Questions about what?"

Levi inched closer. "Monroe, how long have you been seeing him?"

I glanced down at the glossy space tome in my hands. How do I explain all this? How do I tell him I was a fool for staying so long?

"We're not seeing each other anymore," I admitted. "We were on and off for the longest time. But lately, he's been showing up at my door and badgering me to get back with him. I'd say no, I'm done. Eventually, he'd give up and leave. Then we'd do it all over again in a few weeks."

When Levi didn't respond, I raised my gaze to his furrowed brows.

"And you didn't report any of this to your uncle, I take it?" he asked.

My parents had dreamed of relocating to Florida for years, especially Dad, who fished as a hobby. Not to mention, they also wanted to escape New York winters, which were brutal on Dad's arthritic joints. However, I impeded their plans. They worried about leaving me behind, so Wyatt and Peg stepped up and kept an eye out for me. If I whined about my relationship drama, word would get back to my parents, and they'd lose sleep.

How could I do that to them?

"No," I answered. "I don't rely on nepotism to manage my life."

Levi flexed his jaw, as if he was holding himself back from unleashing a few choice words. "And how's that working for you?"

I glued my eyes to the books' spines, because the answer was as plain as day.

Levi read me and nodded, not needing my words.

The quietness between us was starting to suffocate me, and I caved in, letting out a breath of defeat. "Not lately. I'll give you that. Hence, the installation of the alarm system—well, you installed it, but you get my drift. And it was also due to the home invasions. Both reasons, actually."

Levi rubbed his jaw scruff and squeezed his eyes closed.

Dear Lord, how long was he going to continue being mad at me for dragging him into the fight with Monroe?

Before I could even get the question out of my mouth, he said, "Okay, let me ask you this. You're more afraid of Monroe than the invasions, aren't you?"

My heart pounded so hard that my mouth dried to Sahara. I scrambled, "I... ah."

Levi's fist rocketed out like a cannonball, slamming into the bookshelf with a deafening bang. Its impact made me jump.

"Listen to me carefully," he rounded on me, his face inches from mine. "If you need help, ask for it. Don't you dare think you're being a hero by keeping quiet. That's what Monroe is counting on. He wants to intimidate you into silence. He wants you to feel isolated. But you're not. Come to me, and talk about it. Don't let that weasel mess with your head and try to take this on alone. Got it?"

My heart leaped in my throat, flooding me with overwhelming emotion. Tears burned my eyes. Levi's words were the sweetest I'd ever heard, although his delivery rubbed like sandpaper. He was right about me not being alone. But I still needed to find the courage to ask for help.

A daunting task. A nearly impossible one.

Having nothing more to say for myself, I nodded slowly.

Levi expelled a breath, dispersing the oppressive clouds surrounding him since he walked in here. "Good, babe," he eyeballed the enormous clock mounted above the circulation desk. "Listen, got some business to see to. Catch you later."

My pulse pounded as Levi's broad shoulders rippled beneath his black shirt, as he stalked out of the library like a gladiator about to battle in the Coliseum.

Why was he so angry? And why did he seem to care so much about my safety?

The realization dawned, and a slow smile spread across my face.

Did he...?

Did he like me? As more than just a friend.

My heart flip-flopped, and I felt like dancing on sunshine. I had never really thought of Levi in that way before.

Okay, that was a dirty lie.

Of course I had—many, *many* times, but I wasn't delusional enough to think anything would come from it.

As the library door slowly closed behind his departing back, I couldn't shake the feeling that he was on the same page, too.

CHAPTER NINE

LEVI

I CHARGED through the metal doors of the sheriff's station, my blood still seething from the exchange with Abby. The fact that she allowed that weasel to undermine her brilliance nearly made me blow my top. Adding to that was his brazen audacity, threatening her right under her uncle's nose. I bet that rush made him come back for more. Didn't she realize the danger she had gotten herself into? She needed someone at her back. She needed me.

I had been working at Jane's late last night, and the old lady's situation had helped sour my mood even more. When I finally made it home, sleep eluded me because the town's drama plagued my mind. Deciding to come here and talk business with the sheriff eased my conscience enough to allow a few hours of shut-eye.

The station hummed with activity, and heads tracked my movements as I strode to Stone's office, but I paid them no attention, my eyes locked on my destination.

The old man sat behind a desk weathered by years of service. Its surface, a myriad of file folders, documents, and sticky notes. Stone paused scribbling when our eyes met, and his bushy brows arched in surprise.

"I'm here to take the job," I answered his unasked question.

Stone clasped his hands together, and his eyes wandered down to my rumpled clothes. "Well, now, that's an about-face. Yesterday, you were dead set against it when Barns' ribbing got under your skin," he said. "What made you change your mind?"

Hold on a second. Did he interpret Barns's conduct as "ribbing"? No wonder he didn't put the kibosh on it.

I slammed the brakes right there. Enduring pointless assholery, brushed off as mere good-natured ribbing, made me want to cut and run. But the two security systems and bolts I had installed in a single day rooted me in place.

I pressed my lips thin, clenched my jaw, and leaned against the wooden doorframe, shifting my weight to one hip. Just thinking about her situation made my eyes narrow. "A stubborn woman did, sir," I answered my new boss.

Stone's shoulders shook with silent laughter, his coffee-stained teeth glinting under the fluorescent lighting.

I cocked a brow at his puzzling response.

Stone said, "Nothing like a stubborn woman to change a man's mind. Been hitched to one for three decades. Anyway, welcome aboard." He rose, sending his chair sliding backward until it hit the wall. "C'mon, let me show you the ropes."

Tailing Stone through the lobby, I greeted the half-dozen officers I had ignored earlier, now my colleagues of sorts.

Awkward: it's what's for dinner.

Stone introduced me to officers Ramirez, Foster, and Simmons. They shook my hand with varying degrees of enthusiasm. I held my gaze steady, determined not to let their side-eyeing bother me.

Not even when they murmured, "He's not even trained. What the hell?"

If this devolved into junior high school locker room antics, I didn't know how much I could stand before I split town again.

"Levi Cross's here on a consultation basis," Stone explained to his uniformed underlings. "We need his expertise in breaking in to help solve the case."

The officers exchanged uneasy glances, but some patted my shoulder before dispersing to their respective desks.

All but one.

Ramirez stood with his thumbs tucked in his belt, and his legs shoulder-width apart. "Welcome to our humble abode," he said with a smirk, immediately setting off my alarm bells.

I compressed my lips into a thin line and delivered a curt nod. Why did that sound like a greeting in a prison yard?

Want to hear the crazy thing about this whole situation? I returned to my hometown to avoid prison time, only to find myself in the same atmosphere. No matter how hard I had pursued freedom, I faced confinement in one form or another.

Wild, right?

Stone said, "Head on over to the library. They got papers on microfiche. Look through the articles on past break-ins. Remember what I told you. Find the patterns."

I should have been at the crime scene, investigating. Not poring over some dusty relics. But a job's a job, and I couldn't afford to turn it down, with my bank account at scary-low levels.

The kink in my neck ached, a result of couch sleeping. I reached behind and rubbed at what was no doubt the beginnings of a migraine.

Joy.

"Alright, I'll get on it," I said to my boss.

Working at the library meant I had to make things right with Abby. I couldn't stand those terrified eyes. They would haunt me, promising another sleepless night. But I wasn't confident that she'd forgive me for scaring her at this point. I had screwed up royally. Again!

CHAPTER TEN

ABBY

THE SMELL of engine oil in Graham's Auto Shop made me wrinkle my nose, as I hunkered down in the waiting area while they ran tests on my car. If I worked here, I'd need a permanent stash of headache pills. How did mechanics tolerate this all day? Were they nose-blind?

Craig Graham owned this shop. His wife, Deb, worked as our librarian but was currently on maternity leave. I delayed filling her position because the summer lull had reduced demand. Activity ramped up during "back to school," when kids used our library as a gathering spot to do their homework.

I shifted in the hard plastic chair, attempting to peruse social media and listen to my audiobook, hoping to drown out the whirs and groans of machinery working in the background.

Suddenly, a beast of a man swung open the glass door and filled the space. He was clad in a gray compression shirt, black gym pants, and had his long black hair tied in a loose tail.

All I could say was, "Whoa, mama!" The man was jacked up.

I poked at the screen, with the intention of pausing my audiobook, but my fumbling fingers ended up opening the email app instead. I twisted my lips, eventually giving up, and then popped out my earbuds.

Craig, a stout man with his short blonde hair, emerged from the back, wiping his hands on a grease-stained rag. "McGregor! How's it hanging? Heard things at Thompson's have taken a turn for the worse since Lyle got sick."

The man named McGregor replied in a deep, rumbling voice. "Hey, Craig. I'm about done with Lyle's ungrateful brat not showing her face to help her old man. With these bills mounting, I might look into selling off Lyle's hauler to stay afloat. Ain't right piling this shit on me when I'm not even relation. Anyway, I heard about the accident yesterday. If you need more extensive work done, give Thompson's a ring, and I'll send over Carlos with the tow truck."

Craig's lips pulled downward into a frown. "Sorry, man. They didn't bring the cars here. I'll make some calls to see where they are. Maybe the sheriff might know."

McGregor thanked Craig in a quick murmur and headed out. As he passed by, our eyes met, and a bolt of electricity nearly short-circuited my phone. Those striking, electric-blue eyes and sturdy jaw made my breath catch.

Come to think of it, he looked vaguely familiar, but I couldn't quite place him. I'd never seen him before... had I?

"Abs," Craig said, drawing me out of my thoughts. "Camry's ready. That'll be three hundred dollars, please."

My pulse raced as I exited the car and hustled across the parking lot. There he stood, leaning against the library's locked door, holding a steaming cup of coffee in one hand and a paper bag in the other—a complete turnaround from this morning. What in the world was up with him? How could he flip-flop from one extreme to another?

But his eyes, though. His eyes invited me in like a double-fudge brownie. I practically tasted the electricity in the air and nearly melted onto the pavement.

The memories of our last interaction flooded my mind. "Hi, Levi," I breathed out, in a voice barely above a whisper. "Can I help you with something?"

Levi's voice oozed out like honey, sending a delicious shiver down my spine, which eased my weariness. "Sorry for scaring you this morning. Just so we're straight, I will never lay a finger on you, nor threaten you. Not even if my life depended on it. Got it?" Then he held out his stomach-rumbling treats. "These are for you. Heard you were picking up your car, and I didn't know if you had time for lunch."

"I—ah," I stammered, caught off guard by his tender gesture. "Thank you, Levi. That was super kind of you."

"No problem, babe," he said, his laugh lines crinkling at the corners of his eyes. "Now, let's get you inside." He pointed his chin to the door, reminding me that I should be opening it.

I rifled through my book charm keyring, clanging them together as I searched for the right one.

Levi said, "You're looking at the new consultant for the police department. I'm here to use the microfiche."

I tossed a raised brow over my shoulder as I turned the lock. "You've taken the job? Excellent. But I'm curious, how's using the microfiche going to help the police department? Shouldn't you be working on-site?"

I caught his shrug before pulling open the heavy door, revealing the vast expanse of books inside, my happy place.

Levi followed me. "Same thing I asked myself, but at the end of the day, it's a paying job. Can't argue with that."

Totally true. Although it was kind of strange that Uncle Wyatt offered someone with Levi's expertise such a trivial position. Could it be his lack of training, or was Uncle Wyatt keeping him out of trouble by giving him a menial task? Knowing my uncle, I'd lean towards the latter. Still, I didn't have the heart to mention it to Levi. If he was satisfied with the work and pay, why rock the boat?

Levi dropped the food off on my desk. Then, I led him to the microfiche drawer, my heart pounding. He stood so close during the lesson that my breath caught in my throat. The heat of his body radiated along my back, and the scent of his cologne filled my senses. I wanted to turn and look at him, but let's face it, I'd lose my composure.

"So, you insert the slide in here and turn this knob to adjust the focus." I gestured toward the knob, my cheeks flushing like a ripe tomato as I tried to ignore my idiotic response.

"Uh-huh," he said absently, tearing his eyes away from me to focus on the machine.

I cleared my throat. "Right. Then you can use these buttons to move around the image and zoom in and out."

Levi reached out and grazed my arm. "Thanks for showing me how to use this thing. I'll level with you, I had no idea what a microfiche was. I pictured attaching bait on a fishing hook when Stone first mentioned it. Confused the hell out of me."

I giggled at his self-deprecating joke and withstood the tingles that shot up my arm from his touch. The sensation, so intoxicating, prompted me to yank it away, just as I had done the other day when we shook hands. Why did this man have such an effect on me? I needed to get a grip, or this would be embarrassing. "No problem," I said, my voice shaking with betrayal.

The silence between us hung thick. I could feel his eyes, but I didn't dare look at him. Instead, I kept them glued to the machine, determined to finish up our lesson.

"I think I'm starting to catch on," he said finally. "I can handle it from here." He let out a quick breath as though he had let go of his intensity and changed the subject. "Never thought I'd find myself working in a library. Can't help but feel out of place."

I suppose he would. I'd never seen him in the library while we attended school. If he had, the place would've been teeming with girls who suddenly needed to work on their projects. We couldn't be more different. I pursued intellectual endeavors while he chased reckless thrills. But this enchanted place shouldn't feel foreign to him, especially if it'll be his workplace for the next little while.

"Oh, we can't have that," I said, while hiking up the red sleeves of my cardigan and waving him forward. "Come on, let me show you around."

Levi cracked a smile and followed me.

We started in the young adult section, an inviting space adorned with colorful posters and bean bag chairs scattered around low tables. The shelves were packed with a diverse selection of books, from thrilling mysteries to heartwarming coming-of-age tales. Soft overhead lights illuminated the area, creating a welcoming haven for young readers seeking an escape into the world of words.

Levi came to a sudden stop. His eyes lit up like twin super-novas in the graphic comic section. "Woah," he exclaimed, surveying the vibrant array of comics before him. "When I was a kid, I'd spend hours at the comic book store in Union Vale, poring over the pages. But the store owner wasn't too thrilled with my loitering. More than once, I left without spending a dime." He bit his lip, a flush staining his cheeks, as if he had omitted a secret.

Perhaps he had snagged a few books, and the memory shamed him.

My chest clenched for that little boy, and my hand nearly flew out to rub his shoulder, but I swung and grabbed my other arm to cover the movement. *Smooth, Abby.*

I wish I could have offered solace to ease his shame, but my paltry words didn't stand a chance to combat the emotional toll of his memories. We were classmates, after all, nothing more. "They're here whenever you need them," I said instead, gesturing to the rows of comics. "I often do the same with the true crime section before buying it at the bookstore." With a gentle nudge, I steered him away, hoping to soothe his embarrassment.

Levi's coffee-colored eyes roved my face, a question brewing behind them. "You like crime books, huh? So, tell me, what led to you becoming a librarian?"

I smiled as the memories bubbled up. "I used to hang out here all the time. My mom took me here to borrow books as a kid. Just got hooked on the vibe, you know?"

His warm smile, both inviting and unexpected, caught me off guard.

Cool, I wasn't. I knew that.

But for some reason, I thought my reserved nature would offend him, so it came as a surprise that it didn't.

As we approached the back of the library, I gestured toward inside the separate room. "This is our community room," I explained. "We hold all sorts of events here—book clubs, author readings, even yoga classes on the weekends."

Levi's nose scrunched, and his eyes bulged in such a comical way that Deedee could have used it as a reference photo for her cartoon strip. He asked, "Yoga classes...at the library?"

"Yeah," I said through a giggle. "The library is used for more than just reading."

Levi glanced around, his forehead wrinkled. "I don't know about working in the open. Being around townsfolk. The way they'll look at me. Do you think we can move the machine to the back?"

"Most folks around here are great," I said, my voice low and earnest. "All that stuff you did happened in your past. You've grown up since then. Look, I've done things too that I'm not proud of."

He arched a disbelieving brow.

"Not illegal things," I qualified. "Just, you know, dumb stuff." I waved a hand. "Not important. Moving on."

Yikes.

Levi's eyes held a mixture of surprise and vulnerability. "You...you don't judge me for it?" he asked, his voice tinged with disbelief.

My heart stirred, and a smile crept across my lips. Without a second thought, I placed my hand on his shoulder. For a moment, I held it there, feeling his warmth and sculpted muscles beneath my fingertips. Then it struck me that he might interpret it as a come-on.

I began to pull my hand back, but something inside me rebelled. Instead, I fought the urge to retreat and kept my hand in place, willing him to understand the sincerity of my words.

Meeting his eyes, I said, "No, I don't. I see the person you are now, and I believe in second chances. What's important is that we learn from our mistakes and strive to be better. It's how we grow and learn from those experiences that matter most."

As I spoke, a flicker of something shone in his eyes—surprise, perhaps, or gratitude. Hard to tell. But in that moment, there was a definite connection that transcended the awkwardness of our earlier interaction.

Levi's face lit up with a grin, and he placed his hand on top of mine. "You're something else, you know that?"

My breath hitched, and I tried so hard not to swoon. I couldn't suppress my dopey grin, though, even if I tried. This man was too much.

Levi continued, "Hey, listen, since we're going to be working together, how about we grab dinner tonight?"

My smile deflated like Aunt Tess's soufflé she always brought for Christmas dinner. Was that the brightest idea? I mean, we were working together.

I said, "Sure...but just so we're clear, this isn't romantic."

"Wouldn't dream of it. Enjoy lunch, babe." He winked and sauntered back to the microfiche area with the swagger of a cocky teenager, leaving me standing there to pick up my jaw from the floor.

CHAPTER ELEVEN

ABBY

THE AIR CARRIED the intoxicating aroma of garlic, onions, and fresh herbs. My stomach growled as we followed the host through the illuminated dining room of Sapori del Cucina. Thankfully, the soft murmur of conversation and the clinking of silverware against plates provided excellent cover. The stucco walls wore timeless fashions inspired by Italian vineyards.

A gaggle of she-wolves cast their hungry gazes at the handsome devil in the dark suit shadowing me. He was probably so used to the attention, it wouldn't have registered. Me on the other hand? My cheeks flamed and I wished I could've teleported back home. Anywhere but here.

Finally, we came to rest at a table for two by the window, offering a view of the gazebo lit up for the night in the Village Green.

The host placed our menus on the table before leaving.

Levi helped me out of my shawl and draped it on the back of my chair before taking his seat. His gaze lingered hungrily on the spaghetti straps of my blue polka dot dress before descending down my chest. Tearing his eyes away, he clenched the menu, his knuckles turning white.

Being treated like a queen felt downright fabulous. I could totally get used to all this fussing and fawning.

"Wow, this place oozes class. Even the dust bunnies are decked out in tuxedos," I quipped with a sassy grin. "Just saying, this is uncharted territory for me. Typically, when my parents visit, we frequent kid-friendly restaurants. Old habits die hard, I suppose."

Levi, a vision in a casual black suit and gray tie, said, "This place and me go way back. Spent my scrawnier days scrubbing dishes while nursing dreams of a future when I could bring someone special here. The grub ain't half bad either." His gaze skittered over my shoulder as though someone else had captured his interest. "Figured it would be a nice place to talk with minimal interruptions. I thought we should get to know each other better. Helps with work, you know?"

Work. Right.

I should've opted to wear something more sensible and not so low-cut to avoid broadcasting desperation. My insides twisted in anguish as the bitter cocktail of fear and insecurity churned up. All traces of confidence vanished, leaving me feeling like a popped balloon.

While we were out on dates, Monroe rarely locked eyes with me. Instead, he constantly scanned the room to gauge the interest of other women. It didn't matter how sexy I dressed. Maybe this "guy thing" existed beyond my grasp. Or maybe my eagerness backfired and came across as desperate.

I cleared my throat, snapping Levi's focus back to me. "What's up?"

In a heartbeat, Levi's eyes transformed from hawk to puppy. "Nothing," he murmured, barely audible over the ambient noise of the restaurant. "Just... old memories, I guess."

Old memories, or was he warring with demons? His simple explanation spoke volumes. Now I felt like a slug for turning this situation into a pity party, comparing Levi to Monroe while he dealt with his own challenges. A surge of protectiveness made me want to be the superhero that vanquished his emotional villains.

I swiveled in my seat to find a silver fox in a tailored charcoal suit, sitting at a table in the corner. His piercing gaze caught me off guard, sizing me up.

Why, though? I didn't know him from Adam. I returned my attention to Levi. "Want to talk about it? Does that guy over there play a role in your sudden mood change?"

"It's nothing, seriously," he said. "He's an old friend—well, more of an acquaintance, really. He owns this joint. Haven't laid eyes on him since I skipped town after grad. I bet he's racking his brain trying to place me."

Levi puffed out his cheeks and confessed, "He reminds me of the kid I once was."

Compassion washed over me in waves, and I pressed my lips together for that little boy—for the whole family, really. How strapped they must've been for that sensitive child to resort to those tactics.

"I understand. And that kid unsettles you, right?" Reaching out, I placed my palm on his hand, silently offering support.

"More like he reminds me of my parents and all the things I did to help bail them out financially," Levi said, his voice gruff. "Things I never fessed up to. Look, Abs, life got messy. I messed up, caused pain, and kept it bottled—so I didn't incriminate myself."

I squeezed his hands, and his answering sorrowful smile marred his handsome features. "Like I'd said before, we all have our demons. What truly counts is how we face them."

Levi's thumbs caressed my knuckles, shooting a charge through my body. His chocolate eyes widened, but he didn't sever contact. Instead, his grip only tightened.

We stayed locked in that moment, holding hands on our non-romantic date.

His eyebrows arched, and his gaze sparked with curiosity.

"Tell me about your parents, babe. You said they moved to Florida?"

I beamed at the mention of those two—my favorite people. "Yeah. They're retired. Dad spends his time fishing, and Mom works in an animal shelter. They make the obligatory visit once a year, during Christmas. Sometimes I reciprocate.

Let me tell you, witnessing Santa Claus donning a red tank top, red shorts, and a jingle bell is an experience like no other. Shocked the heck out of me during our trip to Busch Gardens. I couldn't help but feel pity for the poor guy. He must have been sweaty."

Levi's laughter erupted, setting off my own. His thumbs ignited another electric jolt through my body as they brushed against my wrists.

I pulled away, but his grip tightened, holding me in place. When would he return my hands, or did he intend to continue our hand-holding session throughout dinner?

The man in question winked, his voice dipping into a velvety purr that sent a delicious shiver down my spine. "Spill, sweetheart. What led you into the world of true crime? No offense, but you don't strike me as the type."

I arched my brow, infusing my voice with sass. "And why's that?"

A mischievous glint sparkled in his chocolate eyes as he leaned in closer, his lips curving into a playful grin. "Because you strike me as the kinda gal interested in gathering cookie recipes than postmortem reports," he teased, his eyes dancing with amusement.

A flush swept over my cheeks like a crimson tide, and my heart pounded with a heady mixture of excitement and defiance. Did he imply that my sheltered lifestyle shielded me from the ugly underbelly of life?

My eyelids lowered a notch, and a smirk danced upon my lips. "Listen here, Hotshot. You can be into baking cookies and interested in whodunits. The world's big enough for both."

Levi's laughter burst forth like a hearty bark, etching crinkles around his eyes, and prompting heads to swivel in our direction. Our antics and hand-holding probably painted a picture of undeniable love to our onlookers.

But my date ignored them, with his gaze fully trained on me and his grip gently tightening around my hands.

"Seriously, baby," he said. "Where did it develop?"

The memory came flooding back, and it brought a smile to my face. "As a kid, my dad watched Unsolved Mysteries. Afraid it would give me nightmares, he'd shooed me off to bed. So, I snuck back down, sat on the stairs, and watched it through the rails."

Levi arched a brow. "You sly little fox. Didn't that show give you nightmares? I can't stomach those kinds of stories. Even a seasoned sinner like me has his limits."

"Initially, yes," I confessed. "It didn't take long to become hooked, devouring every grain of information to assemble clues like a puzzle solver. It became a clandestine obsession. You know, I missed the boat on career choices. Should've become a detective."

"I have full faith you'd solve the crime spree faster than Stone." He winced. "Sorry, baby. Meant no insult to your family."

I reassured him by squeezing his hand, signaling that I wasn't offended. "No problem. I get it. I don't understand why he hasn't solved it yet. Maybe with you on the case—"

Crap.

Regret washed over me in an instant. Levi wasn't actively working the case—unless you counted slogging through grunt work for the department as "working."

Switching gears, I swiftly redirected the conversation, diving into the first purchase that popped into my mind. "Anyway," I said, forcing a smile. "Have you visited your Uncle Al lately?"

Levi's brow furrowed, forming deep lines across his forehead. "Haven't seen nor spoken to him after he turned rogue."

Despite the unsavory topic, Levi still hadn't let go of my hand.

At this point, I couldn't lie to myself that he didn't have romantic feelings towards me, as absurd as that may be. This amount of hand-holding wasn't natural among friends.

"I haven't seen him around town either, not that I frequent the outskirts." I straightened up and leaned in, giddy about my bright idea. "Hey, do you think we should go talk to him?"

"Who, Al?" Levi asked.

Honestly, his reaction puzzled me to no end, but I pressed on because family formed the bedrock of life. "Why not? He's your uncle. You haven't seen each other in a while. Let him know you're back in town."

Levi gawked at me as though I'd sported two heads. "We're talking about Al here?"

My hopes sank like a ship taking on water, and I conceded defeat as disappointment saturated my mood. We don't share family values, and that didn't sit right with me.

"So, I guess that's a 'no,' then," I muttered despondently.

I pried my fingers from his grasp and curled them into my chest, seeking solace in its warmth.

Levi's attention drifted to the crystal goblet, his fingers curling around its clear stem. The liquid reflected a kaleidoscope of colors onto his serious face.

After he returned the goblet to its place on the table, he said, "No, it's not, Abs. I haven't thought of him in ages."

I kneaded the taut muscles in my neck, attempting to loosen the knot that had formed between my shoulder blades. "Is there more to the story? Why did Al move out there, anyway?"

Levi unraveled the fork and knife from the napkin with measured precision and held them up to the light, examining them as though watermarks suddenly became important to him. "He worked for the government as a code breaker. After a while, he spiraled into paranoia, convinced that the government was out to get him. He packed his bags and vanished from town. We'd all written him off as looney."

Something set off my radar, but I couldn't place what exactly. Either Levi was intentionally withholding the juicier bits of this story, or he was genuinely unaware of the entire truth.

My "I see," came out more tersely than I'd intended.

In a one-eighty, Levi said, "No harm in visiting him. Haven't laid eyes on him in years, so I doubt he'll remember me. Aunt Clara and I took off without telling him so it might be good for him to know family is in arm's reach."

Pressuring Levi into something he obviously didn't want to do would be like kicking a puppy, and my conscience would've chewed me out for that one. "Are you sure?" I asked.

"Yeah, babe," he smiled, his warmth returning, much to my relief. "Thanks for asking. No one ever asked if I was okay with anything. Means a lot."

I winked at him and said, "Even Iron Man needs checking in on."

The server came by to take our order.

CHAPTER TWELVE

ABBY

PICTURE AN OVERGROWN LOT. On it, a home on wheels that was one part UFO and one part farm. Satellite dishes sprouted from the rooftop of Uncle Al's Winnebago, eavesdropping on alien chit-chat while a large field of purple grew out back.

The crunch of gravel ceased as Levi parked his car on the opposite side of the road.

Absorbing every peculiar detail of our surroundings, I asked, "Are you sure we've got the right place?"

I hoped he'd be like, "Nah, wrong house," and speed away.

But no such luck.

"Yeah," Levi answered, opened the car door, and vacated the vehicle. I followed suit. Levi waited for me to join him.

We stepped out into the dry air, greeted by the scent of a fragrant aunt, courtesy of Uncle Al's lavender garden.

"My old man brought me here back in the day. Uncle Al gave me candy and comics," Levi began. "Let's say, Pops wasn't too thrilled I'd taken it. He acted like they were laced with poison, and once we got home, he trashed them."

His words struck my sympathy chord. The disappointment

young Levi must have felt at having familial gifts snatched away by his overprotective father—poor kid.

I laid a hand on his arm. "Sounds rough. I'm sorry."

Levi's eyes flickered with a hint of sadness as he brushed his fingertips along my hand. His black tee hugged his toned frame, its faded skull emblem eerily fitting in with our surroundings.

"It's all right," he said, and winked, as if attempting to shrug off the memory.

Dread gnawed at my insides like a rabid dog as we neared the Winnebago. "Would he mind us dropping in? What if he doesn't want to talk to us?"

"Then we'll wish him peace out and dip," he said with a nonchalant shrug, his fingers vanishing into the depths of his black jeans' pockets.

"But I doubt it'll go down like that. From what I remember, he seemed alright. Cray-cray, but alright."

The slam of something in the distance snapped my attention to the Winnebago.

Out of nowhere, a shrill alarm pierced the stillness, vibrating in my skull like a swarm of angry bees.

Frozen in our tracks, Levi and I shot our hands up, desperately trying to block out the sonic onslaught by clamping our ears.

A gruff voice boomed through a loudspeaker. "My gun's aimed at you. What do you want?"

What the—

Did he just say, "gun?"

What did we just walk into?!

Levi's voice, laced with urgency, cut through the ruckus. "Uncle Al, it's me, Levi," he said, hesitating. "Tod's boy."

How Al heard him, I couldn't explain. A miraculous feat over the noise.

Al responded, "Prove it. You could've looked that up."

Levi shot back, "Visited you with Dad once. You gave me a

Superman comic book and Jolly Ranchers. Said the blue raspberries were your favorite."

The alarm fell silent, and the bees eased off.

Al's voice sounded over the speaker. "Who's the woman?"

Levi glanced at me but addressed his uncle. "My friend, Abigail Martin. Her uncle is Sheriff Stone."

For some ridiculous reason, I needed to set the record straight.

"I'm his God niece, not his biological one," I called out. "You might remember my dad, Chet Martin."

"The fisherman's kid? Well, I'll be damned."

The speaker erupted with the wild laughter of a mad scientist, giving me the creeps and making me want to book it the hell out of there.

But before I could act on my primal instinct, the metal door swung open. A grizzled old man emerged from the dimly lit interior, his unkempt dirty gray hair and weathered face told tales of a hard life. He was clad in a stained set of yellow overalls that had seen better days, and a faded denim shirt hung loosely on his wiry frame. His pockets bulged with garden tools. One gnarly hand clung to a jar of peanut butter and jelly, while the other waved us inside.

In an instant, curiosity replaced my fear, anchoring me to the spot. I reverted to my twelve-year-old self, eyes glued to the TV screen, captivated by my unauthorized show.

"Come in," Al said, his voice heavy with cantankerism.

Levi climbed the steps, and I trailed behind.

Books, newspapers, and other assorted junk were tucked in every nook and cranny of the already cramped interior. A person needed to duck and dive to maneuver its tight quarters. The musty scent of old paper permeated the thick air. My years working at the library didn't prepare me for this.

The mold might have something to do with it.

Despite all of that, a strange comfort settled over me. The

chaos created a haven of sorts, and I understood its appeal to a man like Al.

The older man settled into a small booth pushed up against the wall, and we stationed ourselves across from him. He edged out Levi in height, surpassing him by half a head. Both possessed a slender build, suggesting a shared genetic component. Their facial features were a toss-up. Levi's face bore a sculpted, slightly rugged appearance, while Al's sagging skin made it challenging to visualize how he would have looked if he had embraced a more indoor lifestyle.

Al began. "Levi? What are you doing here? Last I heard, you took off after they offed Tod and Marley. Smart move, boy," he growled.

The word "offed" brought my mind to a screeching halt. My brows shot up as I turned to Levi for answers. His expression stayed blank, and his gaze remained locked on Al's, as if those words had no effect.

As far as I knew, a tragic car accident had claimed the lives of his parents, yet Al clearly implied that someone murdered them.

Then I felt it—Levi's feet hooking around mine under the table. A discreet version of hand-holding.

Wanting to alleviate his discomfort, I willingly surrendered my leg, all of this passing unbeknownst to Al.

Levi said, "We're here to talk to you."

Al crossed his arms over his broad chest, his eyes hardened to steel beneath his gray bushman's brows. "About what?"

"There have been some break-ins in town, and Sheriff Stone can't solve them, so he hired me," Levi explained.

The older man's laughter burst out of him like a deranged hyena, brimming with energy. I gritted my teeth, enduring the jarring sound.

What was so amusing about the break-ins? It wasn't the slightest bit funny. Not to be rude, but it clicked why Tod chucked Levi's candy. I would've done the same.

"Wait a minute," Al said with a dying smile. "You're telling me that cock-sure bastard can't solve a crime?"

Levi refrained from joining in on the hilarity, keeping his face a mask of indifference. "Seriously," he said in a sobering tone. "He can't. That's why he hired me to help."

Al's eyes bounced from me to Levi, softening from steel to butter. "What's the real story here?"

I didn't know Al well enough to gauge, but his inquiry sounded like the kind a father might pose to his daughter regarding her relationship status.

Levi hesitated, a brief glitch in his energy, then recovered with a serious tone. "About the break-ins? Not sure. That's why I'm here talking to you."

My gut flipped and flopped, leaving me queasy. It brought back memories of the morning when Rachel proposed they meet up again, and he went radio silent.

But unlike her, I wasn't going to push him for more. My dignity meant something.

I yanked my foot free from Levi's hold without protest from him—thank goodness—avoiding what would have been an awkward situation if he didn't release it.

"I'm the wrong person to ask, son." Al leaned in and lowered his voice as he spoke. "You know my take. Said it before and I'll say it again. Can't trust anyone connected to the government. Stay on guard and don't buy into any malarkey they're feedin' ya."

With my chin propped on my hand and brows furrowed, I tried to make heads or tails of his cryptic words.

Levi said, "I get it. So, how are you holding up?"

Al settled back in his chair, his gaze drifting to the vastness beyond the window. "Simple life, wouldn't have it any other way. Off the grid ain't for everybody, but it's the only one for me. Turned me into a farmer. Grow most of what I need right here."

He turned his attention back to the table, a smile crinkling the corners of his eyes. "Every now and then, I venture into town to buy meats. But not much. I harvest lavender, distill the hydrosol, and sell it. That reminds me, are you two hungry? Got some bread. Lemme whip up some peanut butter and jelly sandwiches."

Oh geez, no!

I sat up straighter. "Ah, no thanks."

Levi grinned. "Dad used to talk about your peanut butter and jelly sandwiches all the time."

Al's face took on a reminiscent quality. "Used to make 'em for your dad and Clara after they came home from school. Those were the days before peanut allergies. I blame the government taking revenge on Jimmy Carter by poisoning his peanut crop."

Oye.

When Al's conversation veered into the treacherous terrain of politics, I leaped to my feet, mentally waving the white flag of surrender. Reasoning with a man who blamed Jimmy Carter's farm for the rise of widespread peanut allergies was a fool's errand.

"Thanks for allowing us inside your home, Mr. Cross. Nice meeting you," I said.

Levi stood up, allowing me to shuffle out of the booth.

"It's good to see Chet's kid grow into a fine young woman. Pleasure meeting you, Abigail. Pass on my regards to your pops."

Al said, "Ah, Levi, now that you're here, I need to have a word with you in private."

Politely excusing myself, I left the Winnebago and sought refuge in Levi's car.

Some minutes later, while scrolling through Facebook, my mind replayed the bizarre encounter. The eccentricities of Uncle Al, the alarming mention of Levi's parents being "offed," and the unsettling laughter all painted a picture that left me questioning the wisdom of this visit.

Five minutes later, the door creaked open, and Levi effortlessly slid into the driver's seat.

"Everything okay?" I asked. "What was all that about?"
"Family stuff," he answered.
Hmm, curious way of saying, "none of your business."

CHAPTER THIRTEEN

LEVI

IN THE LIBRARY'S cozy nook, I skimmed the newspaper article dominating the financial section—rising insurance premiums due to the break-ins.

I wonder, did my wild days cast the same shadow over the community? Back then, I did what I had to do, consequences be damned. With a deep exhale, I flipped to the next page.

My thoughts circled back to Abby. That unsettling, quiet vibe she had when I dropped her off last night really got under my skin.

I suspected that our visit to Uncle Al was the cause of her quietude. After that, she wasn't a fan, but her politeness restrained her from admitting to it, especially considering her spiel about family during our date.

To heighten my annoyance, a group of chatty moms gathered nearby, dissecting a reality show with the insight of Vegas' main event commentators.

Mom #1 said, "He shouldn't have given her the rose. He can't even see that she's playing him. So sad."

Mom #2 responded, "Unless the whole thing is a setup, and he sees it. They tried that last season."

Mom #3 exclaimed, "OMG. Wasn't that fabulous?!"

I rolled my eyes so hard I could've sprained them. Time to check on the foxy librarian.

Hoisting myself out of the armchair, I strode over to the circulation desk. Abby immersed herself in reading her screen and jotting down notes in a book.

She spared me a fleeting glance before returning to her task and casually inquired, "Making headway with the articles?"

Her coolness bugged the hell out of me. I rested my arms on the circulation desk, leaned in, and went for nonchalance. "Other than the riveting tales of the skyrocketing cost of insurance, nothing much."

A patron set her book stack on the counter for Abby to check out while she rooted around in her bag. She lamented, "No kidding. I usually fly out to visit my sister in Altoona for Thanksgiving, but with my premium so high, I might forgo that trip this year."

Abby lifted a sympathetic brow while scanning the lady's books. "I'm so sorry to hear that. Times are growing difficult."

Because I was sitting there in the library instead of doing fieldwork, frustrated as all hell, but this lady needed help.

I asked the patron, "Have you tried installing bolts on your doors? It's a cheap and easy way to make your home more secure. No one will be able to pick your locks."

The patron's lashes fluttered away. "I never considered that. Thanks for the suggestion."

A subtle smile spread across Abby's face. "We have a comprehensive guide to home security in the non-fiction section. I can show you where it is next time you come back."

With a swift motion, she stowed the receipt inside the book's cover and shoved the stack to the patron.

The lady thanked Abs, clutched her literature, bid us farewell, and took off.

I studied Abby's stoic marble facade. She deadlocked her

gaze on the screen, mirroring the same detachment she had displayed the first time I apologized. I gathered my words, ready to broach the conversation, but as luck would have it, Kaminsky strode up to the desk, ruining the moment.

My arms tensed, preventing the instinctual urge to fly out in a gesture of exasperation. Opting for the less offensive route, I stuffed them in my pockets.

The ever-friendly Doug greeted us.

Abby's smile brightened towards her friend, warming her demeanor a degree. "Hey, Doug? How's your mom holding up?"

Doug's sturdy shoulders drooped slightly, yet he maintained a steady tone. "Better since Peg has been keeping her company."

Peg? Who's—Oh right, Stone's wife.

Abby's grin widened, her pale blue eyes sparkling. "That's good. During our last club meeting, she mentioned that she'd check in on her. How are you holding up?"

Was it wrong of me to feel put out that Doug elicited smiles and sparkles in Abby, while all I got was a cold shoulder and curt replies?

Okay, I'll admit to giving her a reason to feel that way, but damn, it stung.

Doug's next words pierced through my haze of self-absorption, dragging me back into the harsh realities of his world.

"I won't bail on Shane," he said. "Sheriff Stone told Mom years ago that missing children usually end up dead, but I don't buy that. I can't shake the feeling that he's still alive. The jacked-up part was my editor refused to let me run the story, saying I can't use the paper as a platform to air out my family problems. So that leaves me pulling double-duty investigating the robberies and hunting down leads to find Shane."

My brows furrowed, and I asked, "Shane?"

Doug explained, "My missing older brother, kidnapped at a mall while Mom was pregnant with me."

That revelation gut-punched me, dropped my mouth open, and robbed me of speech.

Fuck.

I mean—

That was...fucked up on every level. I didn't even know where to begin.

Abby's face twisted into a mask of anguish. She glanced at me, holding contact this time. We both found ourselves at a loss.

I shook off my stupor. Outraged on Doug's behalf, I asked, "And your boss called it family problems? Damn, that's cold. I don't even know what to say to that. Best of luck finding your brother, man."

"Thanks," he rasped.

If I found myself in Doug's shoes, I would quit. Okay, I would be in the slammer after landing a right hook to his boss's jaw. Still, there's no way I would work for someone who would make such a heartless remark about my missing brother.

Far be it from me to tell another man to quit his job, though. Doug's admirable dedication to his work suggests it had to be his true calling, 'cause most folks wouldn't put up with that mess for a job.

Eager to offer help in any way possible, I said, "About the robberies, you could write about the rising cost of insurance. That's where all the buzz seems to be."

Abby put in, "Agreed. A lady just talked about changing Thanksgiving plans because rising premiums made plane tickets unaffordable for her."

Doug said, "Already on it. Found some interesting leads."

I quipped, "Detective Kaminsky on the case. Ever considered moonlighting for the police department? They could use your skills."

Doug chuckled, amusement dancing in his tired amber eyes.

My pocket vibrated. I snatched my phone and read the text notification from Stone.

Stone: Come to the station, quick.

Frowning, I announced, "Sorry, guys, duty calls. Boss's ears must've been burning because he wants to see me."

I rapped on the circulation desk. "Abs, hold down the fort while I'm out. Be back later."

Shooting her a wink, I strode out of the library.

Stepping into Stone's office, I caught sight of Casey, his posture commanding—legs spread wide, and arms confidently crossed.

What the heck is going on?

I positioned myself in front of the desk, while trying to read the room.

Stone stood up, circled around us, and closed the door. "Appreciate both of you answering the call immediately. Levi, I've been receiving some complaints."

About what?

I furrowed my brows at Stone and shot Casey a side-eye. "Enlighten me, sir. What complaints?"

Casey feigned innocence, as though he didn't have anything to do with this.

Stone blew a breath laden with fatigue. "Look, y'all are grown-ass men. Bury the hatchet and stop behaving like three-year-olds because I don't need discord on my team."

"I don't understand, sir," I said, trying to keep my voice steady. "How am I supposed to deal with people talking smack about me? It's out of my control."

Stone dodged my question, providing no insight whatsoever. "Sort this out. Grab a beer," he rumbled. "Do something."

To make matters worse, Casey's hand landed on my shoulder. "Don't worry, sir. We've got this."

Steam practically shot out of my ears, and I would've knocked the smugness off of him—if I could reach.

Redwooded bastard.

Swallowing back my cuss, I forced out the words. "Yeah, we're good."

I couldn't say for certain if Stone bought my agreement to play nice. Most likely, he wanted to address the issue and have done with it.

He responded, "Alright then. Now, go on your way. I still got some paperwork to see to."

Suddenly, a uniformed officer pushed open the door. "Sir, outside, we got an emergency."

The officers jetted out of the room, and I trailed them.

A grizzled man, his salt-and-pepper hair hinting that shaving was his least favorite pastime, stood by the front. Worry lines creased his forehead. His faded flannel shirt, with sleeves rolled up to his elbows, revealed tanned forearms, suggesting he worked outdoors.

Casey immediately greeted the man.

The man said, "I was over by the old mill, and I reckon I found the stash where they'd been hoardin' loot from them recent heists."

Stone asked, "At the mill. You sure about that?"

The guy answered, "Swear on my life, officer. The stuff didn't look old. It's like a load of household junk that don't fit the age of that place."

Stone narrowed his eyes. "What exactly were you doing at the old mill?"

Shifting, the man hesitated before responding, his voice carrying a hint of guilt. "Honest, Sheriff, times were tough. I was just tryin' to scrape together anything worth a buck, for some quick cash. I caught wind about the old mill holding hidden treasures, so I decided to check it out. But what I stumbled on... didn't expect it. I swear!"

"Easy. Easy. I wasn't accusing you." Stone softened his tone.

"You did well coming in and letting us know. We'll take it from here."

The man exhaled a sigh of relief and thanked us before leaving the station.

Stone turned to us. "Alright, boys, move out."

Sensing an opportunity to finally participate in the investigation, I raised a steadying hand. "Before we jump the gun, I have an idea on how we might catch 'em."

CHAPTER FOURTEEN

LEVI

WITH THE CLOSING of the day, the sun dipped behind the cloud cover, casting a warm orange glow across Millbrook as we approached some old train tracks.

The old mill's silhouette loomed in the distance.

Stone and Casey claimed the front seats of the police cruiser, leaving me in the back to fiddle with the drone, preparing it for use.

"You got a plan on how to use that thing?" Casey's skepticism sliced through my concentration as I studied the diagrams in the drone's instruction manual. "I'm curious to hear it because that thing isn't exactly discreet. You can't just fly in hot."

"Sure thing," I replied, my thumbs rolling the joystick control as I read the diagrams.

This critical moment in our pursuit of the case fueled my resolve to not let my lack of knowledge be the weak link. Trust me, it's not just the tech geek in me talking—I seriously think our shot at nabbing these crooks hinges on staying low-key.

Stone's contemptuous glare seized mine in the rearview mirror while he grumbled behind the wheel.

I squarely met his stare, narrowing my eyes at him, refusing to back down—not a damn inch.

My drone pitch at the station made the boss man blow a gasket. His preference for old-school grit made him dismiss my idea as "kid-foolery."

From where I stood, his tried-and-true methods yielded nothing. Deploying different tools could change their luck, given that they have exhausted traditional methods.

So yeah, that suggestion landed like a lead balloon at a hot-air balloon fiesta.

And Casey, well, he blew me away when he stepped into the role of peacekeeper between Stone and me.

How's that for a turnaround?

I had expected him to wear a shit-eating grin while I chased after Stone after he stormed out of the room, but he didn't.

Surprise, surprise.

"You ready?" Casey asked.

"Let's do this," I replied firmly.

We exited the cruiser. The men slammed their doors and approached me while I carefully extracted the drone from the back seat.

Stone radiated unease as his hawk-eyes swept our surroundings. He was out of his comfort zone, and it showed in the clenching of his jaw and the fists balled at his hip. But I had to give him props. He kept his cool despite it.

I'll tell you one thing; this game plan better deliver, or I'll stare down the barrel of unemployment yet again.

With a tap of the power button, the drone's motor buzzed in my hand. I set it on the ground, some distance in front of us, and then turned on the controller. As it lifted skyward, the live feed of the drone's camera appeared on the controller's screen.

A thrill of anticipation shot through me, and I fought the urge to jump up and down like a kid again. But I checked that impulse.

The lawmen flanked me, craning their necks into my personal space to view the screen.

As the drone closed in on the mill, the setting sun cast an

eerie glow over the dilapidated structure, transforming it into an almost haunted presence in the fading light.

Wicked cool, if you asked me. The younger me and my friends would've gathered here to play TIE fighters.

"Alright, old girl, let's see what secrets you're hiding," Stone muttered as the drone hovered closer, its camera panning across the area.

I maneuvered the drone around the perimeter, carefully noting any potential hiding spots.

"Fly it over the back entrance," Stone directed, his voice picking up with excitement. "It's farther from the road and makes a better access point."

"Good thinking, sir," Casey said, kissing up to Stone.

Working independently allowed me to avoid stooping to playing those games. I would've shot Casey a hard side-eye if I didn't need to keep my eyes glued to the screen.

Executing Stone's orders, I readjusted the drone's position to focus on the rear entrance. When the camera zoomed in, I noticed an oddity: a smudge of paint on the doorframe, as if someone had accidentally brushed up against it.

"Looks like we've got something," Casey murmured.

I squinted at the screen, adjusting the drone's camera angle to sharpen the focus on the door.

"Come on, bud," I coaxed the drone as it hovered silently above the mill's back entrance. "Give us an inside peek."

Responding as if it heard me, the camera feed flickered for a moment before revealing a shadowy figure heading toward the mill.

The men beside me snapped to attention.

Instinct kicked in. My thumbs urgently manipulated the controls, trying to bring the figure into focus.

The figure donned a hoodie, gloves, and carried a bag—attire I knew well.

My finger pushed the joystick to its limits as I tried my damnedest to zoom in for a closer look, but the distance prevented a clear identification. The dying light didn't help any, either.

As much as I would have loved to swoop in and tackle that man to the ground, wisdom prevailed.

Stone, on the other hand, was a hair-trigger away from launching into a sprint. He ordered, "Keep eyes on him and see where he goes."

The figure slipped inside the mill through the rear entrance.

My curiosity burned like jet fuel. I couldn't imagine what Stone or Casey might be wrestling with right now.

Stone said, "Alright. Retreat. That's as much intel as we're gonna get."

He called the shots.

A heavy dose of letdown weighed on my chest as I piloted the drone back to us.

CHAPTER FIFTEEN

LEVI

LATER THAT NIGHT, the frosty bottle of beer chilled my palm as I sauntered away from the bar to join the guys at a table tucked in the corner. I gulped down a hearty swig of the bitter-sweet liquid, craving temporary respite from the day's drama.

I kept my relationship with alcohol in check, opting to toss one back every now and then, but too much of a good thing led to trouble. Dad's sage advice echoed in my ears, even after he'd been gone for so long. His struggle with the bottle had cost him jobs and, ultimately, led to the car accident that robbed me of my parents.

Needless to say, I steered clear of that destructive path.

And chose another.

Dad's led to my parents' demise, while mine would land me in a jail cell.

Funny how life worked out.

The joint buzzed with energy, courtesy of raucous game night patrons hooting and hollering like wild beasts. Games were never my cup of tea... or rather, bottle of beer.

Casey chose this place. I gathered he wanted something to watch in case our attempt to bury the hatchet went sideways. I invited Doug to join us because he needed a distraction from his obsessive search for his brother.

Doug's long brown hair was tied back in a ponytail. He said, "Levi, you need to talk to your girl to convince Lex to go to that book fair, or else Deeds won't stop talking about it. Apparently, she was all in until she learned that Oli would be there."

A couple things threw me off, but I zeroed in on the most crucial one. "My girl? Bro, what are you getting at?"

Casey, who sported civilian clothes, comprising of blue jeans and a black t-shirt, scoffed. "Oh, come on, man. Don't play dumb. Word is you and the librarian are seeing each other."

Word is?

Don't tell me we're water cooler talk already.

My eyes ping-ponged between these two nut jobs.

"I assure you, we're not an item. Abby is just a friend. She likes it that way." I replied calmly, hoping to squash that rumor before it circled back to Abs, potentially bruising her feelings in the process.

Doug shot Casey a dubious glance before returning to me.

It pissed me off, so I pointed out the obvious. "Honest. Why would I bother lying? I'm a grown-ass man. If I want to see someone, I would."

"Alright, if you say so," Doug said, then he changed the subject—sort of.

"She's a firecracker, anyway," he continued. "You'd have your hands full." He caught his slip, turned red when he realized what he said, and raised his bottle to his lips to conceal it.

No lies detected. What I wouldn't give to cup her masterpiece of an ass.

Damn it! Did it again. My mind battled against itself for the umpteenth time. I need to stop fixating on her. To sate my thirst for her, I took a swig of beer.

"Abby's cool. I like her, but we're working together, so..." I clarified with a shrug and tackled my other issue. "Now, what's this about Oli? You mentioned he's showing up? How did you find out?"

Doug responded, "Through the paper. We're covering the event. Anyway, turns out he wrote a book about his P.I. adventures, and he's promoting it at the fair."

I blinked, trying to register his words. All those years, I believed Oli had died. Even shed a few tears for him.

And here he stood, not just alive but knee-deep in police work.

Casey chimed in, "Who's Oli?"

"My friend from high school," I explained to Casey. "He disappeared not long after we graduated. Hadn't heard from him since."

Casey's ginger brows pulled together. "What, did you two have a fight or something?"

"Naw, nothing like that," I said casually, careful not to say anything too incriminating.

This moment struck on why I avoided forming friendships with men in uniform. Constantly monitoring my words is headache inducing.

"After grad, everyone scattered," I said. "I hightailed it to the city, so we lost touch."

Casey nodded, satisfied by my vague explanation. He returned his eyes to the TV screen.

Doug and I shared a quick glance, and I could practically hear the gears turning in his head as he pieced together the puzzle. I rolled my eyes, and he dropped it.

"So, how's the investigation going?" he asked.

Recalling the day's drama, my spirits nosedived into a pit of anxiety. "Stone's climbing the wall. He needs answers soon."

I gulped down a pull.

Doug pressed his lips into a firm line, likely from disappointment that I hadn't divulged details about the case.

"Yeah, I can imagine," he said. "Hopefully, you'll uncover some solid leads soon."

I grinned. Can't fault him for trying.

Casey scratched the side of his face, his attention returning to us.

"I've been meticulously going through the evidence," he said, "but honestly, there's nothing concrete so far. It's like these break-ins are happening without leaving a single trace."

Without a trace?

My lips tightened, and I sipped.

Was he at Jane's, or did I imagine him there? Because, bro denied the existence of any shred of evidence amidst that mess. Who was he foolin'?

Doug crossed his arms.

Without even looking at him, I could sense he felt the same. My fingers dug into the label, peeling away the edge.

Casey's and Doug's attention drew to the door.

My gaze followed theirs and snagged on a voluptuous redhead, Doug's girl, and a dark-haired woman who stirred a flicker of recognition, all ambling towards the bar.

Wait.

Isn't that—

Waving his beefy arm, Doug caught his woman's eyes. She smiled at him and whispered to her crew.

Abby's gorgeous, pale blue eyes honed in on me. I offered her a playful wink, and she gifted me with a bashful smile in return. This woman had no clue what a knockout she was.

And I desperately needed to show her. But we work together. I'll tell you one thing—I'm itching to wrap up this case and be on the lookout for another job. Maybe then, Abby'll entertain the notion of seeing me.

My attention shifted to the familiar woman standing beside her.

Lexy Edwards maintained her worried expression. She resembled a cornered animal, ready to bolt when our eyes met.

I pressed my lips together, guilt seeping into me for upping and leaving without a word. I should've handled things differently back then. As a dumb kid, my focus was solely on saving my own hide rather than extending a helping hand.

The women gathered their drinks and joined us.

Doug and I sprang into action, liberating unoccupied seats from fellow patrons after seeking their permission and expanding our table's capacity. My hand reached out to find Abby's delicate fingers and interlaced with them.

"Well, look who decided to grace us with her presence," I said.

With a gentle tug, I guided her towards the vacant chair beside me. Delilah settled beside her man, and Lex claimed the seat beside Casey. She set her drink down, and her weary blue eyes met mine before quickly averting them. She couldn't be that way all night.

We needed to hash this out.

"Lex," I said, then motioned my head towards the door. "Talk to me outside for a sec."

Lex nodded, the skin on the ridge of her nose bunched up like she smelled something foul.

After planting a kiss on Abby's hand, I said, "Back in a jiff, babe. Save my seat." With a reassuring wink, hoping it conveyed that my chat with her friend—formerly mine too—was strictly platonic.

Rising, I led Lex outside into the warm summer night. The door swung shut behind us, muffling the cheers and chatter of the bar.

Lex wrapped her arms around herself, despite having no reason to be cold.

I broke the ice. "Long time no see. How've you been?"

Glancing down at her scuffed white flats, she brushed a few strands of her black ponytail away from her cheek.

"Getting by," she said and used the toe of her shoe to paint invisible designs in the ground. A pause hung in the air, heavy with unspoken words, then she asked, "You?"

"Got a job working for Stone," I deadpanned.

Lex's eyes met mine, her lips curved into a grin that swiftly swept across her face like wildfire, culminating in a burst of laughter. It was so contagious, I couldn't help but join in.

Yeah, me working for the police was ludicrous. Just like Oli becoming a P.I.

I mean—what the hell was this world coming to?

I said, "I take it you're still pissed that we left town."

Lex seized up. "Not pissed. Just hurt. Okay... pissed too, if you want the truth. You two left without a word." She shook her head. "I could see why you did. You were always a lost soul, even while your parents were alive. After they died, you took it really hard. But Oli? I don't understand that. It was cold."

I rubbed the back of my neck, loosening my corded muscles and said, "I get you. All I could tell was something went down the night we pulled off that last job for Enzo. He must've had some side deal going that I didn't know about."

Lexy's eyes widened. "So you don't know where he went, either?"

Ah, now I get it.

The realization struck like a thunderbolt. Her question, her reaction, it all made sense now. She assumed I knew of Oli's whereabouts but withheld that info from her.

I softened. "No, babe. Promise I don't. When I left, I made connections with some guys in Brooklyn, and they found me work. Eventually, I branched out on my own and partnered with one of the other underlings to form an agency that specialized in—"

The cameras mounted over the entrance gave me pause. "You know," I finished vaguely.

Lexy nodded. To her credit, she refrained from prying further because she knew me well enough to understand my meaning.

"So," I began. "Heard Oli's coming back. You planning on seeing him?"

Her eyes widened with disbelief. "Not you too. I don't wanna lay eyes on him. He took off, not even bothering to give me a heads up about his exit. Why should I give him the time of day now when he didn't return the favor back then?"

"Babe. Maybe it's time you two hash this out. Get some closure. No pressure. Just think about it."

Lexy glanced at the door of the bar, then back at me. "Fine. I'll think about it."

Bullshit.

She threw that out to get me off her back. But I wouldn't push it further. Instead, I opened my arms to her.

Lex flashed a warm grin and wrapped her arms around my waist.

I quipped, "You got shorter. What the hell happened?"

She needled my side. "You shot up after high school, moron. Quit rubbing it in."

I cracked up and slung an arm around her shoulders. "Lets go back inside."

We returned to our table, and Abby's questioning eyes moved from me to Lex. When her expression fell, I fought the instinct to shove Lex away.

Settling beside Abs, I contemplated taking her outside to talk, but that notion was promptly squashed when Abby's gaze drifted towards the bar's entrance, her expressive eyes widening in a mix of fear and recognition.

I swiveled in my seat and spotted Abby's ex swaggering towards the bar, his arm draped around a woman with wavy brown hair. He reeked of entitlement like cheap cologne.

CHAPTER SIXTEEN

ABBY

TROUBLE ON TWO LEGS, also known as Monroe, advanced toward our table with sights locked on me like a heat-seeking missile. His hunched posture showcased his well-earned beer gut, enhancing that trollish charm. And then there was the hair. Good Lord, the hair. It was slicked back and glued to his skull, revealing recently installed plugs.

Wasn't the point of those things discretion and not to be a neon sign screaming, "Hairline? What hairline?"

Despite his ridiculous visage, my spine clicked upright like a flagpole, and I braced myself for his verbal impact. No doubt he'd unleash grade-A mortification.

Lexy's reassuring words came from behind me. "Deep breath, Abs. We've got your back."

She ranked low on the list of people who could fortify my resolve at the moment. Her chummy embrace with Levi still sat heavily in my stomach.

Monroe's narrowed eyes shifted to Levi before returning to me. "Abby! Imagine running into you here with your new man!" he said in a mocking tone.

Mustering up my conviction, I shot back, "This is none of

your business. We're no longer together. Please, go back to your date and leave us be."

"Not together?" he had the gall to say, "You moved on so quickly? How could you?" sounding like a victim.

I made a point to glance at his date, who stood at the bar looking like a deer in headlights, before returning my attention back to Monroe.

"What's with the drama? Abby has moved on. She has the right to, just as you clearly have," Levi stated, his words cutting through the tension like a sharpened blade.

Fuming, Monroe's eyes flashed with anger as he was called out on his hypocrisy.

I recognized that face all too well. I called him out constantly.

He hated looking like a fool. Odd when you think about it, because he had a knack for acting like one.

"Do I look like I need pearls of wisdom from her rebound? If I need your opinion, I'll ask for it!" Monroe said.

A wise-ass smirk graced Levi's lips. "I'm her personal life coach, teaching Abby how to go from dial-up to fiber optic."

His words slapped me in the face, and I sucked in a breath.

Life coach? What the hell was a life coach?

I thought we were more. Was that why he asked me out to the restaurant? He wanted to give me pointers on how to improve my life?

My gaze dropped to the buttons on Monroe's lavender shirt. Humiliating tears pricked my eyes, threatening to spill over. Why did those words hurt?

They shouldn't. I mean, we were friends. Being a glutton for punishment, I chanced a peek at his date again. You would've figured with her doll-like beauty, she could have snagged any man in the room, even Levi, if I were being honest.

I—

I wasn't so blessed in the figure department. Looks-wise, I landed squarely in the realm of "meh." Daily, I dolled up my face with makeup and tamed my hair into a semblance of presentabil-ity. But I'd never be considered a knockout by any standards. So I settled for this troll because no one else noticed my bait.

And evidently, Levi was my friend, which translated to him not being interested either.

My spirits sank like the anchor of a docked ship, and my throat tightened. Suddenly, the urge to be anywhere but here—the lady's room, preferably—hit hard.

Lexy drove us here, leaving me stranded without a getaway car. This conversation needed to stop before I started bawling.

While steadying my shaky voice, I said, "Monroe, I get it. Watching me move on stings, but let's face it: our relationship wasn't working. It's time for you to leave."

He wanted to have his cake and eat it too, to have flings while I pined away for him in the wings. Now that he suspects I'm with someone else, he's disgruntled because he lost his fall-back girl.

Cringe.

Settling for Mr. Wrong opened the doorway to being tram-pled on.

Casey rose to his feet, his basketball-playing size made him tower over everyone. "I believe Abby has made her intentions clear. You need to leave now."

Monroe's lip curled into a sneer. "And who the hell are you?!"

Casey calmly reached into the back pocket of his jeans and pulled out his wallet. He flipped it open, revealing his deputy's badge.

Levi beamed and nodded slightly, thoroughly relishing this.

Monroe's pupils dilated as the gold-plated badge twinkled back at him. His sneer quickly transformed into alarm. He moved backward, clearly taken off guard by the turn of events.

Levi said through a smirk, "Guess you picked the wrong person to mess with, bro."

Monroe scrunched his face as though he caught the smell of

something unpleasant and retreated out the door, having forgotten about his date.

As much as it shouldn't, I couldn't help but feel sorry for her as she stared after him with her mouth agape.

Her body jolted in hesitation until she took off after him.

There will come a time when she catches on to his drivel and leaves him. Fingers crossed, her insight won't take as long as it did for me. No one deserved to have their time wasted by a weasel. *No one.*

The thick tension that had saturated the air moments ago popped like a balloon, leaving behind a sense of triumph.

Without the help of Levi and Casey, I couldn't have gotten through this. Facing the men, I said, "Thank you both."

Levi grinned, his eyes sparkling. "Anytime, Abs. That's what friends are for."

Casey issued a curt nod. "No problem."

Levi gestured with his bottle at Casey. "Nice having that badge to settle things down."

Casey grinned. "It has its uses."

Doug's mouth tightened, and he sipped his beer.

Levi frowned. "What do you mean? You don't like being on the force?"

Casey twisted his lips and leaned in. "Between you and me, not really, but don't repeat that to Stone."

I gulped down my coffee martini quickly to steady my nerves during their exchange, but my throat remained tight as I fought back tears.

Stay focused on the conversation. You can cry later.

Levi nodded at Casey. "Why do it, man? It's tough work."

Casey blew out a breath, then casually shrugged. "'Cause it's the viable option. Not like I can play basketball again and this line of work ain't exactly physical around these parts."

My insides quaked. Unable to maintain the charade any longer, I stood up. While shuffling out of my seat, I announced, "Excuse me, please. I need the bathroom."

Snatching my bag from where it hung on the chair, I hurried to the restroom, tears already streaming down my face.

The sanctuary of the empty lady's room drowned out the chaos of the bar.

I darted into the first unoccupied stall; my trembling hand turned the lock, securing it with a click. Pressing my back against the door, I released the miserable sob I'd stifled for far too long. Tugging on a roll of toilet paper, I blotted my tears away. The once pristine tissue now bore black stains of mascara.

The ambient noise of the bar swelled as the door of the bathroom opened.

"Abs?" Lexy's voice called out. "You okay?"

Delilah added, "Wanna talk about it, chicky poo?"

My throat burned, and my voice betrayed a tremor. "I'll be okay. Everything got too intense for me out there, and I needed a moment to collect myself."

"That jerk!" Lex shouted, her voice filled with indignation. "He can't just have a drink with his stupid date; he had to come over and pick fights."

Shivering under the overzealous air conditioning, I folded my arms, trying to warm up. Levi's words about being my life coach hurt worse than anything Monroe had dished out. He implied that I was some loser incapable of getting her life on track, so he generously stepped in to save me.

Alright, fine.

Maybe he didn't mean it that way.

But in the midst of Monroe taking a wrecking ball to my feelings, all while parading around with his drop-dead gorgeous date, that was how it landed.

You know what, though?

I'd sooner chew broken glass than admit that to any of them. My pride might be tattered, but I possessed enough of it to keep that humiliation to myself.

Releasing a measured breath, I unlocked the door and found

my friends' concerned faces waiting for me. "I wasn't expecting any of that, so it took me off guard. And with an audience, it became too much."

Lexy's eyes, almond-shaped and blue narrowed with a hint of fire behind them. "Next time that fool starts anything, I'm going to get involved. I won't just sit back and watch. So glad Casey sent him packing, though. Impressive," her voice sounded hopeful.

Delilah's long, red hair fell to one side. "We're here for you, whatever you need."

Pasting on a weak, brave smile, I said, "Don't worry, I'm fine. I need to do some damage control on my face, though. I look like a raccoon just attacked me in an attempt to steal my mascara."

Their chuckles echoed in the tiled bathroom.

I rummaged through my bag to retrieve my emergency travel-size repair kit. While I dampened a tissue in the sink and scrubbed away the runny mess, Delilah said, "As long as you're good to go, we'll take off."

They smooshed me into a group hug, delivering a cozy blend of warmth and comfort. Then, they took off, leaving me alone in the bathroom. I spent a few more minutes fixing my face, trying to salvage what was left of my carefully applied makeup.

Stepping out of the restroom, I discovered our deserted table, with the exception of the last person I wanted to see. Clad in an army-green shirt, he sat with folded arms. Then, his head swiveled, concern etched in his eyes as they locked onto mine.

My girls and their guys had disappeared, leaving me stranded and reliant on Levi for a ride home.

Fantastic. Just what I needed to make this night even more perfect.

CHAPTER SEVENTEEN

ABBY

I FOUND myself in Levi's car outside the bar. His refusal to let me call a taxi for a ride home irritated the heck out of me. What I really craved was alone time to wallow in peace, but nope, he wasn't having any of that.

Levi opened the door and slipped into the driver's seat with purpose. He paused for a beat and glanced at the darkened light. After clicking the belt into place, he said, "Babe, we need to talk. I was hoping to get you alone all night."

"What's on your mind?" I asked, curiosity battling with annoyance.

Levi sighed, his shoulders slumping slightly. "Listen, Abs," he began, his voice laced with apology, "about what happened at Uncle Al's..." He paused, searching my face for any sign of forgiveness. "I'm sorry about all of that. I know it freaked you out."

Oh, so *now* he wanted to talk about that, did he? After a day of radio silence. His uncle pulled a gun on us yesterday, and all Levi did was drop me off at home, afterwards. No talks, no apologies, no nothing.

My eyes narrowed, the resentment churned in my stomach, and spilled into my voice. "Took you long enough to bring that up," I spat. "You think a simple 'sorry' erases having a gun being pointed at me?"

Levi's jaw clenched, his eyes flashing with a annoyance. "I was trying to come to grips with everything that happened," he said. "It was tough for me too."

I moved my gaze outside the window, tracing the murky tree contours in the night's darkness, and formulated my words. "I never had a gun pointed at me before," I confessed in a quiet voice. "It more than freaked me out. I understand that you had nothing to do with that, but. Well. I don't know. It just shook me up. What hurt was that you weren't there for me. And tonight," I added, laying it out because I couldn't stop the deluge once it started. "That whole life coach business really hurt. You kicked me while I was down."

Tears welled up in my eyes, blurring the world around me and threatening to spill mascara down my cheeks. Honestly, I should just give up having mascara in my life.

Levi's hand paused on the way to the ignition.

His eyes roamed my face, and anguish laced his voice. "I didn't handle things in the best way, baby. I have a knack for that," he admitted, his voice gruff with emotion.

"Fear got the better of me, and I had no idea what to do. But I should've been there for you. Shielding you. As for what I said at the bar, I said it because we were together too often, and people might start talking. Since we're friends..." he leaned in. "But just so we're straight, I want more than just friendship. I want you."

For a long moment, we stared at each other, his charged words hung in the air.

My heart raced as I tried to process them. The implication of his confession sent me into a tizzy.

Levi ripped his eyes away from mine, flung his gaze out of the window, and gripped the steering wheel like he wanted to crush it.

I placed a hand on his arm, summoning his attention, and confessed, "I want you too."

Levi's head jerked back like he received the shock of his life.

Why though? Wasn't my feelings obvious? I wore them like a sign.

"Really? You're sure?" he asked.

My brows furrowed at his unexpected reaction. "Of course, I'm sure. How could I not be?"

Levi's gaze searched my face. "After your ex left, you were pretty shaken up," he explained. "I figured that seeing him with someone else poured salt in your wounds."

"The only thing that bugged me was her prettiness and how she resembled—"

I pressed my lips together, side-stepping a near blunder.

Ugh, mental facepalm.

"Reminded you of what, baby?" Levi prodded.

Heat scalded my face, leaving it tingling as if I'd fallen asleep in a tanning bed. My lashes flickered, buying precious seconds before admitting, "Of that lady I saw you with," I said, my voice strained, "when I came over to offer you the job..."

"Ah, so that's what's going on. Well, you can rest assured she was a hookup, a flash in the pan," he put in quickly. "Never saw her again. I went strictly no-strings after my ex left me for my associate. Up until now, I wasn't interested in seeing anyone."

His words soothed my soul, chasing away lingering doubts, but in their wake, new questions arose. My brows shot up so high they nearly merged with my hairline. She left him for his associate? What was she smoking, 'cause in what world did that make sense? Succumbing to my dorkiness, I blurted, "She left you? You? I mean, seriously...who does that?"

Levi erupted in laughter, its rich, resonant sound filling the car. "You're too sweet Abs, making me feel like a king. But you'd be surprised. I worked nights; he worked days. While I was grinding away, they'd spend time together."

"Sorry. That must've been tough." I reached out and smoothed his arm sympathetically.

The familiar ghost of shame coiled around my insides, triggered by memories of dating that louse, but I swallowed it back. Levi deserved a chance to speak his mind without me monopolizing the airtime.

"Tough, humiliating, rage-inducing, you name it." He paused, then added with a note of finality, "Anyway, baby, that's over with. Back to us," he said, undoing his seatbelt and reaching across to undo mine.

Tilting his seat back, he asked, "Ever been naughty in a car, Abby?"

Giddiness shot through my chest so intensely that a Cheshire Cat's grin stretched across my lips. With a subtle nip, I clamped down on the bottom one and teased, "Nuh uh." Anticipation practically hummed throughout my body as I awaited his next move.

"Come over here, foxy," he patted his lap and hiked up his brow suggestively.

Foxy?

Did he just call me foxy?

Holy smokes!

My brain just about short-circuited, struggling to process this rugged Adonis's words.

Wait! Why was I still sitting here?

Like a rocket, I sprang into action, not caring how goofy I looked.

How I managed to climb over the console without kicking the gearshift out of place, I don't know, but I'll credit my lust-filled haze.

Levi settled me on his lap and placed a hand on my cheek. "Do you have any idea how crazy you drive me? I struggle so damn hard to just be friends with you, when every ounce of my being fights tooth and nail for more."

The world tilted on its axis, and my heart bloomed in my

chest. His words were a revelation. The idea that he reciprocated my feelings hadn't occurred.

Goodness, this completely changed everything.

With more guts than I'd ever possessed in my life, I settled a trembling palm on his cheek, mirroring his movements and meeting his gaze. "Then lets be more."

Levi's smile bloomed beneath my touch. I caressed his cheek, and he turned, his lips meeting my palm in a tender kiss that spoke volumes without a single word.

My heart liquefied, warmth spreading throughout my body at his sweet gesture. Unable to resist the magnetic pull of those pillow-lips, I placed a shy kiss on them. Their softness, so intoxicating, made my skin tingle.

Levi emitted a deep, almost inaudible groan, and he rubbed my back, soothing me and turning me on at the same time. An erotic energy built low in my stomach, and I leaned in again, kissing him, opening my mouth to him.

His hands tangled in my hair, urging me toward him. He delved his warm tongue into my mouth, devouring every inch of me in a primal play that left me dizzy. He demanded everything, and I willingly surrendered myself without hesitation.

And then disaster struck. My phone's ring doused a bucket of cold water on us. I swear, I could've hurled the incessant thing out the window.

We broke apart, our chests heaving as we reclaimed the air we had deprived each other of moments ago.

"They'll call back if it's important," I said, as though I'd just completed a marathon.

The ringing stopped.

A mischievous grin spread across my face as I tilted my head, pressing my lips against Levi's before the ringing started again.

I cursed under my breath, grabbed my bag, and snatched the maddening device from the side pocket. My face fell when Sheri Martin's name appeared on the screen.

"It's my mom," I said to Levi as I swiped the screen.

Before I could even greet her, she said, "Abby, are you okay?"

"Chill, mom. I was just..." I looked at Levi, and he shrugged. "Out on a date?" I asked.

"Chet, she's fine," Mom called out to Dad.

As I climbed off Levi's lap, Mom asked, "So, how is Monroe? Tell him Dad and I say hi."

Startled by Mom's mention of my ex, my leg twitched and I kicked the gear shift, then mouthed "sorry" to Levi.

He helped by moving my legs. Oye, if this didn't qualify as awkward, I didn't know what did.

"Ah, Mom, Monroe and I broke up. I'm seeing someone else. You remember Levi Cross, Clara's nephew?"

Clara's sweet demeanor made everyone like her. Her brother, Al, on the other hand—

Ah, *Yeah.*

Better not bring him up. My dating Levi probably shocked her enough, anyway.

"Abby, are you sure about this? He's... he's... you know. From the wrong side of the tracks."

I shot a quick glance at Levi and found his jaw clenched, and he stiffened his body in a rigid line. He clearly sensed Mom wasn't exactly thrilled with the news. Needing to reassure him, I grabbed his hand, hoping to comfort him. He held it, but his mood didn't budge.

"I'm all in, Mom. Levi's been incredible, treating me like a queen. It's like someone finally cracked the code to my happiness." I squeezed Levi's hand and winked at him, eliciting his shy smile.

"Are we talking about the same Levi Cross who stole from the food stalls in Union Vale? Wow, I didn't think you two ran in the same circles," Mom said.

"We do now. He's been working at the library for Uncle Wyatt. That's how we met."

"So he lives there?" she asked. "He's not just making a temporary stop?"

A simple enough question, but it set off my warning bells. We never discussed his intentions for the future. What if I became too invested in our relationship, and he didn't feel the same, enough to stay with me? What then?

I untangled our interlaced fingers and pressed my back against the seat. "The truth is, Mom," I admitted, my voice laced with uncertainty, "we haven't broached that conversation yet. We're still new. This is our second date."

Kinda, sorta, date. More like a make out session, but she didn't need details.

"Well, if he makes you happy, that's all that's important, darling. I'll admit that I'm worried about you. I remember what a headache he was when he was younger, but I trust your decisions. If you say he treats you well, then I believe it. At the end of the day, that's all your dad and I want."

I grinned, a weight lifting off my shoulders. "Thanks, Momma. So how are you and Daddy doing?"

Levi started the car, and the engine did absolutely nothing.

I faded away as Mom droned on about training Milo to pee on a tree. She worked at an animal shelter, so I assumed Milo might be a hound and not some poor soul with bladder issues.

"Mom, I have to go. Levi is having trouble with his car, he might need help."

CHAPTER EIGHTEEN

LEVI

DESPITE MY SIMMERING temper and stress levels fueled by this hunk of junk Subaru, I forced myself to suck back my anger into the pit of my stomach and popped an antacid in my mouth. Abby needed me, and that outweighed my inconveniences. I draped a protective arm around her shoulders. After everything that had gone down between us before my car betrayed me, she became the one bright spot in this whole mess.

Funny how life worked out.

Just when I had everything figured out, it threw me a curveball.

At least we were in the parking lot of the bar and not stalled at the side of the road. Small miracle, but I'll take it. The lot had been nearly deserted, save for a few cars that I figured belonged to the bar employees still inside.

I'd popped the hood of the Subaru, exposing its mechanical innards for someone with more know-how than me. Times like these, I wish I'd honed more practical skills than the ones I'd sharpened over the years, but hindsight was twenty-twenty.

Just then, a tow truck rolled into the lot, its headlights sweeping across the desolate area.

I waved the driver down, so relieved I could've fist-bumped the moon.

Rhythmic beeping noises erupted from the truck as it reversed in front of my car. Moments later, the driver, a massive figure, approached. Long black hair, tied in a loose ponytail. Square jaw. His white T-shirt showcased his brute strength under wraps.

As a straight man, I could admit his physicality. Unconsciously, my grip tightened on Abby's shoulder, subtly staking my claim.

"Hey, man. Thanks for coming. My car won't start," I explained.

The driver's glacial blue eyes darted from me to Abby, noting our closeness.

My jaw tightened. Didn't care for the way his gaze lingered on her, his brows pulled together as though he tried to place her.

He gave a sharp, decisive nod. Tearing his eyes away from Abs, he switched on his flashlight and swept the beam across the engine block, pausing over the battery.

This guy moved with the purpose of a freight train, all business and no bull. A man who didn't waste time on pleasantries, preferring to get down to business.

"From the looks of it, you got a dead battery," he rumbled in a deep, resonant voice. "When was the last time you replaced it?"

Good question.

I scratched the back of my head, my mind dredging up the distant memory. "Uhh, about six years ago."

The driver straightened. "Six years?" he shook his head, clearly annoyed. "Count yourself lucky it didn't give out sooner. I'll drag it to Thompson's Garage and take a look first thing in the morning. Sounds good?"

My old man never taught me how to maintain cars, leaving me helpless in that department. Damn it to hell! I had hoped to conceal my flaws a bit longer before Abby caught sight of the wreck that was me. I swallowed down my embarrassment.

"Yeah, that works. Thanks, man."

The driver's eyes bounced between me and Abs. He asked, "You two need a lift?"

Did I want to share space with this guy?

Hell no.

Not when he outshined me with his expertise. But I needed to see to Abs. She needed to get home.

"Appreciate it," I said. "You can drop us off at my place, and I'll take Abby home on my bike."

Pale blue eyes shimmering with excitement, Abby looked up at me, a grin blossoming on her face.

The driver slammed my hood with a bang, snapping my attention back to him. "Alright, climb into the rig. Give me about ten, fifteen minutes, and we'll be on our way. After I unhitch your car at Thompson's, I'll give you a lift in my pickup." Without a backward glance, he marched toward the truck, cutting off my response.

I guided Abby to the tow truck and placed my hands on her ample waist, hoisting her into the vehicle. With a lithe maneuver, I climbed in after her, squeezing myself into the grease-stained seats.

Closing the door behind me, I mumbled, "Sorry about the crazy night, baby. Definitely not how I planned our evening."

Abby let out a small laugh. "Oh, don't even think of apologizing," she said, making a shooing gesture. "It's an adventure, right? I haven't had this much fun in ages."

This woman. This sweet-natured, beautiful woman.

With a low chuckle, I slipped my arm around her. Her head found its resting place on my shoulder, and her warm palm anchored itself on my chest, like she belonged there. The scent of her fruity shampoo filled my senses.

We fit. We just fit.

"Consider this chariot our temporary love nest," I declared, watching her eyes sparkle and a smile bloom on her face.

My mind took me back to just after she ended the call with her mom. In a bid to clear the air between us, I said, "I hope I didn't scare you when I punched the steering wheel earlier."

Abby's lips pursed into a thin line before she spoke. "It shocked me at first, but I understood your frustration, so don't lose any sleep over it. Honestly, I was more worried about you. That call with Mom left me wondering if you were okay."

Leaning in, I kissed her forehead to soften the blow. "Initially, it stung. But hey, I get it. Worried parents, right? Heck, I'd probably be flipping out too if my daughter started dating a guy like me." I winked. "But I gotta say, baby, that bit about treating you like a lady? That was gold."

Abby rubbed my chest.

I don't know if she was aware of it or not, but it felt *so* good.

She said, "All of it is true, you know? No one has ever been so kind, looking out for me, whether I had lunch or not. It's those gestures that make a huge difference."

I met her shimmering eyes and leaned in for a real kiss. Her lush lips drove me wild. With a groan, I yanked myself back before I lost control and buried my face in the curve of her neck. The faint scent she wore made my mouth water. A shiver ran down me and I murmured, "Damn, girl, you smell real good."

"Coconuts," Abby replied.

Huh?

Before I could even ask about her meaning, she said, "Now that you're in a good mood, I have to apologize for messing up your car when I kicked the gear shift while climbing off your lap."

I raised my brow. "Baby, don't worry. The car was already messed up when we were in the parking lot. Something was off when the dome light didn't turn on when I opened the car door."

"The dome light?" she asked.

I pulled away and explained, "Figured the battery gave up the ghost as soon as I turned off the ignition. All those years spent in stop-and-go traffic contributed to that."

"So, my ninja kick didn't actually cause this?" she asked.

"Nah, not this time, baby, just shit-timing."

Our laughter filled the cab.

Suddenly, the heavy metal door groaned open. The driver hoisted himself inside, his work boots thumping against the floorboard. With a flick of his wrist, he awakened the engine and turned toward Abby. "You look familiar. Been trying to place you but I can't."

My arm involuntarily flexed around Abby's waist.

Abby studied the driver. "Wait, aren't you... McGregor?"

The driver circled the steering wheel, turning us onto the dark, tree-lined road. He flicked a glance towards Abby, his voice tinged with suspicion. "How do you know my last name? Only guys at the garage call me that. My given name is Blake."

My jaw clenched as my jealousy flared to life.

Abby answered Blake. "I remember you from Graham's Garage. I was waiting for my car, and you strode in and mentioned something to Craig about an accident. You offered to tow the car over if he needed extra detail work done."

"Right. Now I remember. For a moment there, I thought you were a customer at Thompson's that I couldn't place," Blake said.

Feeling out of place, I did what any man would do and hijacked their conversation. "So how long have you been working at Thompson's?"

Blake puffed out a sigh. "Too damn long. But if you want specifics, around ten years. Been holding down the fort until Thompson's daughter decides to come back and take the reins."

My head spun, trying to piece together his words. "Wait a minute, Thompson's got a daughter who's a mechanic?"

Bitterness tinged Blake's smirk. "Nah. She's just some spoiled city princess. Never lifted a finger to help her old man when he was fading away. Left me to handle everything – the burial, the heartache, the whole goddamn mess. Now, I'm stuck babysitting his shop, waiting for her royal highness to decide to grace us with her presence. And let me tell you, she can't come soon enough. The landlord's got his eye on selling this place, and the whole thing has left a sour taste in my mouth."

I glanced down at Abby and found her eyes clouded over with sympathy.

"Geez, that sounds like a nightmare, Blake. I'm sorry," she said, her voice soft with sincerity.

No lies. A heatwave of embarrassment swept over me for flexing like that, kind of like I did every time I opened my mouth around Kaminsky. Seriously, I felt like a total doofus. I need to get it together.

"Yeah, man," I said, in an attempt to smooth things over. "I'd offer a job at the police station if I could. That's where I work. They could use big guys like you."

"Believe me, with the way things are going at the garage, I might take you up on it," Blake quipped. Then he asked, "Hey, you a cop?"

"The official title they gave me was police consultant," I clarified. "Name's Levi Cross."

"Cross?" Blake furrowed his heavy brows. "Say, you wouldn't happen to be related to Al Cross, would ya?"

Abby rolled her eyes, and I flexed my arm. Uncle Al didn't make it into her good books.

"Yeah," I answered Blake. "He's my uncle. You know him?"

"Built him custom cabinetry to outfit his Winnie a while back," Blake said, shaking his head. "No offense, but that guy's a trip. Kept me entertained with his government conspiracy theories during installation. Anyway, you mentioned having a bike. What kind is it?"

The man builds furniture too?

What the hell?

Next, he'll demonstrate that he's more powerful than a locomotive. Just watch. Luckily, he steered the conversation back to familiar territory.

"A Sportster, '07," I answered with a smirk.

Blake shot me a glance with arched brows. His head bobbed rhythmically with the truck's sway. "An '07? That's a classic. How'd you come across it?"

"Inherited it from my old man," I answered, my chest puffing with pride. "He owned it before he passed. Big motorcycle enthusiast."

"Solid. Any modifications?" Blake asked.

"Swapped out the handlebars for more of a custom feel and added a Sundowner for my lady's comfort." I gave Abby's shoulders a reassuring squeeze to remind her that I hadn't forgotten her.

She rewarded me with a pink stain on her cheeks. I considered kissing her but refrained, unsure if she welcomed PDA.

Before I could loose track in the moment, the tow truck rumbled to a stop outside Thompson's Garage.

"We're here, folks. Home sweet home, at least until the Park Avenue princess decides to grace us with her presence." Blake opened the door and climbed down from the truck.

Something uncanny about his demeanor struck me as strange.

His mannerisms—I met him before?

CHAPTER NINETEEN

ABBY

AFTER REPLYING to Doug about my whereabouts, I slipped my phone back into my bag. Levi's hand cradled mine as he led me into the deli for lunch. I'll admit that I felt a tingle of excitement when people craned their necks at us.

Their cartoonish eyes took in our linked hands and our proximity, meaning that we'd no doubt become the topic du jour around town. I anticipated it, so it didn't bother me much.

Honestly, it would've freaked me out if Levi hadn't confessed his feelings in the car. I'm relieved we addressed that before we realized his car battery kicked the bucket.

And that ride home from his place on the back of his motorcycle.

Confession time: I'd never ridden on a motorcycle, and the thought of falling off scared the bejeezers out of me. Thankfully, my bad balance didn't come into play. I clung to Levi like a Koala at first, but eventually exhilaration replaced my terror. The speed of the bike blurred the country road. Simply put...magical. Loud and windy too, but magical. I totally get bike enthusiasts now. They're onto something good.

Levi scanned the menu. "What's good, baby?"

My insides did a pirouette at his casual use of the endearment, but I schooled my features into a nonchalant mask.

"Hmmm," I said, placing a playful finger to my lips. "Depends. Are you a pastrami kinda guy, or do you prefer the smoky kiss of lox?"

A slow, sexy grin spread across Levi's face as he lowered his gaze to meet mine. With twinkling eyes, he lifted my knuckles to his lips and placed a feather-light kiss on them.

"Pastrami. I dig the classics," he declared with a wink that could melt butter.

I furrowed my brow.

The classics?

Oh wait! He meant me. My rockabilly style.

My grin lagged behind a beat too late. Levi was already at the counter putting in his order. He glanced back at me with an expectant expression. I asked for the same. Minutes later, sandwiches and chocolate chip cookies in hand, we found a table and got settled, ready to dig in.

In the midst of unwrapping our lunches, Doug appeared at the deli's entrance. His sharp, golden-hazel eyes located us immediately. A laptop bag slung from his shoulders, and he carried a stack of papers.

My friend's demeanor set off my alarm bells. His determined strides that parted the crowd as he made his way to our table made my gut drop. I sat up straighter and braced myself for whatever he was going to say.

Doug pulled out a vacant seat, occupied it, and dropped his papers on the table. Upon closer inspection, they appeared to be printouts and newspaper clippings.

"Got some news," he said, his voice dropped to a near whisper.

Levi peered at the stack. "Sure looks like it. What's up, bro?"

"Found out who's behind the break-ins." He leaned in. "The police."

Levi's brows bunched up, and his forehead creased. "What are you talking about, man?"

"Some officers are working with criminals to break into homes and have people make insurance claims. The police officers banked the extra money. That's why the cases aren't being solved. They aren't trying to solve them," Doug said as he unraveled the papers containing his research.

My mouth dropped open.

I—

What?

Geez Louise.

"It all makes sense when you think about it." My mind flashed to Uncle Wyatt. That's not the man I knew—the man who became a second father to me. Sure, I could see Casey pulling this crap, but not my uncle. I shook my head, dispelling the notion.

"Do you know how far in the department this has spread?" I asked, distilling it to the more pertinent question. "Like which officers are receiving kickbacks?"

"Don't answer that!" Levi said.

Doug and I reared back.

"Don't drag her into this," Levi continued. "You and I can talk about it later at my place, not out in the open."

My friend's face flashed in my mind, and I instantly felt my mood plummet. "My God, Lexy. This is going to crush her. Seriously, the girl was practically bursting when she texted me and Deedee about Casey."

Out of nowhere, Levi's foot nudged mine under the table. I loved the secret little connection, his subtle way of saying, "I'm here for you." A grateful smile spread across my face.

"Right," Doug said. "You and Deeds are going to have to talk her out of that one. She's playing with fire."

Levi cussed under his breath.

"But...God. I was hoping this one would work out," I said, my hatred for this situation growing by the second. "She needs to forget about Oli and move on with her life. I mean, I don't like Casey, but I was hoping he turned over a new leaf. Once a double-crosser, always a double-crosser, I guess."

Doug's heavy brows pulled together. "What are you on about?"

I waved him off, playing down my failed attempts at love. "Oh, nothing. Just some unresolved beef I have with Casey for ditching me on a group date way back when."

"You dated Casey?" Levi asked, his eyes widening to the size of dinner plates.

This was the second time I'd seen him get worked up over me talking to other men. Last night with the truck driver made sense because that man was too handsome for words. I still preferred my guy, though.

I tilted my head at the man sitting across from me. "Seriously, Cross? We went out when we were twelve. And it was a group date, not some whirlwind love affair. Don't get your jealousy in a twist."

Doug's eyes bounced back and forth from me to Levi. Then he muttered, "Knew it."

"What?" Levi scowled.

"You two," Doug answered. "After everything happened at the bar, Deeds and I figured you two were seeing each other. Anyway, back to this," he said, gesturing to his papers. "Levi, when you want to meet up?"

"After work this afternoon. It'll be hell going back to the station to face those thieving bastards and act like I don't know what they're up to."

Doug said, "Whatever you do, don't breathe a word of this until after we know for sure that Stone is involved."

Levi nodded. "Ten-four."

I pushed away my lunch, no longer hungry.

CHAPTER TWENTY

ABBY

I RAPPED RHYTHMICALLY on Lexy's apartment door, shooting an anxious glance at Delilah. The thumping bassline of Bruno Mars emanating from inside abruptly softened, and the persistent hiss of a vacuum cleaner cut off.

A moment later, the door swung open, and our friend met us, her long black hair frayed in a ponytail, her blue eyes popping wide as they registered our impromptu visit.

"Hey, squad! Come on in," she exclaimed, her voice bright with excitement. "Give me a sec to dial down the volume, so we can hear ourselves think."

With that, she hurried off to her kitchenette, fiddling with her phone, as we ventured further into her sanctum, closing the door behind us.

Lexy's tidy nature shone through. Not a single cobweb or dust speck in sight. A wooden dining table replaced the kitchen island to the right, while the left side of the room housed an army-green couch and TV in the living room. On the crisp, white walls, an eclectic collection of flea market finds proudly displayed itself.

Our host gestured expansively, her arms stretching wide. "Find a perch wherever you fancy. I decided to tackle cleaning the fridge as my extra task. You're welcome to join in on a charcuterie dinner. I'm finally going to crack open the bottle of vino birthday present from the guys at work."

We approached the farm-style table, graced with meticulously arranged piles of fresh cheeses, their sharp and creamy colors contrasting with the vibrant hues of grapes. The aroma filled my nostrils, making my stomach rumble.

Thank goodness she offered for us to partake, because I was seconds away from gnawing on her furniture.

"Thanks, Lex," I said. "Your place always feels super cozy."

Delilah eyed the walls while settling into the seat opposite me. "Oh my gosh, are those the sconces you were talking about? They're adorable! Seriously, your place is like a real-life Pinterest board. I'm stealing inspo as we speak!"

Lexy practically glowed. "Aw, thanks. Snagged those babies last month at Stormville. Felt like they belonged with the rest of my shiny hoard, you know? You should've seen how I nearly threw down with that stingy old codger to buy them at a decent price."

She shook her head, a wry smile playing on her lips. "He pouted the whole time I paid. I swear, some folks price their wares so high, you'd think they'd rather keep it than make a sale."

Lexy sighed, drumming her fingers against the table, bringing her story to an end. Her smile dimmed, and her thin black brows pulled together as a shadow crossed her eyes. "Anyway," she said, her voice quieter now, "spill it. What's got you two looking like storm clouds rolled in on your picnic?"

Her joke landed flat, met by our silence, and her cheeriness vanished instantly. "Uh oh. What's going on?"

My teeth sank into my lip as I fumbled with my gold bracelet. "It's about Casey."

Lexy's smile faltered completely as her gaze met mine and Deedee's. Then, a smart-aleck grin raised one corner of her mouth. "What about him? Don't tell me he gave ya'll a speeding ticket."

Deedee and I exchanged a panicked glance. The pit of my stomach bottomed out. This was so much more awful than I anticipated, and I didn't have high hopes to begin with.

With a resigned sigh, Deeds said, "I wish it were that easy, then we won't need to have this conversation."

"Casey's in hot water," I blurted out. "Like boiling hot. Like, investigation-and-possible-jail-time hot water. Don't breathe a word of this to anyone."

Lexy's jaw dropped open like a puppet's, her gaze darting between Deeds and me as silence stretched out. "Wait, what?" she finally asked, her voice cracking. "How did you find out all of this? What happened?"

Delilah explained. "Doug found out who's behind those break-ins in town. Levi is helping to uncover how far the problem has extended in the police department."

"Are you sure he has the right guy?" Lex asked, trying to make sense of it all. "Casey? No way. He couldn't steal a candy bar, let alone orchestrate home invasions. After Ethan and Oli both turned out to be disappointments, I thought, I don't know, Casey would've been the safer option."

It's understandable that she missed the red flags. Casey resembled a caricature of the 50s: wholesome, with family values. His rat-like qualities weren't apparent to the naked eye.

"Yeah, babe," I said, reaching across the table, squeezing her hand gently. "We're positive. We don't want you getting hurt when everything goes down."

Watching hope die from her eyes left me feeling like the world's biggest goon.

She stood up and walked over to the window, crossing her arms while gazing outside.

Deeds and I frowned at each other.

I hated this.

Lexy mumbled, "Every time I think there's a chance for

something healthy, it all falls apart. First Ethan, now this. Swear, I'll snap a rubber band across my wrists next time I consider getting into a relationship."

"Don't fret, hon," I soothed, resting my folded arms on the table. "Relationships are basically like assembling an IKEA desk without the instructions. You think you're doing everything right, then BAM! Missing dowel, wobbly table, and tears. Monroe was a nice man, in the beginning, until he wasn't," I admitted, telling them something I swore I wouldn't.

But Lex needed to know she wasn't the only one who screwed up royally in companionship choices. My very public fights with Monroe made me feel like a poster child for bad decisions.

Deeds dragged her finger on the tabletop, and worry lines marred her smooth forehead. "Speaking of relationships, how are things with Levi, Abs?"

The change of topic flustered me for a second. With a silent "why go there?" directed at my fellow ginger, I shook my head and answered, "Good, so far. I'm taking things slowly. I've learned to approach love with a hard hat and caution tape."

Rubbing my blissful relationship in Lexy's face?

Absolutely not.

I'm not heartless.

Delilah said, "Yeah. Even when you think everything's going great, something unexpected always pops up that takes you off guard."

"What are you talking about?" I asked her.

Turmoil flickered in Deed's eyes, hinting at a dark secret she was hesitant to reveal. Then she gave in and said, "Since we're sharing, Doug doesn't want kids. That's why he hasn't proposed yet. To me, it goes deeper than not wanting kids. It's like a phobia."

My eyes widened; that didn't compute at all. Doug had always struck me as a family man. I envisioned a picket fence and a minivan kiddie parade in their future, so I had to check.

"Seriously, Deeds?" I asked. "What could have scared him? He'd make an awesome dad."

Delilah swallowed the question whole, offering nothing in return. Instead, she folded inward, the vibrant life in her eyes replaced by a dull ache.

I cringed at my careless comment, which had the sensitivity of a rampaging bull in a china shop, shattering whatever fragile comfort she'd built.

If that wasn't unfortunate enough, the gods decided to soundtrack my misstep with Adele's *Hello.*

Lunging for Lexy's phone, I swapped the song with an emotionally neutral Jazzy playlist. The smooth, muted notes were a welcome reprieve from Adele's mournfully melodic voice.

I offered Deeds an apologetic smile, hoping to mend fences.

Delilah shrugged at me and winked a teary eye.

Relief flooded through me at the return of her spirit.

Next, I crossed the space to Lex, and rested a hand on her shoulder. "How about we indulge in some charcuterie therapy?"

Delilah sprang into action and readied the cheese plates, pouring wine into glasses, the whole bit. She probably needed therapy more than anyone.

Lexy shuffled towards the vacant chair, lowering herself onto it with a flop. "What do I even say to him? How do I end it?"

Deeds suggested, "Be like, 'I'm sorry, but I'm not feeling this relationship right now.'"

I winced at her blunt-force-trauma approach and countered, "That's a bit harsh, don't you think?"

Deeds hiked a brow, challenging me. "She needs to be straightforward. No room for negotiation or he might try to talk her out of it or humor her so she'd change her mind. I'm not saying that I know him well enough to suggest he might do that, but preparation is key."

Lexy popped a few grapes in her mouth, mindlessly chomping away as her face transformed into a wry grin. "Don't worry. I'm an expert at repelling men."

At least she could joke about it. That's a good thing, right? Count on her to inject levity into any situation.

I grinned and popped a soft piece of Brie in my mouth, then chased it down with a hearty sip of fruity wine. The unexpected taste took me by surprise. I scrutinized the label, committing it to memory for future reference. The inn always has the best of everything.

"So," Deeds said. "Dish on this Ethan fella. Don't think I missed that snippet." She winked and sipped her wine.

A grin spread across Lexy's face. "He's the head chef at the inn who looks like a sexy metro mountain man. Bonus points for the leather jacket, motorcycle, and swagger. Needless to say, every woman, including yours truly, had tried and failed to land him. We're strictly friends now. He's a sweetheart to me, but he's got a temper in the kitchen that would put Gordon Ramsay to shame."

Deeds straightened. "Ooh, color me officially intrigued. Point him out when we go to the book fair. I gotta see."

Lexy rolled her eyes. "Nearly forgot about the book fair. Thanks, Deeds."

CHAPTER TWENTY ONE

ABBY

AS SOON AS I set foot into Levi's home, his strong arms wrapped around me, pulling me close. His faint cologne of leather and spice filled my head like a fog machine. I nuzzled the crook of his neck and inhaled so hard a snort nearly came out, 'cause I'm suave like that.

Lex's soiree's lingering buzz left me pleasantly woozy. I should've known brie and Pinot wouldn't prepare me to weather this level of Levi-alanche.

My guy withdrew, and his gaze meandered down to my mouth. "You're lookin' damn good there, sweetheart. You had dinner?"

Inwardly, I practically turned to Jell-O, but coolness prevailed, and I merely shook my head. "Already demolished at Lexy's."

A single eyebrow arched upward on his lean, handsome face. "Dessert, then?"

My lips stretched into a slow, provocative smile. "Wouldn't miss it for the world. Lead the way, dear captain."

Levi's eyes crinkled at their corners as he swept my hand into his, guiding me past the living room, deep into the heart of his kitchen. He swung open the turquoise relic of a freezer and plucked out a carton of my favorite—vanilla, still crisp with frost.

Sweet! His love for the classics extended to a shared flavor of kryptonite. Why am I getting so excited over ice cream?

Blame the wine. And the cheese...

Wait, can a person get drunk on cheese? Maybe.

He rummaged through cupboards and drawers, gathering his tools for creating our sweet repast. Scooping generous mounds of ice cream into bowls, he finally looked up, eyes twinkling with question. "So, how did it go with Lex? You two talked to her?"

"Yessiree," I answered, earning a quiet chuckle from Levi. "She didn't take the news about Casey well. Let's just say an impromptu wine party formed a temporary truce with heartbreak. She's good for now. I just wish I could make things easier for her."

Levi said, "This might sting, but trust me, she's tough. It's a setback, not a breakdown. Unlike Oli, she wasn't hung up on Casey for ages, you know?" His gaze met mine, curiosity in them. "Anyway, talk to me about this wine and cheese. That how girls deal with the sting?"

It's how girls might deal with everything, but I didn't offer up that newsflash. 'Cause girl code. Instead, I flashed a Mona Lisa smile and said, "Something like that."

Levi stowed the tub back in the freezer, swung it closed with a thunk, and handed me a chilled bowl. With a silent invitation, he gestured to join him in the cool haven of the air-conditioned living room. The window unit churned away in the corner.

Sinking onto his couch, I watched dust particles dance in the dying sunlight. Turning to him, I asked, "How did it go at the station today? Was it weird working with them?"

Levi settled next to me on his couch, scooped a spoonful, and answered, "No clue where to start. Gotta find out if Stone's involved, but how? And should I even touch this mess? I'm no detective."

The thought of my uncle defrauding insurance companies, facing possible jail time, and losing his pension knotted my stomach into a ball. None of it made sense. No matter how hard I tried to banish the thought, it would boomerang back. Swear it, this whole fiasco might land me in the madhouse.

Levi eyed my untouched bowl. The vanilla ice cream melted slightly at the edges. With an inward sigh, I scooped the slurry mixture, the taste bland and unappealing on my tongue.

Being his ever-supportive girlfriend, I suggested, "How about going to internal affairs? Let them handle it."

"Evidence, babe. We need to present some to internal affairs, but we have nothing to go on. Those burglaries are common knowledge for everyone at this point. However, linking it back to the police? That's a whole other ball game, because they're experts at cover-ups." His spoon scraped against the ceramic bowl as his brow furrowed in thought. "Let's table that for now. How're you holding up?"

Offering a pitiful imitation of a smile, I admitted, "It isn't just him doing it that cuts. It's the 'why'? Every time I picture law and order, my mind conjures up Uncle Wyatt." I shook my head in defeat. "Breaking into people's homes, stealing from folks who trusted him to protect them... none of it adds up."

Levi's spoon halted its ascent to his mouth, and he lowered it. "For what it's worth, I can't picture him being embroiled in this chaos, either. He's too hell-bent on nabbing the perp. If he were involved, his deflection game would be off the charts."

Makes sense. Levi had a knack for reading people, which was a lost art for me. I should hold off on jumping to conclusions. Uncle Wyatt deserved the benefit of the doubt. I could give him that much.

Offering a feeble smile, I inquired through a mouthful of icy vanilla. "Will you be continuing your employment there?"

"Not for long. They haven't axed me yet, but it looks like I'll be job hunting soon. Probably will head back to the construction company and ask again." Under his breath, he murmured, "With my tail between my legs this time."

Hmmm. What's the story behind that?

"Whatever happens, you've got this. Sign up at job banks and see what comes up. Be a temp if you have to. Heck, come back and work at the library. I'll check if there are job openings. Maybe there might be something in the line of custodial work if you don't mind."

Levi grinned. "Not at all. Anything but my former line of business." Then, with a playful wink, he added, "Too much to lose."

Not gonna lie, that tidbit lifted a weight off my chest. It brought out a mile-wide grin. I jabbed him with an elbow and sassed, "Glad to hear it, Iron Man."

Levi gathered our empty bowls and stacked them on his coffee table.

The air buzzed with electricity, raising the flesh on my skin as if someone threw a switch on an invisible generator.

Those chocolate eyes of his held a promise to make my heart race. A slow smirk played on his lips, and a playful challenge laced his voice as he drawled, "Like what you see, sweetheart?"

Ah, wasn't that obvious? My eyeballs almost popped out of my head, and my tongue forgot how to function past a pathetic waggle from day one. But was I going to admit it and stroke his Texas-sized ego?

Not in this lifetime.

Playing it cool, I nonchalantly shrugged and replied, "Maybe."

My fingers explored his denim-clad leg, tracing a path down as if deciphering clues to the hidden strength beneath.

Levi's gaze dipped straight to my lips.

My tongue flicked out to moisten them, eager for what was coming.

Levi emitted a rumble, and the divide between us disappeared as our mouths met in a kiss so fevered it felt like I had swallowed fire.

Then, he withdrew and searched my face. Whatever he found sparked a gleam in his brown eyes before diving back in.

The next thing I knew, we were back at it, tongues tangoing like we'd won a free cruise.

Levi's hand snaked into my hair, his fingertips dancing across my sensitive scalp. Tickle zone engaged.

Laughter bubbled up, the sound muted against his lips. I felt, rather than heard, his own amusement reverberate in the warmth of his chest.

The touch vanished when he withdrew his fingers.

Who knew making out with a hot guy could be so much fun? Maybe it was only fun when the guy in question was Levi.

He had a way of erasing the canyon-sized gap between our leagues. My hair, which I swear took seventy-ten hours taming, likely resembled the loser of a badger battle royale.

But, I couldn't give two figs. Horn—ah—passion had that effect.

Levi, on the other hand, his hair was also messed up, thanks to my handsy exploration. But somehow, the man still managed to look sexy.

Being with Levi has taught me that my life felt like a beige turtleneck compared to his leather jacket and ripped jeans. Sure, the turtleneck provided warmth, but the leather jacket? That promised adventure.

He undid his shirt in one swift motion, revealing an ex-girl-friend's name inked in dark medieval font, complete with infuriating flourishes.

My breath hitched, and I jerked back like Rachel's phantom hand slapped me. Yes, weird of me to have that reaction considering I saw it that first time we'd met, while his one-night stand did her walk of shame from his house. But for some reason, my brain had filed it away under "irrelevant information," lost in the chaos of everything else going on.

A stupid tattoo. Who cares, right?

But a wall towered between me and acceptance. Every ounce of my being wanted to climb it, but something deeper held me back.

Unconsciously, I jerked away.

Levi's brows shot up. "Whoa, hold on there. What's with the sudden ice age?"

"I... I... her?" I stammered, my brain working overtime to form words of everything I was feeling, resulting in a jumbled mess.

Levi mashed his lips in a grimace as he refastened his shirt, his fingers fumbling with the buttons. "Blinded by hormones when I decided to get it. Stuck with it now."

Well, that explained it. Dumb youthful decision? Check. Relatable? Unfortunately, check. My throat tightened, and I tried swallowing to loosen it.

"She's part of your past, right?" I asked, my voice embarrassingly pitchy.

"Absolutely," he answered instantly. "Haven't talked to her since I left the city. Clean break, the whole shebang."

I crossed my arms. Sure, he plied me with things I wanted to hear. No messy exes, no lingering attachments, right? Yet, my stomach churned, throwing a full-fledged rebellion.

Nope.

Not happening. No more playing happy-go-lucky when my gut tells me otherwise.

I shot up from the couch, my feet already propelling me toward the door.

"Gotta go," I blurted, grabbing the doorknob.

Levi raced after me. "Wait, Abs!"

But the door swung open as I whipped around, my voice steely. "Promised myself: never again will I settle for anything that makes me feel small. And pretending that tattoo doesn't twist my insides? Yeah, that breaks that promise big time."

"Abby, don't!" Levi pleaded.

My feet hesitated, then I backed away, shaking my head

involuntarily. "Promises matter, Levi. And I deserve better than staring at another woman's name on your chest, night after night."

Turning away, I stepped double-time toward my car on shaky legs, with a mix of anger and humiliation. One thing was clear, though: the game of pretend had run its course. I won't do it.

CHAPTER TWENTY TWO

ABBY

LEVI'S BIKE sputtered into silence, leaving a thick hum of tension in the air.

I rolled my eyes so hard, I swear they nearly got stuck that way, proving Grandma Martin's warning true. Unease chomped at me as I grappled with the cold metal of the house keys, eager to escape this drama.

With each step of his heavy boots up the walkway, my chances of that diminished. Levi didn't frighten me; I just had allergies to confrontation. Seriously. Itchy nose, the sweats, and a sudden urge to sing show tunes. All that.

Despite it, I worked up my will and addressed him. "Don't even try it," I said, my voice tight. "Spare me the declarations. I'm done."

Considering the man trailed after me on his bike, the gentleness of his tone took me off guard. "Words are cheap, I get it. Let me show you I'm not all talk."

Caught in a moment's hesitation, I didn't reply.

Levi used that opportunity to advance into my space. "You're the most beautiful thing in my life, and losing you isn't an option. And frankly, that tattoo is a daily reminder of a bad call. I'm gonna fix it, and I need your input. Come with me."

Stuck firmly on the Halloween doormat, a permanent upgrade from the bland original, I gaped at Levi as if he'd sprouted horns. "Levi—I." My tongue tripped over the words of rejection, until his request finally broke through.

A bewildered laugh escaped my lips. "Hold up," I said, shaking my head. "You want my input on your tattoo cover-up? Seriously? Mine? You should know I once proudly presented macaroni art smothered in glitter and declared it a masterpiece."

The image of him permanently etched with a botched cover-up, inspired by my dubious artistic choice, flashed in my mind. "What if you end up looking like a Pinterest fail?"

Levi thrust the helmet at me, his gaze pleading, like a lost puppy's. "Painting new pictures with you," he mumbled, smooth as butter.

His sweet words melted the frost around my heart and coaxed a genuine smile. Taking a leap of faith, I accepted his offer. Helmet secured, we clambered onto his motorcycle, and I clung to him like a koala. No shame.

Levi turned his head and tossed over his shoulder. "Ready?"

Although curiosity gnawed at me, if I ended up face-planting on the asphalt, he owed me a lifetime supply of tacos. Just saying. And him being drop-dead gorgeous might've also factored into my embrace. I mean, the last time I checked, I had a pulse.

Levi's bike snarled like a hungry beast as we rocketed down the road. The yellow streaks from the street lamps morphed into occasional dots as we arrived at the edge of town.

We rolled to a stop in front of this cool tattoo parlor with a glowing neon sign illuminating the night. After he cut off the engine, heavy metal music blasted from inside the shop. Our fingers intertwined as we made our way up the gritty path that led to the entrance.

Stepping into unknown territory jangled my nerves. To drown out the jitters, I blurted, "So, how'd you discover this hidden gem?"

A smirk played on Levi's lips as he recalled a memory that put it there. "Used to work here as a teenager. Had a brief stint trying to walk the straight and narrow."

Poor little boy.

The uphill battle he must've waged to avoid his addiction to stealing might have been worse than he mentioned.

It's a terrible thing to survive for someone so young.

My fingers tightened around his hand. "This place is cool," I said. "I'll admit, it isn't my usual stomping ground, but it grows on you. Rough around the edges."

Despite feeling out of place, a strange sense of comfort settled over me. Someone willing to give a boy a chance couldn't be that bad. Suddenly, the weeds poking out of the cracked pavement no longer felt like neglect, and more like character, adding to its overall charm.

With that in mind, I loosened my hold on Levi, and my wooden steps adopted a smoother rhythm.

Levi leaned in closer, his breath tickling my ear. "You never had a man like me giving you a taste of the darker side, have you?" The wolfish flash of a grin lit his face, sending an odd thrill racing through my bloodstream, causing my heart to stumble and my neck to warm.

Before I could respond, Levi opened a creaking wooden door, revealing a dimly lit room.

A mosaic of inked stories adorned the walls, each one waiting to be etched onto flesh. Some depicted ferocious beasts, while others showed delicate creatures, showcasing the artist's undeniable talent.

I swallowed, my heart thrashing in my chest like a humming-bird trapped inside.

Okay, Abby, breathe.

Needles. Ink.

Totally chill, right?

Disinfectant, tinged with an unidentified aroma, filled the air.

This is probably what rebellion smells like.

Behind the counter, a tattoo artist hunched over his sketch-pad, his brow furrowed in concentration. He reminded me of Delilah, who often immersed herself in the world of her sketch-book. The difference was his arms exhibited a rainbow of his own creations. He paused when he spotted us and reached out to mercifully lower the music to decent decibels. His piercing gaze met Levi's and softened into a knowing grin.

The artist boomed, "Levi, my man! Long time no see. Who's this porcelain doll you brought with you?"

Levi met him, palms slapping together in that manly, tough-guy way. He grinned, turned to me, and said, "Rex, this is Abby. The bravest little firecracker you'll ever meet."

Firecracker? Me?

Since when did I come off like a firecracker?

Unless he counted me storming out of his house, forcing him to chase me down the street like a lovesick fool.

Okay, maybe he had a point there.

Still a weird nickname, though.

Rex's bloodshot eyes sized me up. He embodied the biker stereotype: black leather vest, tatts crawling up his neck, nick-named after a mean dinosaur. You know the type.

His voice, though, had a surprising amount of lilt which soft-ened the harshness of his appearance. "Smooth skin, sweet-heart. You got ink?"

"Um, no," I stammered. My skin burned under his scrutiny, like he'd taken his tattoo gun to it already.

Rex's lips parted, showcasing yellowed and uneven teeth. "That Rockabilly style you're sporting would be fire with some ink. Think about it, yeah? Don't worry, I won't butcher it."

Needles? More like miniature harpoons puncturing me for the sake of art.

The idea sent an icy ripple down my back, but I suppressed my shudder to not be rude.

Yeah. Sounds like fun. I'll stick to temporary tattoos.

Rex directed his attention to Levi. "How can I help you, bro?"

Levi rubbed at his faint five o'clock shadow. "Looking to trade up for something a little less... embarrassing, but I don't know what."

"Let me see the tat, so I can make suggestions," Rex said.

He squinted at Levi's chest like a plastic surgeon eyeing his patient, then he pointed to sheets mounted on the wall that might provide a suitable cover.

One in particular caught my eye: The phoenix. It practically glowed. If I weren't such a chicken, I'd contemplate snagging that one, because the thought of a bird rising from ashes is awesome. More dramatic than the butterfly.

Levi examined the sheets, mulling over his options. Then he dipped his head and whispered, "Pick something, baby. Anything. I'll wear it with pride. Make me look less like a walking bad decision and more like... your man."

His words sunk into me, a weight so heavy it twisted my gut. I couldn't believe the sheer amount of trust he'd placed in me. Back at my place, he'd declared his intentions, but standing here now, I yearned to backpedal right out of here. The enormity of his request slammed into me hard - there were no do-overs if I messed this up.

"I... I don't want to choose something that doesn't jive with you, and then you end up hating it," I squeezed his arm while speaking, my voice tight with worry.

Levi's gaze scorched into mine, his voice a low rumble that made my insides squirm like a basket full of kittens. "I trust you'll do right by me. That said, Abs, if you choose a skull tat, I'll question that decision." A mischievous twinkle lit his eyes, then he winked.

This man, this walking GQ ad on legs, knew exactly how to disarm me. A giggle tumbled out of my mouth, grateful for him narrowing down my choices without directly voicing it.

With a wall of options overwhelming us, each design vying for attention, a black wolf with hypnotic eyes jumped out at me. I pointed to it and said, "That one's pretty cool. Kind of reminds me of you, actually."

Levi's lips quirked, brimming with a touch of intrigue. "Fascinating. Why's that?"

I explained my rationale. "He marches to the beat of his own drum, yet understands the importance of aligning with the right pack. Strong, resilient. Beautiful. You. Plus, it's way cooler than that butterfly I was eyeing," I joked.

Levi didn't join in the laughter. Instead, his fingers drifted to the back of my neck, kneading out a soothing massage that had me wanting to melt into his touch. Holding my gaze, he called out to Rex, "My mind's made up. I want the wolf."

Janky teeth stretched across Rex's grinning face. "Solid pick! Let's rock and roll. Follow me."

He ushered us into a small room dominated by a reclining chair. I perched nervously in the corner, eyes glued to Levi. My fingers twitched instinctively, mirroring the grip I wasn't allowed to take. Ignoring my own anxieties, I relished my front-row seat to this intriguing process.

The low whir of the tattoo gun hummed through the air, punctuated by the quiet exchange of memories between Levi and Rex. Rex filled Levi in on gossip about the people they'd known. I have to admit, for a scary looking man, Rex had an awesome bedside manner.

Despite occasional winces, Levi's eyes never left mine.

After what felt like an eternity, Rex finally rolled his stool back, revealing the masterpiece on Levi's chest. A magnificent wolf, its gaze both fierce and serene, adorned his skin. No sign of Rachel anywhere.

CHAPTER TWENTY THREE

LEVI

I STOOD BEHIND CASEY, who heaved open the mill's door, sending a plume of choking dust into our faces. Instinctively, my arm shot up, shielding my nose and mouth. Stone mirrored my action, but Casey plowed ahead, unfazed by the grit. His boots creaked on the half-rotted floorboards as he made his way inside the cavernous building.

Inside, light invaded through boarded slats, casting ominous shadows on cobwebs that hung like drapes.

My hairs stood up, and the urge to swat off phantom bugs nearly took over. I almost bailed. Screw street cred.

But turning back now wasn't an option, especially after all the hoops we jumped through to secure a search warrant with the property owners. So I thugged it out and joked it off. "Man, nothing but tumbleweeds. The vultures already picked the bones clean. We got here too late."

Disregarding my quip, Casey focused on the rafters above. He glanced at Stone for a fleeting moment, their eyes locking in a silent exchange.

A thought struck that iced my spine as I shifted on my feet. What if they were setting me up to take the fall for the break-ins?

Both Casey and Stone were now scouring our surroundings

with as much curiosity as I was. That threw me off. Now I couldn't tell if I'd misinterpreted their exchange because I felt uncomfortable here, or whether they were just better at hiding their motives.

"Procedure, Cross," Casey snapped, his voice grating like sandpaper. "Remember? No cowboy showboating. We need solid evidence that'll hold up in court, or this entire investigation will go tits up."

What the hell was bro's deal? Why was he talking down to me?

With my luck, I'll probably end up in jail for decking an officer before the day is over. Just wait.

I wonder if Casey or Stone gutted this place while we waited on the warrant. It all started to add up. Sticking me in microfiche hell wouldn't exactly light a fire under this investigation. Not that I minded spending extra time near Abby.

Stone grumbled, "Enough yapping. We're on the clock. Let's get a move on."

He didn't need to tell me twice. I patrolled the interior, each shadow scrutinized for any hint of missing furniture.

My foot, oblivious to the treacherous floorboards, snagged on something, sending me lurching forward. Before I could regain my balance, I found myself crashing onto the dusty floor. The rough grain bit into my palms, flaying them like a mother.

I lay there, squeezing my eyes shut while my hands burned. For some reason, the memory of falling off my bike came to mind and my dad's paternal advice of, "Walk it off, kid. Builds character."

Well, Dad, you said it. Consider my character officially built.

Gritting my teeth, I peeled myself off the planks and stood up. A glint of color in the far corner drew my attention.

As I scrubbed off the smoky dust, I squinted at the source, trying to bring the thing into focus. Maglite in hand, I trained the beam at the spot, oscillating it back and forth, hoping to reproduce that glint and to prove my mind wasn't playing tricks on me.

My heart thumped like the savage beat in a Necrophagist song. Inch by inch, I pushed deeper into the obscurity and swiped away the snagging cobwebs, grimacing at their creepy threadiness.

Jackpot! Tucked deep in the corner, out of view of anyone who might've swept through with a cursory inspection, was a painting of a woman. Her eyes were like sapphires, her hair of gold, and a smirk potent enough to make a man rethink his priorities.

The grin stretching across my face rivaled the one I wore after pulling off my first successful heist. All the bureaucratic BS had been worth it for this moment.

"Well, I'll be damned," I said, my voice holding a smile. "How'd they miss this beauty? Must've had cataracts or some-thing, 'cause it's freakin' huge."

Casey shifted, a muscle twitching in his jaw. He removed one hand from his belt loop, rubbing his temples as though trying to ease a brewing migraine. "Just snap the photo, Cross. We'll deal with the 'whys' later."

My jaw clenched until the muscles locked tight. Every fiber of my being wanted to shred him with words, but instead, I forced myself to kneel and snap the picture.

Adding to my irritation, Stone said, "Casey's right. Bag it, and let's get it back for analysis. Every minute we spend here is another minute closer to losing this case."

We spent a half-hour more walking around before we called it a wrap and left. No one said a thing as we made our way to the car.

But Casey said a hell of a lot in the tightness of his shoulders when he carried the painting to the cruiser. I'm no body language expert, but even I noticed it. Which meant Stone defi-nitely picked up on it.

That wasn't even the strangest part. While we sat inside the cruiser, Casey pulled out his phone, his fingers flying across the screen. He angled it away from Stone, but its reflection in the window caught my eye. It looked like he was using ASCII in some kind of code.

I opened my phone, copied down the code as best as I could into a notepad, then reached into my pocket for an antacid.

Back in the station, the atmosphere was stilted since we'd arrived. Casey left for patrol, and Stone poured himself a mugful of stale coffee from the communal pot out front.

Strange because he had a coffee maker in his office, so it stands to reason that he had something he wanted to say.

I was proven right when he turned, making eye contact through the steam rising up from his dark blue ceramic mug. He walked towards me and said, "We need to talk about the painting, son."

Suddenly, Robson materialized from the back.

My gut churned. It felt like they were ganging up on me. But I didn't get a chance to reply because the door swung open.

A whirlwind of gray hair and polyester, draped in a muumuu worthy of Woodstock, slammed a purse on the counter with a force that could have broken her valuables inside.

She burst out, "Bloodsuckers! This town's gone bat-guano crazy! Some lowlife stole my vintage record collection! Every piece, gone! Hendrix, Joplin, even my Elvis first pressings."

Robson raised his hands in a placating gesture. "Alright, ma'am. I understand why this is upsetting," he whipped out a pen and pad from his notebook holder, clicked the pen and said, "What exactly was taken?"

"Lilla?" Stone asked, eyeing the woman up and down. "Lilla Reed, that you? Dammit to hell, what happened?"

Now, I was sure he directed that question to the lady, but

Robson shoved his way into the conversation and answered for her. "Break-in, Cheif. We need your insight."

"Got it," Stone said, dismissing him. "We'll get right on it, but you need to start from square one. Exactly what was stolen?"

The lady placed her hands on her hip. Her stormy blue eyes fixed Stone with an odd glare, like she knew him and wasn't going to back down.

"You need an itemized list, Wyatt?" she scoffed. "My vinyl had been raided! My Hendrix originals, Joplin's Pearl, even the Zep Four album with Jimmy Page's autograph."

Her voice cracked for a second before she recovered her bravado and jabbed a finger at Stone. "I'll tell you one thing, you better find this fool before I do, because he made it personal."

Robson scratched the nape of his neck, impersonating a stray plagued by fleas.

I smiled, tossed in a wink, and said, "Bet they dug your taste in music."

Her lips twitched into a fleeting smile, momentarily banishing the storm in her eyes. Even Stone chuckled.

Robson, douche almighty, said, "Real professional, Cross."

What is with these chastising assholes today? I swear!

Stone snapped a serious look at Robson that could have stilled the Hudson.

I smiled down at my feet, loving it.

Stone continued, "Don't pay heed to my deputy's lack of sensitivity. Now, Lilla, can you give me your address? We'll check things out ASAP."

Lilla rattled off her address, and Robson's pen raced across his pad.

After she left, Stone said, "Check it out, but ease up on the way you talk to her. She's sensitive." Then he walked back to his office.

Robson snapped his notepad shut with a decisive click, tucking it securely onto his belt. He shook his head and said, "Bet her kid probably hocked them for weed."

I didn't react, because his comment was uncalled for. Yeah, she dressed weird, but she didn't deserve that.

My lack of response must've bugged him, because Robson eyed me. "You're real pals with the Sheriff, huh?"

"Just work," I shrugged, my voice nonchalant. "Nothing personal. We're not exactly BFFs."

A smirk spread across his face, like he was supposedly in on my secret. "Don't get too comfortable. Eyes everywhere, bro."

"Let 'em watch," I fired back.

Robson kept that smirk on his face while strutting out the station like some kind of big shot.

CHAPTER TWENTY FOUR

LEVI

SLIPPING PAST THE CIRCULATION DESK, the clack of keyboards grated on my nerves. Some did it way too hard, like maniacs carrying out a vendetta. And don't even get me started on the overachievers who pounded out two million words per second. Let's just say, I didn't miss that.

Faces close, Abby and Kaminsky murmured in hushed tones, their heads bent together as though they were hatching a secret plot.

Bile ran up my throat, but I checked the knee-jerk reaction. Doug's girl was a real stunner. After seeing them together, he didn't strike me as a man who'd risk flirting with another woman and ruining what he had. So I wasn't too bothered…ish. The fact remained that Abby and Doug had known each other for years, a lifetime in small-town terms, and nada ever happened between them.

Deep breaths, Levi. Keep it cool.

Abby and Kaminsky's heads snapped apart like startled deer caught in headlights the moment I strolled up.

A spackled smile animated my face. "Keeping the peace in library land, beautiful?"

Abby quirked her red lips to the side, and her brow raised.

"The usual," she said. "Wrangling the desperados with a disapproving glare and rescuing our paperbacks out of the wet hands of teething toddlers. Same old, same old."

A grin tugged at my lips. "Sounds rough. Maybe you need a bodyguard? I'm fluent in librarian intimidation." My gaze lingered on her flushed cheeks a beat too long before I winked. "Anyway, just dropped by to fill you in. Think you can handle a ghost story? Or are you all talk and no spine?"

Doug shifted uncomfortably, seeming unsure of where to direct his gaze during our exchange.

Whatever, man. My lady's allure overpowers my resistance.

She straightened, and a spark lit her gray eyes, triggering my delight. "Don't underestimate a librarian, cowboy. Now spill. Does this story contain a haunted mill or talking paintings like a good ol' Scooby Doo Mystery?"

I snapped my fingers and pointed at her with a theatrical flare. "Bingo! Your psychic prowess amazes me." My hand ached with a sharp throb, and I flinched, reminding me of the tumble at the mill. Apparently, walking it off only works for the feet. Thanks to my text while driving back to HQ, Abby knew about the mishap.

Doug, on the other hand, blinked and furrowed his brows at us like we were a particularly hairy calculus problem. I'd bet he didn't get the joke, although he probably heard about the forgotten painting via Abs. "Anything new at the precinct since the mill?" he asked.

The crapfest of a day replayed, leaching off my mood. Did I want to spread gossip that the precinct devolved into locker room bs with a reporter?

Not happening.

Telling Abs about the painting had already pushed that line. The potential backlash from Stone alone triggered a shudder. I sidestepped that landmine and provided Doug with information he already knew. "Stone's a riddle, that's for sure. I'm like a behavior analyst trying to read him but can't."

Doug's brows shot up, and his voice carried an undercurrent of disappointment. "So, nothing new then."

"Slow day," I shrugged. "Most of the guys are out on patrol."

"How's this whole mess sitting with you? Knowing your family's right in the thick of it?" Doug shifted closer to Abby, his voice dipping to a murmur.

A frown replaced Abby's playful smile as she fiddled with the mouse. "It's been weird, you know? Watching what I say, afraid something might slip."

"And then there's the book club." A sigh escaped her ruby lips. "The girls know what's going on but I didn't tell them about my uncle's potential involvement. They figured that me and Levi are hitting a 'rough patch' because I'm so cagey."

Rough patch? The rough patch had nothing to do with us, but the vultures circling our perimeter.

Balling my fists, a cuss slipped out from under my breath.

I circled behind the desk, and gathered her in my arms. Looking down into her trusting eyes, I cupped her face and vowed, "Whatever it is, baby, we'll face it head-on, alright?"

Abby smiled and wrapped her arms around my hip. Just the feel of her made a warmth bloom in my chest, and I had no doubt that everything wrong in my world would sort itself out. She calms me. No one I'd ever been with had that effect.

No one.

"Sorry, Abs," Kaminsky chimed in. "I forget how stressful it is for people who aren't used to guarding info."

Doug's eyes flickered to me for a brief second before returning his gaze to Abby.

A barbell of unease settled in my stomach. Was his comment directed at me? Was he throwing shade at my past, or maybe admitting how hard it is for him to sit on journalistic secrets?

Confronting him ranked far down my to-do list. Calming Abby's anxiety did. Reassuringly rubbing her arm with one hand, I reached into my shirt pocket for an antacid roll with the other—as a preventative measure.

"I bet being at the precinct beats microfiching any day," Abby said, her voice laced with a forced lightness that didn't fool me.

The whole damn situation elicited an eye roll. Leaning down, I planted a quick kiss on her forehead. The way her eyes fluttered closed made my insides churn. Seeing her this way never got old, but I shifted focus and got down to business.

"Don't remind me," I said. "Speaking of interesting situations, maybe a Winnebago trip will be less intense this time. I'm hoping Al can help me figure out this stumper I'm dealing with."

Abby's smile went the way of a snowball on the fourth of July, replaced by a tight line across her brow. "Does that mean I have to go too?"

Selling her a politician's promise made my skin crawl. "He phoned me and said he wants us to go back to his place. Says he feels like shit about—well, you know. He offered to make us dinner. Come on, babe, second chances, right? Where would I be without yours?"

Dang! That came out wrong. Using "shit" and "dinner" close together didn't exactly make the offer appetizing.

Abby's shiver was a dead giveaway that she recalled the memory of the gun incident. Then she shook her head. "I don't know, Levi. After what happened last time... I'm not sure if I can handle being there again."

Squeezing her shoulders, I tried to project a confidence I didn't entirely possess. "I get it, baby. More than you know. But this time will be different. I won't let anything happen to you, and the old bastard genuinely wants to make amends."

After a moment, she put on a brave smile. "Alright. If it means that much to you, I'm in." Her smile faltered, and she whispered, "Peanut butter and jelly," under her breath.

Seeing her lighten up, even a notch, soothed the knotted ball in my gut, and I chuckled.

However, Doug bit his lower lip as his eyes wandered to the dusty old globe behind us. His vibe screamed of unspoken questions, but politeness, a trait I appreciated for Abby's sake, kept them corked.

Giving Doug a quick chin jut, I asked, "You crack that code yet, bud? I took a run at it but didn't make any headway."

Doug shook his head, his eyes glazed over. "Same. It made my brain itch, so I passed it on to the puzzle department at the paper to see if they have a clue."

Wall-to-wall book cases, here I come. "Maybe the answer's somewhere in this paper jungle. Time to get cracking."

CHAPTER TWENTY FIVE

ABBY

DREAD BALLOONED IN MY CHEST, growing to the size of a Thanksgiving turkey as we neared Uncle Al's chrome monstrosity.

I gulped so hard, I could've swallowed my Adam's apple whole. My slick hands nearly fumbled the cherry pie plate, almost dropping it onto the dirt path.

Next time, I'll bring a fruitcake instead.

Flashbacks of our last visit rushed in, making me clamped the pie plate tighter. Who in their right mind welcomed their estranged nephew with a firearm?

I mean, call me crazy, but a simple 'Hey there, partner! Long time, no see,' has a better ring to it than 'stick 'em up.'

Levi kept pace beside me, his still-calloused hand resting on the small of my back. That nasty fall he'd taken at the mill really did a number on them. Last night, at my place, his hand froze mid-reach for a can of beer. With a grimace, he nearly retracted it.

I grabbed his hand, found welts, and begged him to have it x-rayed, but the stubborn fool refused.

He laughed it off and said, "Relax, foxy. It's just a flesh wound. Besides, there's no crying in baseball."

Seriously, what's the deal with guys and the ER? They have a universal allergy.

If that happened to me, I would've jetted to the hospital like I was hopped up on Red Bull, but Macho Camacho over here preferred to tough it out.

I didn't pry deeper into his refusal of medical treatment, because it likely stemmed from a lack of insurance.

Whatever the reason, it wasn't any of my business.

Yet.

"Abs, chill," Levi murmured, his voice a low rumble of reassurance. "It'll be alright. He just wants to patch things up, remember? He's expecting us."

Right. This was for Levi, for his chance at deepening family ties.

You can handle this, Abs. It's only Al Cross.

A flash of movement in the garden sent my hand darting towards the pepper spray stowed in my purse. "Whoa, did you see that?!" I blurted out.

Uncle Al materialized from around the bend of his home, his gardening gloves caked in mud. He held a hand shovel in one hand, while the other clutched a peanut butter and jelly jar.

"Well, lookie here!" he boomed, his voice surprisingly jovial. "Didn't hear you pull up. Them garden gnomes took off running while I was reaping my tomatoes." His eyes twinkled as he delivered his puzzling joke.

Smile, Abby. Think happy thoughts... like puppies and rainbows. Not being chased off the property by a delusional old coot brandishing a shotgun. You can do this. It's a piece of cake.

Listening to myself, I plastered a tight smile on my face, or grimace, however you choose to look at it. But hey, at least we didn't set off the alarm this time.

Small victories.

"Ah, hello, Mr. Cross. Sorry if we took you by surprise," I managed, extending the plate as rehearsed in the mirror before leaving the house. "We brought a cherry pie for dessert."

A tough smile, testament to his dentist-free lifestyle, split Al's face. "Nah, darlin', don't sweat it. Anyway, you're just in time for dinner. Burgers are sizzling as we speak. Used your Grandma's recipe, Levi. The first bite will have you swearin' they came straight off a Conestoga wagon." With his rusty spade in hand, he waved us forward. "Come in, come in!"

At least he behaved in rare form this time around. Promising. Thank goodness he planned on serving Levi's grandma's burgers instead of his sussy PB&J. My stomach unclenched as we stepped into the cramped interior of Al's abode.

Books, faded maps, and trinkets from Al's life spilled out everywhere. All the same as the last time, but it felt surprisingly cozy. He ushered us to the same booth we'd occupied during our last visit, except for one addition, a manila folder sat like an unwelcome guest on the table.

Al plopped down opposite us and unfurled the folder with a theatrical snap. "So, Levi, my boy, ready to inherit your vagabond uncle's kingdom?"

My brows pulled together in confusion and twisted to Levi. "What's this?" I asked him. As far as I knew, this was a reconciliation dinner, not a notary signing.

"Thought I'd make things official while there's air in my lungs. Provisions in case the reaper comes knocking unexpectedly," Al replied, thumping his chest playfully. "Just tidying up loose ends, sweetheart," he winked at me, in the same way Levi often had.

Charm, it seemed, ran deep in their family.

Levi inked his signature on the document as his uncle watched with a satisfied smirk. Afterward, Al rose from the booth and tucked the folder between a row of magazines before tending to his sizzling patties.

Securing his future wasn't something I could hold against him. My parents had me sign similar documents during visits to Florida. Retirement definitely fueled that worry, so I readily signed whatever they needed to provide them with peace of mind.

A silent understanding passed between us. Levi's arm found a casual rest around my shoulders, a familiar gesture he'd enacted since the night he'd gotten the tattoo.

I ate it up and burrowed closer, welcoming the reprieve from the earlier tension.

As Al flipped the burgers, his voice rose over the sizzle. "Speaking of reapers, did Matty ever tell you about the chili ointment I used to make? Cured just about anything."

"Dad swore by it. Said it patched him up better than duct tape, more than once, on camping trips," Levi responded.

Al shook his head, a wistful smile playing on his lips. "We were thick as thieves back then, me and Matty. He was always tinkering with his car or motorcycle. I preferred dirt under my fingernails, working in Ma's garden, content with the simple things. A hobo by nature." He chuckled at his self-deprecating joke.

"Anyway," he continued, "I still got some ointment stashed somewhere in the back. I'll hunt for some later. Your hands look rough, kid. What's the story? Bike accident?"

"Work mishap," Levi answered. "Whining won't fix it, and Dad always said nothin' heals better than rubbing dirt on it."

I pressed my lips together in a tight line and shook my head, unable to reconcile this brand of logic with the coddling and care I benefitted from as an only child. It felt utterly alien to me.

Levi's lips tugged into a lopsided grin as he leaned in and planted a sweet kiss on my temple.

Al laughed while chopping the veggie toppings for the burgers. "Sounds like my little brother, alright. So, Abigail, what's Chet been up to?"

With a smile, I said, "He's been all about competitive fishing lately, even gearing up for a tournament next season."

"Good for him. Me? Retirement?" Al snorted. "Not for this old dog. Too much fire left in my belly. Wouldn't know what to do with myself idle. Anyway, enough about me. Son, how's the business at the precinct?"

Levi's arm became a ghost on my shoulder as he disentangled himself and crossed them. He scratched at his five o'clock shadow and muttered, "Confusing as hell. Don't know which way is up or down or who to trust. Every time I think I have it figured out, something else makes me suspicious."

Al grunted, flipping a patty with a practiced flick of his wrist. His gaze flitted to his nephew and then back to the sizzling pan. "That's a murky pond you're wading through, kid. People doing dirty behind the scenes ain't fond of having their secrets come to light. Take it from me, I know a thing or two about that."

"Speaking of which, there's something I need to ask," Levi said. He pulled out his phone from his pocket and scrolled through it. Rising from the booth, he joined Al. "This message is a cipher. Can't crack it for the life of me. Any chance you have some insight?"

Levi held up the phone to his uncle's scrunched face. "Ah, cryptograms," Al said. "Hold on a sec, I think I got just the book for that."

The stove clicked off. Al's fingers traced across worn book spines like a man reading Braille. Finally, he snagged the one he wanted.

Thank goodness. The ravenous grumbled that erupted from my stomach could have rivaled a banshee's wail. Levi caught it with a wince. I offered a sheepish shrug, twisting the chipped silver of Granny Martin's post-war ring between my fingers.

"Aha!" Al boomed, brandishing the book like a trophy. "This bad boy might get you started. Not sure if your specific code's in there, but it could point you in the right direction." He plopped it in front of Levi, then reconvened burger duty.

Levi cracked open the book and skimmed its yellowed pages. The info must have been relevant in the 80s. He skipped the copyright page, so I didn't get a chance to check. Something about the pages nagged at me, but I couldn't put my finger on it.

What concerned me the most was whether Levi could find information here that might help him in the case.

Al placed plates stacked with mouth-watering burgers on the table and said, "Chow time, kiddos. Eat up."

Unable to contain my delight, I snatched up the burger, my famished insides erupting in a wave of gratitude.

CHAPTER TWENTY SIX

ABBY

I GROANED, sinking deep into the plush, blue velvet of Levi's couch, my focus riveted on him. Our lips met with such urgency, you would think we had been separated for weeks.

My fingers, no longer concerned with propriety, mussed his gel-stiffened hair with the urgency of an animal in heat.

Drawing back, our lungs scrambling for air, he methodically released each obsidian button of his black, tailored shirt, exposing the wolf tableau spanning his toned physique.

Driven by curiosity, my fingers reached out with a mind of their own, tracing the edges, careful not to smudge it.

Months ago, the mere idea of being this close to Levi would have sent me running for the hills. Not because I didn't want him. Between you, me, and the birds, this man starred in my dreams—only wrapped in a blue towel, but I digress.

Truth bomb. His past intimidated me.

We were brought up galaxies apart. While I set our table with silverware for family dinners, Levi probably filched ripe tomatoes from street vendors just to fend off his family's hunger.

How could I possibly look down on that? My heart ached for the boy he used to be, and I'd defend his actions against anyone who hadn't walked in his tattered shoes.

Through that lens, it's understandable how desperation molded his life choices. Although I wouldn't have shared his course, it didn't take a genius to see how the hardship of his family's dire circumstances forced him toward unlit alleyways, so to speak.

"Still tender?" I asked, referring to the wolf sprawled across Levi's chest.

His lips quirked up in an alluring smirk that pushed the pedal on my heart rate. "At first, yeah. It felt like fire knives," he admitted, eyes meeting mine with a depth that pierced straight through me.

"But my old man used to say, 'Beauty ain't handed out like candy, you gotta bleed for it sometimes.'"

Levi's espresso-brown eyes regarded me with an intensity matching the wolf's. His gaze seared into mine as though he drilled a silent confession into the marrow of my soul.

Heat seeped into my heart, intertwining with a tremor of something profound. As his words settled in my consciousness, my throat burned.

"That's..." I whispered, searching for the right expression, "that's beautiful. Touchingly so. It's awesome your dad's wisdom impacted you after all these years."

Levi's fingers, rough and calloused against mine, tightened their hold. A slow smile played on his lips, teasing and dangerous.

Then, in a breathtaking gesture, he lifted my hand to his mouth, his lips lingering on my knuckles like a searing brand.

"You made up your mind about getting a tat?" he asked.

"Kind of. The phoenix from the shop is stuck on repeat in my head," I admitted, a blush creeping up my neck. "The idea of it became an obsession, honestly. Rising from the ashes... needing fire in your soul to be reborn. It resonates with me, you know?"

I sighed, the tug of war raging in me since I laid eyes on it. "But where to put it? I have second thoughts on placing it where everyone can see."

"So, you're fixated on the phoenix, huh? I pictured you more of a hearts and roses kind of girl."

I gestured to my hair. "Nah, I've got the market cornered on red."

Levi grinned as his thumb brushed mine, sending a zing straight to my core.

A self-satisfied chuckle escaped him, leaving no doubt he knew exactly what he was doing.

The fiend.

"Why don't we find a secluded spot? I'll make sure you're properly searched," he said, his eyes twinkling with mischief.

Jolt number two, with an added clench of my lower lips.

Game on, sir.

"Hmm... let's see," I said, attempting a seductive purr, but the Christmas Eve giddiness in my voice fooled no one.

I coughed, clearing my throat, then shot up, and wiggled to shed my dress until I stood there in just my modest bra and panties—vulnerable and exposed, yet strangely empowered.

Levi's fingers found the rest of his buttons, popping them open in record time.

Just when bravado bloomed in my chest, someone banged on the door.

Levi growled out a cuss and said, "Who the hell...?"

He stood, moving to the door, and grumbled along the way, "Can't leave a man in peace."

Panic-driven, I hustled with the speed of a film stuck on fast-forward, practically jumping into my dress. An audible tearing sound made me almost start bawling. This blue number held the crown jewel spot in my wardrobe, saved for special events, dang it!

"For the love of God, what the hell are you doing here?!" Levi boomed.

His reaction momentarily froze my hand, midway through righting the shoulder strap.

"Can't a girl visit her ex?" Her saccharine voice dripped with mean-girl venom.

"I see you painted over my name on your chest. Guess true love doesn't last long after the thrill of the heist, huh?"

It clicked. Rachel. Well, joy to the freaking world.

"Seriously, Rach?! Haven't we done this already? You said it yourself, we're done! What part of 'over' don't you understand? Just go!"

"I came to find you. Rick needs your help with a testimony."

Maybe I'm off my rocker, but if you were going to request a favor, wouldn't flattery be a smarter tactic? Not exactly 'damsel in distress' vibes. More like 'temptress with an agenda.' Total B.S. on her needing help with testimony.

A laugh tore from him, a nasty, mocking one that broke my heart he had that in him. "Have you completely lost it? Hell no! I'm not getting mixed up with you two again. I made that crystal clear the first time you asked back in the city. That answer still holds."

Even with a frown twisting her luscious lips, Rachel, all porcelain skin and killer cheekbones, was still radiant. I mean, her chestnut curls defied gravity, without a hint of product.

My victory rolls suddenly felt like a costume gone wrong, transforming me from Levi's girlfriend into a backup singer for the Andrew Sisters. And him being older than me by a few years didn't matter one bit.

A flush engulfed my entire body. I snagged my handbag and tried to slink past Levi's solid frame and Rachel's surprised expression. "I'll just, uh, make myself scarce," I mumbled, desperately wishing the floor would open up and swallow me whole.

An arm, firm and warm, snaked around my waist, stopping me cold. "No," Levi's voice rumbled, a possessive edge. "You stay. This is your turf, too."

I practically melted into a puddle, loving him for defending me. If I had pom-poms, I'd be leading a celebratory cheer right now!

Without a single tassel in sight, I beamed and asked, "Have I mentioned how much I appreciate you?" I grinned, soaking in the moment. "Not many guys would extend an invitation for their date to linger after... well, you know."

Levi casually flexed his arm, a playful smirk on his lips. "Fill me in on those details later, 'kay baby?"

He shifted his attention to Rachel, and his no-nonsense edge returned. "You've got what you came for. Now scat."

I rested my hand on Levi's wolf tat, and he winked at me.

Rachel snorted like a prize-winning hog; her arms folded across her chest.

What the—

I didn't think pretty women made piggy noises in front of the opposite sex, much less her ex, who she obviously wants to lasso back into her convoluted web.

Color me intrigued.

"Ugh, why couldn't you treat me like that when we were an item?" Rachel asked, narrowing her eyes. "So preoccupied with planning your jobs, never any time for an actual chat. You were practically a ghost in your own life. No wonder I ran to Rick!"

I bit down on my bottom lip, not giving two hoots whether it stained my teeth cherry-red.

Reminders of his unwavering dedication to his former occupation—like, planning heists—didn't sit well with me.

I understood why he went down that road in the beginning. But after all these years?

I shivered.

It's not like I didn't know what he did. But hearing about it from her made it more real.

Levi rubbed my back. "Things were different then. But you know what? We've been over this a million times. It's getting tired. Let it go. I'm with Abby now."

Rachel raised an impeccably groomed brow at me, no resignation on her face, just an expression of confusion.

She'd insulted me without even trying, and I had to fight to stay rooted and not to slink away.

Donning a mocking smile, she jibed, "Seems like you've got quite the romantic here, sweetie. It's a shame you didn't meet him sooner. Maybe you could have schooled me on being treated right."

My mouth dropped open, and I clenched my fists.

Levi's fingers tightened around my waist, silently communicating he'd handle this. "Some people just bring out the best in me."

Rachel's expression soured.

Why, though? That wasn't a fiery clap back. Unless it meant more between them.

Rachel raised her defiant chin. "And others... missed their chance."

Levi rolled his eyes. "You said what you came here to say. Now get out, I have to tend to my woman."

Rachel about-faced and stormed off.

Levi slammed the door and turned the locks. "Sorry about that weird-ass interruption, Abs. She's been after me to testify before I left the city. I don't know why she came here."

My feelings were so jumbled about the realities of his past. I stepped back from him, putting distance between us, needing space while questioning him.

Levi's forehead scrunched up like an accordion as he studied me, and his expression grew concerned. "Come on, let's talk," he said, and ushered me back to the same couch where we were about to share a different kind of experience.

As we sank into the cushion, he said, "Just FYI, I haven't been talking to her. My guess is she's probably lonely because Rick is in jail, and she's using that 'testify' bull as an excuse to scope out where my head was at."

Hold on. Did he genuinely believe Rachel's sudden appearance was an attempt at an attention grab? Didn't he consider there might be more complications?

My mouth turned Sahara. I swallowed and folded my hands on my lap, my nails forming tiny crescent moon indentations in my skin. "What if this visit wasn't solely about getting back together? Are you in some kind of trouble? Was that why you came back to Millbrook?"

"Look," he blew out a breath, placed his palms together, and gestured with them as he spoke. "I saw how her visit twisted you up, and yeah, I get it. We haven't exactly dissected this whole ex-thing, so hear me out. Things with Rachel were complicated because she's tied up with my ex-partner. True, I raised the alarm when I botched the last job. But when Rick went instead of me, he stole the documents I was supposed to. He got tagged for the whole mess. That could've been me, but since I wasn't technically there, I wasn't charged with it."

That didn't add up. A furrow creased my brow. "But doesn't that still leave you open for a conspiracy charge, even if you don't testify?"

Levi pulled away, a fraction. Then he glanced upwards, as though he wrestled with how much he'd share. "The feds want Rick. He waded neck-deep in the money laundering swamp. See, they go after big fish, and Rick is practically a whale. Rachel chose him over me because she's a sucker for flashy cars, fat diamonds, and enough cash to rival Scrooge McDuck. I couldn't compete with that. My offerings were far more modest —like keeping the fridge stocked and rent paid."

Absorbing his revelations, the white-knuckled grip on my lap relaxed. Levi's account cleared things up, and Rachel's probably designer outfit underscored his claims.

But there was still that gremlin whispering sweet nothings in my ear. So, in the spirit of hashing things out, I admitted, "She's definitely pretty, though."

I must have turned as red as my lipstick. Pointing out how I wasn't some fabulous upgrade from his ex stung like a squirt of lemon juice on a fresh cut. Me strutting down catwalks? Ha, not in this lifetime! I knew that. But despite the outlandish comparison, it smarted.

Levi gently tilted my chin until our eyes locked. "She might be a looker, darlin'," he said, "but it's still a smoke show. You're a whole different kind of beautiful. From your fiery spirit to your loyalty, you're the real deal. You want me, not all the plastic junk I could buy you."

His gaze bore into me like a black hole, pulling me in. "Since I've been here, I've seen you prioritize everyone else's needs over your own. You won't believe how rare that is, baby."

Speech abandoned me, and I dropped my chin to my chest, hoping to formulate them. Denial sat on the tip of my tongue, along with all that stuff about me being beautiful.

Levi cradled my cheek. Likely sensing my hesitation, he said, "Stealing, hurting others... that wasn't who I wanted to be, but it's all I knew. I built a life out of it. Then you showed up, glowing with kindness and forgiveness like some kind of angel."

"Look," he paused. "I'm no saint, not even close, and I sure as hell don't deserve you. But if you give me a shot, I'll fight to be better. It'll probably take me a lifetime—"

Like a heat-seeking missile, I crushed my lips onto his before he had a chance to finish.

Levi might not have been perfect, but neither was I. Maybe, though. Just maybe, our imperfections could fit together like a pair of mismatched socks, forming something unique, something real, something us.

CHAPTER TWENTY SEVEN

ABBY

LEVI SMOOTHLY LIFTED my dress and allowed it to cascade onto his hallway floor. Pressing me against the wall with his solid frame, he kissed, trailing down my neck until his journey halted at my bra strap. With skillful movements, he slid the straps from my shoulders, unhooked the clasp, and removed it, leaving me exposed to his hungry eyes.

His voice rumbled with a lusty growl. "You're gorgeous, baby. Absolutely delectable."

A hot flush erupted throughout my whole body. "Thanks," I gasped, my racing heart caused my chest to rise and fall with each audible breath. "You're not too bad yourself."

Levi's face transformed into a devilish grin, accompanied by a primal gaze, which electrified my core. His fingertips traipsed unhurried circles around my now hardened nipple before taking it into his mouth with the greedy moan.

The flicker of his warm, silky tongue gliding against my sensitive skin made me shut my eyes and rest my head against the wall.

Withdrawing abruptly, Levi cut off our connection, leaving the air to cool my skin.

My body buzzed, every nerve alive. Craving more, I reached out and placed my hands on his chest. Locking eyes with his, I inquired, "May I?"

Levi's eyes flickered with emotion before giving me the green light. "By all means, my love; have your way with me." His words resonated deeply, causing my world to shift.

His...love.

I beamed, soaking those words into my being, allowing them to light the dim corners of my insecurity.

Levi's sincere gaze never wavered, hammering home the point until I felt it in my marrow.

I savored the salty tang of the wolf, while my impatient fingers struggled with the button on his pants, eager to taste more of him.

Seeing my struggle, Levi took over and quickly freed himself, dropping his pants and briefs to his ankles, and then divesting himself of them.

Levi's fingers found their way to the apex of my satin under-wear, his thumb applying pressure to the damp spot, as a guttural growl, raw and possessive, rumbled deep in his chest.

Before my hazy mind could process what was happening, my panties hit the floor. Levi helped me step free of them and led me into his bedroom.

The click of my stilettos echoed on the hardwood as he twirled me and kissed me, backing us towards his bed.

"So, darlin'," he whispered, "have you figured out where that tattoo's gonna go?"

"What?" A breathless laugh spilled from my lips as my body sank into the yielding mattress.

Levi leaned down, dragged his tongue across my nipple, then peered at me. "I'm not cool with anyone touching you here."

He moved to the other one and did the same, sending shivers down my spine. "Or here."

Although I seriously wanted him to qualify more areas, I kept it together and admitted, "Well, it's a good thing because I don't think I can withstand needles harpooning my flesh or exposing myself to Rex."

Levi settled beside me, propping himself up on his elbow. "In that case, where's your comfort zone?"

The wolf's silhouette took form beneath my fingers as I mapped its outline on his skin. "Any suggestions?"

Levi enclosed my fingers, drawing them to his warm lips, and pressed a gentle kiss on them. "This is your call, darlin'. I won't take that from you. But I want to be there when it happens, because it's not safe for a woman to be alone with a man, exposed, for hours."

Emotion constricted my throat, sending a sharp sting to my nose, leaving me teary-eyed. For the first time in my life, someone wasn't dictating my path. He loved me. He loved me enough to trust my decision. Silent, warm tears flowed down the sides of my face. My heart swelled with love and gratitude, overflowing with emotions. Words were too flimsy to capture how I felt.

Gently, I cupped his rough cheek, feeling the coarse caress of his stubble against my palm. "This probably won't get you out of dish duty, but, I love you," I whispered, putting my soul into it.

Levi's soft brown eyes searched mine, speaking volumes without uttering a single syllable. "The feeling's completely mutual, Foxy," he replied, his warm breath dancing against my skin.

He leaned in, bringing our foreheads together in communion. Then, he pressed his lips against mine and claimed my mouth, possessing me. I willingly participated, pouring my all into it.

Because I knew. I just knew with complete certainty he'd keep me safe.

Severing our connection, Levi traversed down my body until his head reached my wet core. He spread my legs wide and groaned as he inhaled, taking my scent into his lungs.

Whoa! My breath hitched, and my brow shot up to my hairline.

Flipping heck, who does that?! This guy was a revelation on all accounts.

I dropped my head on the mattress and fixated my attention on a wooden ceiling fan above his bed. My center pulsated with anticipation.

And then it struck—his tongue.

Wiggling my nub, releasing shockwaves of pleasure that jolted my body. Something between a moan and a cry escaped my lips. No one had ever done this to me. It felt unreal. A thousand times better than my hands.

He relentlessly lapped at me, making my legs tremble as I edged towards release. Just when I was about to tip over, he pulled away.

A sob ripped free. I gave zero cares about how desperate and pathetic I sounded. I clenched and twisted the cotton sheets until my knuckles lost color. Damn him!

Levi growled, "You're gonna come with me inside you on our first go-around. You're too damn foxy... swear I'm about to burst."

Jeez, this man drove me insane, pushing every button I never realized I had. He was too much.

Levi repositioned himself over me.

My hand dipped down, guiding him just outside my entrance. With a swift thrust, he entered me, a gasp escaping my lips as our bodies collided with a delicious slap.

Levi circled his hips, loosening me until the burn subsided, leaving behind an intense erotic heat from his rock-hard girth.

Legs locked around him, stilettos rubbing together, as he kept up his sensual dance. "I'm dying here," I moaned, on the verge of whimpering.

"Right there with you," he gritted out, as if lifting a heavy weight.

I dared him by digging my nails into his back. "Then do something about it."

Please, please do something about it.

"Tell me, baby, what do you need?"

"Move—I need you to move."

Levi whispered, all choked up. "Don't hold back. Tell me what you need. Trust I've got you."

His intense gaze riveted me, paralyzing me in place, as I felt an invisible band tighten between us. Then, he'd follow through on his promise.

Without further ado, Levi repeatedly slammed into me, moving at mach one speed.

My throat constricted as pleasure overwhelmed me.

He cursed through gritted teeth, his face contorted with effort.

I curved my back, determined to prolong the moment for as long as humanly possible, but I didn't stand a chance. Out of nowhere, a wave so violent overtook me and left me pulsating around him.

Levi stilled, spilling his warmth inside of me. For a long moment, our eyes locked in a silent conversation before he whispered, "You're something special." Levi said, his voice husky and tender. "Inside and out."

I basked in his words, my heart swelling with happiness, as a lazy, satisfied smile formed on my lips. "You're not too shabby yourself, hotshot."

Levi chuckled as his lips met mine once more, unhurried and filled with tenderness.

His gradual withdrawal left me aching. I groaned at the loss of intimacy.

It was remarkable how seamlessly we fit together, like puzzle pieces slotting perfectly into their rightful place.

In a dulcet tone, he asked, "You prefer to clean up now, or would you like to rest first?"

"I'd like to freshen up," I replied.

Levi said, "Cool. You can take the bathroom first."

I rose from the rumpled sheets, collected my cast-off clothing, and headed for the bathroom.

After a quick clean-up, I re-donned only my undergarments. No point in getting all dolled up at this hour.

After emerging from the bathroom into an empty bedroom, I hurled the dress on a nearby armchair and I set off to find Levi.

He sat hunched over his kitchen table, brows nearly meeting in concentration, as he compared the cryptic contents from his uncle's book with his phone's screen.

My heart went out to him. He couldn't put the mystery to rest and accept that some things might go unsolved.

"Any luck?"

Levi's head snapped up, and a slow smile curved his lips as he took in my nearly nude appearance.

I couldn't resist tiptoeing behind him and wrapping my arms around his broad shoulders, planting a quick peck on his neck.

The scent of his cologne now mingled with the potent musk of sweat.

Loving it, I buried my face and inhaled deeply. Maybe not the most ladylike move, but hey, a girl's gotta do what a girl's gotta do. Right?

"Nah, still spinning my wheels," he answered, leaning into my embrace.

Sliding into the seat beside him, I held out hopeful hands toward the vexing contents. "Mind if I take a peek?"

"Nope," he answered, then slid the book to me. "Two heads are better than one."

I squinted at the jumble of ASCII symbols on his phone. My forehead creased in concentration, and my brain kicked into high gear, recalling a case in one of my true crime books.

"You know, I read something once," I explained, my voice gaining a touch of excitement. "Where a serial killer—this total psycho—used to send symbols to the FBI before he struck.

Apparently, it's not even that uncommon, messed up as it sounds."

Levi's grin morphed into a skeptical frown. "Why would anyone tip their hand to the people trying to stop them? That's like...the height of dumbassery. And here I thought they were pretty sharp."

"Power trip, honey," I explained, crossing my arms and resting them on the table. "They like playing twisted games with authority. The rush of almost getting caught, the ego boost of outsmarting everyone. The key to solving this is using a keyword, that's if they used the Playfair cipher."

Levi's eyes lit up like a kid who scored a prize in a claw machine. "You have any idea what keyword he used?"

With a nonchalant shrug, I replied, "Something relevant to him."

As his face took on a distant look, he named his first guess: "Millbrook."

I twisted my lips as my gears turned. "Too many double letters. He'd use something longer. Probably even his own name."

Levi retrieved his phone, and his thumbs flew across the screen so fast I swore I saw sparks. He finished his task and declared, "Stone'll be thrilled."

A rustling noise outside stilled us. Levi shot up from his chair and strode to the window. Moving the blind aside, he swept the darkness until locking onto a target. "Package on the doorstep," he announced.

My brows knitted together. They made deliveries at this time of night?

"Did you order anything?" I asked.

"Nope," Levi responded, hauled open the front door, poked his head out, and scouted the dimly lit street.

Nothing but a distant dog bark. Then he bent and retrieved a box, bringing it into the house and kicking the door shut.

I walked up behind him as he placed the box down on his coffee table. "What's that?"

"Beats me. Maybe Rachel dropped off my stuff," he said, half-jokingly, as he pulled the lid off the box.

Levi jumped back.

I mirrored him.

His face turned horrified.

My heart rate kicked up several notches, and my hand instinctively flew to my chest. "What happened?"

CHAPTER TWENTY EIGHT

LEVI

PANTING, I barged into Stone's office, splintering the door against the wall. Stress twisted in my gut like a relentless python, turning my vision crimson with rage.

Stone hunched over his desk with a pen in his liver-spotted hand. He paused writing, his eyes questioning as he straightened in his chair.

I rested my hands on my hip.

Rehearsing this would have been a smarter move, but panic and anger had short-circuited my usual foresight.

Hell, I'd practically shoved myself into the driver's seat this morning, taking Abby to work.

Leaving her unguarded while goons played dead rat games was beyond stupid—it was straight-up reckless.

"Pull me off the damn case!" I barked, my voice rough with barely controlled fury. "It's a dead end, and that rodent on my porch last night wasn't a prank. They're sending a message, loud and clear: either me or Abby next. And I won't lose her. Not now. Not when I just found her."

Stone's gaze swept my face in a calculating assessment. A single eyebrow lifted, hinting at curiosity rather than concern. "I don't follow," he said. "What makes you think this has to do with Abby?"

Annoyance ate away at my insides as I mashed my lips. This man had worked in law enforcement since Noah built the ark, and he needed me to spoon-feed him logic?

I sucked in a lungful of air, and hopefully, patience. "Something bad will happen to me or Abs if I continue to work here. I want out. I've crossed paths with people who send messages like that. They ain't bluffin'."

Stone hitched himself up from his creaking leather chair, circled his desk with the lethargic grace of a hibernating bear, and landed on the edge. Folding his arms across his sagging chest, he said, "Message received, son. But listen closely because this is crucial. Fear will distort your judgment. Our job requires a cool head, not a hot temper. One wrong move and we're all screwed, understand?"

Tearing my attention from him, I refocused on the nondescript water cooler. His nonchalance, his whole damn attitude, sent my pulse into overdrive and flared my nostrils. Concealing my emotions went far beyond my capabilities at this point. His niece could be in danger, and he was dragging his feet. Ensuring her safety ranks as job number one, not this damn case.

"We've been chasing our own tails here," I burst out. "Those assholes aren't playin' patty-cake. Someone wants me out of the picture, and none of this is worth losing a life for."

"We both know there's rot in this department," Stone said, his attempt at soothing words only raised red flags all over the place. "Deeper than you think. But I can't just point fingers and clean house without solid evidence. Internal investigations are underway. We're close, son. You just gotta stay cool. Any change in the wind might spook our snakes."

Stay cool?

Seriously?!

He gets to go home safe, no threats delivered on his doorstep. Easy for him to preach patience.

Stone moved to the water cooler, then turned back with a questioning tilt of his head, offering a paper cup filled with tepid water.

I nodded.

"Think about it, son," Stone said as he poured water and spoke over the sound. "You got skills and raw intuition. This department could benefit with a man like you on our team. Training's no cake-walk, but the pay's steady, benefits decent. Consider it an option down the road."

He handed me the cup.

The water hit my throat like a lifeline, quenching the dryness. I dragged the back of my hand across my lips, drying them.

After crushing the paper cup in my grip with a satisfying crunch, I said, "I came here to assist on that one case. But let's not forget that you sidelined me to keep me out of your hair. You think I'm chomping at the bit to sign on for years of that?"

"The difference you've made runs far deeper than you realize," Stone said. "Barns never tagged that painting I left for him. Instead, he was texting his buddies, blaming them for leaving it. That led us to everyone involved in the ring. And that code you broke. Keen deduction. We could use you around here permanently. Sometimes, the best cleanup happens from the inside. Especially since we're going to be losing half the force after internal affairs wrap up the case."

My brows disappeared beneath my hairline, and my eyes bulged out of my head.

He knew.

All of it.

That bit about cleaning from the inside? The whole thing was a setup. The painting to get Barns talking.

Damn.

He played us.

Stone reached across the desk and snapped up a framed photo. He studied it and flashed a soft grin.

I'd bet it was a family snapshot. That expression was saved solely for them.

"Stubborn woman, that one," Stone said. "Mind of her own. We've been married for thirty years. Says I tamed her wild streak. But I see it the other way around."

Stone spun the framed image in my direction, confirming my guess.

My throat closed up, making me regret chugging that water back, because I could've used some of it now. I clenched and unclenched my jaw before finally forcing out, "Appreciate the offer, sir. But my past... it wouldn't fit into that picture. I was a criminal, and no one will respect me if I work on this team. Hell, they barely give me the time of day now."

Stone set the picture down on the desk and perched himself on the edge, his side facing me. His tone seemed conversational, and he even cracked a rare smile. "Some of the toughest trees grew from twisted roots, son. Don't let your beginnings hold you back. This town needs what you got: grit, guts, and yeah, maybe a touch of that outlaw spirit."

The smirk returned, this time, with an accompanying glint in his eye. "You think they'd accept a choirboy on this team? Hell no. But a man who's navigated the underbelly and comes out swinging? Now that, son, that's sheriff quality right there."

I paused. What the hell was going on here? He wanted me to work full time when all I wanted was out? I stared out his window, not focusing on anything in particular for a moment. Then I said, "Just a few weeks working here. That's all I promised."

Stone countered, rasping with years of chasing criminals. "You saw the possibility of what your life could be like with steady pay, and things changed. It's okay to want that. With training, you can work here, no longer needing to look over your shoulder. Build a future for yourself, for your family. Something solid, something safe."

Suddenly, the shrill ring of the phone shattered the moment.

Stone snatched the receiver, his entire demeanor hardening like concrete. His troubled eyes met mine, the concern deepening. "Damn it! Cross is here with me. We're on our way!"

My blood ran cold. Abby's face flashed in my mind. Images of what might've happened to her choked me. Terror clawed at my throat, tighter than any antacid could remedy.

Stone slammed the phone down. "Son, you need to come with me. Your uncle's dead."

CHAPTER TWENTY NINE

LEVI

YELLOW CAUTION TAPE cordoned off the once lively Winnebago, now desolate under the ambulance's insistent lights. The scene was painted with morbid blue and red.

Stone advanced, but my attention hitched on the EMTs rolling out a gurney.

I stood petrified as they worked, ambushed by memories, sharp and brutal, from the night my parents' lives were ripped away in a car crash: screeching tires, the sickening crunch of colliding metal, the blood running down their mouths. Rex and I heard it. We ran out of the parlor to investigate.

At eighteen, my world fractured beyond repair.

They carted Uncle Al's lifeless body onto the ambulance, covered under a white sheet.

Another loved one lost, another wound scored onto my soul.

A guttural sob tore from me, raw and jagged, tears distorting my vision.

"Steady on, son," Stone murmured as his hand landed on my shoulder, but I barely felt it. "Phoned Abby. She's on her way here as soon as she finds a ride."

Fragments of moments came rushing back. Al hugging his beloved PB&J jar. Him doubling over with laughter in his booth over dinner. Him flipping burgers, asking about my messed-up hand.

That one twisted like a serrated knife – a cruel echo of Dad, another life cut short.

Choking back a sob wracked my body. The weight became too much, causing my knees to buckle, and I sank to my feet.

Stone's hands squeezed my shoulders, repeating his mantra. "Easy, now."

"Can't handle any more loss," I said.

"Losing family never gets easy," he responded, sober.

"We got a damn curse on us. This family can't live in peace," I dragged my sleeve across my nose. "Was it cause of me? Is this why they sent that dead rat to my house?! Is this some messed-up payback because I'm connected to this goddamn investigation?"

While trying to pull myself together, Stone spoke. "Hold steady. We don't know anything yet. Just tell me what happened with Al. When was the last time you spoke to him?"

Primal sirens blared in the back of my mind, twisting my stomach in response. Shaking it off, I sucked in a breath, stood up, and attempted to jog the memory of the other night. "Abby and I had dinner with him a few nights ago. Al seemed in good spirits throughout. He grilled us burgers, gave me a book, asked about Abby's dad, and had me sign his will."

Stone straightened, his wayward brows pulled together, which had the effect of making me feel guilty for nothing. He asked, "Hold on, what's that about his will?"

My mind said, "Oh shit." The sirens cranked up a notch. Damage control mode activated, and my mouth spewed out explanations before I had the chance to decide whether it was sensible. "He was finalizing his will," I explained. "He chose me as executor. Kinda weird, right? But hey, everything Al does is weird."

Biting down hard, I forced my eyes to stay open, refusing to give in to the urge to blink away the horror. Sometimes you just wish you could turn back time to shut the hell up.

Stone, with the sharp instincts of a veteran lawman, picked up on my unease like a bloodhound on a scent. Duty flicked his switch, transforming him into a stranger. Jaw clamped shut, his eyes narrowed, etching canyons around them.

Sheriff mode, activated.

Directed solely at me, he turned a casual dinner into a crime scene, with me being the prime suspect.

"Did anyone witness the signing?" he asked.

"Just Abby," I responded reluctantly.

Stone cursed under his breath before he pivoted toward the Winnebago, his back tense. "What about this book, Levi? What was in it?"

Levi. Not son. This was shaping up to be a real mess. "It's the Rosetta Stone that cracked Casey's cipher."

Interest lit up Stone's eyes. "Got the book on you?"

"No, it's at my house. I could get it—"

"You're waist-deep in a maelstrom," he interrupted. "And I didn't see it comin'. Keeping Abby safe is my priority. It'll benefit her if you keep your distance. I'll get the book from your place. You stay put. Understood?"

Stone's words hit my gut like a heavyweight champ, knocking the air out of my lungs. My relationship with Abby might've put a bullseye on her back. I thought it had to do with me working this case. That angle didn't cross my mind. But it all made sense now. People close to me were dropping like flies.

He said, "Alright, son, hate to cut this short, but homicide's got me by the short hairs now. You good?"

Stone's bombshell detonated a million questions.

The shout nearly let loose. "Hell no! Not even close to good."

"Homicide," I stammered past my tight throat, the word sounding alien on my tongue.

"Yeah, kid. That's the classification." And with that, he vanished into the swarm of brown uniforms.

My phone buzzed. Abby. My fingers twitched, yearning for her voice, for the warmth of her laughter. But Al's still form beneath the stark white sheet, coupled with Stone's warning, locked my fingers in place.

A storm cloud settled over me, swallowing the sun and leaving behind disillusionment and bitterness.

I let the phone ring.

CHAPTER THIRTY

FROM THE MOMENT Doug slammed on the brakes across the road from Al's Winnebago, the sight curdled my blood.

Cops swarmed everywhere.

Panic hijacked my brain, rudely shoving aside the "thanks for the ride" I'd planned for Doug.

The car door flung open, and I ejected myself, spotting Uncle Wyatt standing with his hand on his hip.

But Levi's stance really alarmed the hell out of me. His shoulders slumped, drained of his usual cocky swagger.

Fueled by adrenaline, my feet pounded the asphalt in a sprint towards them. The tail end of their conversation had the same effect as having a bucket of ice water dumped on my head.

Uncle Wyatt said, "You were the last person with him, so that implicates you. Now, I'm not saying you did it, just that we have to investigate your whereabouts. That's all."

Levi's head dipped to his feet, his hands shoved into the pockets of his black jeans. Dark circles lived under his red-rimmed eyes. The despair etched on his face foretold that his five o'clock shadow wouldn't see a razor for the rest of this ordeal.

None of it made a lick of sense. We were both there. So, why exactly were they pinning this on him?

Confused, I called out to my uncle, "If that's the case, then does that apply to me too? Because I was with both of them the whole time."

For the first time since my arrival, Levi met my gaze, and in his eyes, I saw something different—dark and distant.

That passionate man who made love to me last night had vanished. This man wasn't Levi. This stranger usurped him and inhabited his skin.

A lump formed in my throat, and I faced Uncle Wyatt, pleading for answers.

His forehead scrunched into a map of worry lines, and his eyes drooped. "Unfortunately, Mops, it does."

Doug's voice came from behind. "Are they being charged?"

Levi's gaze shifted towards Doug, as though he'd just registered his presence.

He suffered from a clear case of stress-induced tunnel vision, for sure.

Taking a step closer, I wrapped my arms gently around him, but his body stiffened at the contact, refusing any attempt at solace.

Alarm constricted my chest, racking my body with tremors.

Trying again, my hands moved in soothing, circular motions on his back, but he shrugged away from me.

This was grief, laced with something else too. Something cold and dark under the surface.

Tears welled up in my eyes, but I blinked them back. Taking a deep breath, I squeezed Levi's arm, desperately searching for any flicker of recognition.

Nothing.

His spark had died, leaving behind a hollowed-out version of himself.

Dammit! This was a nightmare.

Uncle Wyatt had one hand anchoring his phone to his ear,

and the other cautioning Doug. "Hold your damn horses, Kaminsky! No press leaks until we conclude our investigation, got it?"

He said into his phone, "Can't talk now, Peg. Duty calls."

Levi looked off at the Winnebago. "None of this would be happening if I didn't show my face back here. This town has got a vendetta against us, and my family pays the price."

The emptiness of his voice freaked the hell out of me.

At least he had broken his silence. Now I could figure out what ate at him. Although, hearing him regret returning home shattered my heart.

To ward off my worry, I squeezed my bicep against his, silently reminding him that he wasn't alone.

"Life throws punches," I said gently, "and lately it feels like you're catching them all. It's okay to not be okay. I can't take what happened away, but I'm here to listen if you want to talk. No judgment, just an ear and an open heart."

Uncle Wyatt seemed like he had aged ten dog years since I last saw him. His hair, usually neatly combed back, now stuck out at odd angles.

This man, a fixture in my childhood memories, bore the heaviest weight I had ever seen him carry. It broke my heart.

"I know this looks bad, son," he said to Levi. "But a quick property search and you'll be cleared. Gotta check your place too, Abby. Just procedure."

"You're arresting us?" Levi asked, snapping out of his daze.

Uncle Wyatt put out his hand in a pacifying gesture. "Detaining. Protocol. I'll personally search your place. No funny business that way."

Doug's hands rested on his hip. A fleeting grimace marred his features before he said, "You two need a lawyer. This is serious."

I wanted to scream, feral and high, and pour every ounce of hurt and frustration into it. Then, I'd hitch a ride to Nowheresville.

This was madness.

Having dinner with a man automatically qualified me as a murder suspect.

Before losing it, I handed Doug my phone. "Call my dad. Chet Martin. Key West, Florida."

With a nod of understanding, Doug began scrolling through my contacts.

Uncle Wyatt cussed before exploding, "Don't call Chet! He'll be on the first damn plane here, spitting fire and demanding answers. I can't handle him breathing down my neck while I'm trying to do my job. Let me take care of it first. I'll call him after."

Alone and adrift, I hugged myself.

CHAPTER THIRTY ONE

ABBY

DAYS OF RADIO silence culminated in my finger hovering over Levi's doorbell, my stomach churning with dread.

Swear it, if another woman were to strut out the door, like the first time we met, I would have a full-blown meltdown. Because right now, my patience with this man has disintegrated to shreds.

I jabbed the doorbell button, holding it down a beat too long, my jaw clenched the whole time. No answer. No sound came from inside.

Taking a step back from the door, I bit my lower lip.

Okay, this plan amounted to an epic fail. He wasn't even home. At least, I can finally evict the fear that he left me for another woman.

Mrs. Henderson, Levi's neighbor, rounded the corner of her house, dragging a green water hose towards the bed of pink and magenta peonies under her front window.

We'd exchanged smiles in passing during the multiple overnight stays, so my presence wouldn't have alarmed her.

She waved.

Hope, no bigger than a spark, lit in my chest. With a strained smile, I called out, "Sorry for the interruption, but by any chance, have you seen Levi?"

Her gardening work paused while she considered the question. "Not since the police swung by here last week," she finally said.

That spark sputtered and died, plunging me back into the deep rut I'd been wallowing in for days. To ward off the emotional frostbite, I wrapped my arms around myself, creating a makeshift haven.

My voice verged on pleading. "Well, did he at least say anything about where he was going?"

The neighbor shook her head, and her smile evaporated as she probably sensed my desperation.

"Nope. He tore out of here shortly after the police cleared out, carrying a duffle bag. Never saw him since. We figured he went back to the city," she wrinkled her brows in contemplation before adding, "Although he took off on his motorcycle. He usually uses his car for longer trips and his bike to boot around town."

Despair sapped my strength, so I shifted on my feet to mask the wobble. I'll never find him at this rate.

Why would he opt for his bike when his car made practical sense for a long trip? Not to mention, the noise would draw unwanted attention. Maybe he'll come back to swap it for his car?

Or maybe he doesn't care anymore.

That thought had a depressing ring of truth to it.

A lump constricted my throat, threatening to choke me. Tears stung my eyes, blurring the world. Before they could spill, I forced out a watery thank you to the neighbor and a brittle wave goodbye.

My restless spirit obstructed the course back home. Fuming and fretting wouldn't change reality: Levi wasn't returning. On top of that, I'd depleted my supply of chamomile tea.

This led me to Wyatt's house. Desperation drove me to gamble on my uncle. He and Aunt Peg were tight-lipped about work info, but this stone—no pun intended—I hadn't unturned.

Aunt Peg's cornflower-blue eyes widened like decorative dessert plates when she opened her door. "Abby, dear! What a lovely surprise. Come in."

The aroma of cinnamon and apples filled the air, luring me from the living room straight into her kitchen. Baking was Peg's domain, a kingdom ruled by legendary pies that consistently won blue ribbons at the county fair. But Aunt Peg abdicated her throne years ago to give others a chance.

Fighting the tug of the delicious scent, I turned my attention to the decor for distraction.

A framed photo of me as a kid, fishing with Uncle Wyatt and Dad, still held a place of honor on their mantle.

Laurie Ann, their daughter, blossomed within the loving walls of their home. Her interests never extended to outdoorsy stuff, save for our swashbuckling battles in the backyard. She preferred playing with her dolls and crafting miniature furniture for her dollhouse, which paved the way to a thriving career as an interior designer out in Cali.

"Hey, Aunt Peg," I said and scrunched my nose. "Sorry to bug you during dinner prep, but..."

I swallowed. "Have you seen Levi?"

Aunt Peg ushered me to her well-worn, flowery couch and situated herself in the armchair opposite.

"I'm sorry, honey, but I haven't seen him," she tilted her head, her gaze searching mine. "You're worried about him?"

"Yeah. He hasn't been himself since his uncle died. Based on what Lex told me about how he reacted when his parents passed..."

My voice trailed off, the memory of his vulnerability a sharp pang in my chest.

Peg's brow creased with curiosity. "What did Alexa share with you?"

"About how Levi fell apart after his parents died," I confessed, drudging up an image of teenaged Levi, crumbling under the weight of grief. "He might be spiraling again."

"Oh, darlin'," she murmured, her voice thick with compassion. "I can see why that would cause worry, and I wish I had answers for you."

A worn book perched on her coffee table drew my attention. Al had gifted that code-breaking book to Levi.

Didn't they take it back to HQ when they searched our houses? Why would they have it? What in the heck was going on here? Good Lord, did I stumble into some bizarre parallel dimension?

"That book," I pointed to it and asked, "is that...?"

Just then, the deadbolt turned, and the front door swung open. Disheveled in his sheriff's uniform, a worn-out vibe clung to Uncle Wyatt like he'd been wrestling alligators all day, pretty much in the same state I'd seen him last.

"Mops?" Uncle Wyatt drawled, raising his bushy brows. "Fancy seeing you here. Book club business, I take it?"

"Looking for Levi," I replied, my voice tight with worry. "I hadn't seen him since we got cleared."

Surprise, mixed with something nondescript, crossed Wyatt's face before he schooled it and said, "Skipped town, did he? Didn't peg him for such a drama queen."

I zeroed in on his words like a dog spotting a bone. My lids narrowed to focus on the man before me, seeing him as unsavory, for the first time in my life. It shattered my belief that there were decent people left in this world.

Wyatt, utterly devoid of a soul, answered my unasked question. "Canned him even before you two were out the station doors."

Bile rose in my throat. I slammed my eyes shut, willing it back down.

Everything clicked into place. The sudden death of a family member. No job. No security.

And so, Levi snapped.

Not giving him a free pass for ghosting me, but it painted a brutal mosaic of his mental state. No wonder he took off.

I bolted from my seat, jaw clenched so hard, it probably carved several cavities.

"You fired him?!" I shrieked, the question laced with disbelief and betrayal. "You just tossed him out like trash when he needed you the most?"

"Mops, it's not what—" Wyatt began, approaching me with that placating tone that usually made me cave.

Not this time.

"I'd always given you the benefit of the doubt because I thought you were a decent man. But this?" A sob wracked my throat. "This is beyond reprehensible. You'd choose thugs over a man clawing his way out of the gutter? All he needed was a fresh start, and you couldn't even give him that!"

Wyatt reached out, but I recoiled, my entire body buzzing with betrayal.

Seeing his true nature for the first time shattered my heart.

Poor Aunt Peg sat frozen like a vintage doll, eyes wide as she watched the scene erupt in front of her.

"Look, Mops, I know you're upset, but you gotta give him some space."

"Space?" I spat with venom. "That's all he'd ever known, and where did it lead? Stealing to put food on his table. He needs a helping hand, not more of nothing!"

Throat ablaze and frustrated beyond belief, I came up empty. With a silent scream, I tore out of their house, slamming their door with a thud that probably alerted their neighbors along the way. The sound offered the only catharsis I'd get.

With my foot on the gas pedal, I didn't care about the destination, so long as it wasn't home. The engine hummed a lullaby, quelling my rioting thoughts.

Streetlights blurred orange as I turned corners, oblivious to the markers.

Millbrook's comforting scenery gave way to singular country roads, flanked by expanses of green on either side. Every now and then, the flicker of a neon sign from a lone store, or a burst of laughter from a passing car, would briefly pierce the fog in my brain.

Eventually, my tires crunched on the familiar gravel, pulling me to a stop in the same spot from that one forgotten evening.

Before Al's life was cut short, one thing consumed my mind.

Pushing open the tattoo parlor door, a bell jingled in response.

Rex leaned against the counter, all hard angles and grandpa bad-boy charm. He raised a brow, and his gaze flicked over my shoulder, looking for someone else to follow through the door.

"Well, well, well. Didn't think I'd see your pretty face in here again after you almost passed out during Levi's tattoo session. To what do I owe this second honor, sunshine?" A glint lit his eyes. "Need a tramp stamp?"

Sunshine? Odd choice.

Given the current state of my emotional weather system, "stormy" might have been more fitting. Unless the man had a taste for irony, then it made perfect sense.

Rex motioned to the pre-designed tattoo options on his wall and said, "Have a look at the flash, and pick one."

The wolf tattoo I'd chosen for Levi—back when I'd clung to the delusion that my feelings actually mattered to him—hung mockingly on the wall. Now, the wolf sneered back, telling me that I could kiss that future goodbye.

I offered a half-hearted smile, but the result likely warped into a grotesque distortion. "Actually, I wondered if you'd seen Levi over the last few days."

Rex's brow furrowed like a confused bulldog. His gaze flickered over me for a moment. "Haven't seen him around, darlin'. What's cookin'? You two having a lover's spat?"

Lovers' spat? I wish.

Unless, by his definition, ghosting counted as a proper goodbye.

My hand fisted, nails digging into my palm.

Spats were attributed to couples who fought over burnt toast, not whatever was going on with Levi. But venting my wayward love life to this stranger wasn't exactly top-tier on my to-do list. So, I replied, "You could say that. He's been MIA for days."

Rex crossed his arms and leaned back, causing his stool to squeak in protest.

"Maybe he's somewhere clearing his head. That's what I do when me and Shayna hit a rough patch."

Rex's words calmed the beating storm in my chest.

Uncle Wyatt, bless his loving heart, had suggested the same thing earlier, but it only served as provocation. My cheeks burned hotter than Florida's midday sun, and the corners of my mouth turned down. Jeez, I seriously owed an apology to my uncle and aunt for the nuclear meltdown I'd unleashed in their living room.

Rex said, "Tell you what. How about a little distraction? You ever consider getting a tattoo?"

I arched a single brow and recoiled a touch. His pushiness to get me into his chair caught me off guard. Than again, sell, sell, sell was the name of the game, and the man had to eat. Guess I couldn't blame him.

The blazing symbol of rebirth roared, and I couldn't resist its pull.

✷ ✷ ✷

Avoiding my house, still, I drove to the bar the girls insisted on dragging me to. Not ideal, but better than the steady drone of my own unhelpful thoughts.

I swept the room. A jolt ripped through me, sparking my dormant heart back to life.

Levi slumped at the far end of the bar, a lone figure, his eyes pinned to his glass of half-drunk beer.

Feet frozen, I stood at the threshold. Rushing to him dueled with the ironclad grip of pride. But answers wouldn't come with me standing here, so I stifled the latter.

Lifting my chin in challenge, I marched forward, determined to get what I came for. My hand trembled as I rested my bag down on the bar top and lowered myself onto the stool, careful not to invade his personal space too quickly.

Levi stiffened.

Sigh.

Not that I waltzed in here expecting a brass band and a confetti shower, but this? Talk about a major buzzkill. Every muscle screamed "run in the other direction," but I forced myself to stand my ground and weather the storm.

"I'm glad I found you," I said, breaking the ice.

Levi didn't so much as spare me a glance. Instead, he tipped his glass back, draining the amber liquid down his throat.

His glass hit the counter with a dull thud. "Glad you made it."

My brows shot up at Levi's monotone response.

Abandoning me, putting me through this hell... and now 'glad you made it'? Take a bow, sir, for the best performance in emotional whiplash!

I swear, he might have been a matador waving a red cloth. Every fiber of my being wanted to unleash a good old-fashioned cuss-out he deserved, but that wouldn't get me anywhere. I needed him to say it, face-to-face, to rip the Band-Aid off this thing. No more silence. Just the cold, hard truth, even if it shattered me into a million pieces.

At the end of the day, this wasn't about getting even; this was about closure, and for that, I'd play nice.

"Really?" I mocked. "Because after everything you put me through, I find that hard to believe. You just... disappeared, Levi. No calls, no texts, not even a whisper. Is this how you deal with heartache? Shutting me out? You treat me like some doormat you can just walk all over."

I bared my teeth. "I. Deserve. Better!"

Levi's gaze finally landed on me, but the warmth I craved for days was nothing more than a ghost town, leaving behind this hollowed-out version of him. Stains ringed Levi's troubled eyes, proof that he hadn't slept for days.

Dear God.

"I can barely handle this mess right now. It's a damn nightmare," he said, his voice low and strained. "You don't have a clue what you're walking into."

Yeah, he had me there. I didn't know anything. But who's to blame? He went off the grid for days, and now I'm the clueless one? Give me a break. If he bothered explaining the situation, I wouldn't be here fishing for answers.

Levi's muscles flexed under his shaggy jawline. He muttered a curse and raked through his usually styled hair, leaving it in a disarray.

"You know what? This isn't a good idea. You deserve someone with a normal life, not me."

There it was. That train ran like clockwork. "Normal life?" I snorted, wiping furiously at my wet cheeks with my thumb. "Since when were we ever normal? Don't you dare try to play the martyr card now. Remember who helped you during the investigation. This disappearing act? Cowardice in a nutshell, and that, my darling, is so not you. Or at least, it wasn't."

After a moment, I continued, "Levi," I forced out. Even saying his name hurt. "I can't shake the feeling that you're feeding me a lie. I don't know why, and mysteries don't sit well with me. You know that."

"Damn it, Abby," he growled, running a hand over his face in frustration. "This whole thing is bigger than both of us. Someone tipped them off, and now..." Levi's voice trailed off.

Wait, tipped them off about what? The investigation? But who could have...? Unless he meant Rick or Rachel... No, that can't be it. This felt bigger. Besides, they wouldn't have known about the police politics around here.

My head spun, trying to weave together bits of information. Before I could start down that path, a man slid onto the stool by Levi's other side.

Recognition dawned. This guy. The one from the restaurant. The one Levi couldn't seem to tear his gaze away from during our date.

Looking from the man to Levi, I demanded, "What's going on?"

Levi directed his icy stare at me and said just two words. "You're leaving."

CHAPTER THIRTY TWO

ABBY

I STEPPED out of the stifling bar, the cool night air embraced me like a long-lost friend.

Power-walking to my car in the parking lot, my heels clacked out a pissed-off rhythm on the pitted pavement. A frustrated grunt escaped my lips as I flung myself into the driver's seat. The slam of the door shattered the night's quiet.

My leg bounced like mad, and my molars ground together. Five minutes on the dashboard clock felt like an eternity waiting for Mr. Broody.

Hand to God, if he showed up with another woman, I'd call it quits and leave without causing drama or sparing them a single backward glance.

That "bigger than the both of us" line he fed me stuck in my craw. What the heck did that even mean? Bigger than what, exactly? And seriously, why did he act like he was psyching himself up to throw down with Thanos? None of it made sense.

Levi emerged from around the corner. Even from a distance, the hunch in his shoulders signified a man burdened by far too much. He didn't even recognize my car, a dead giveaway of his mental state.

Instinct kicked in. I slumped down as he stalked toward his

ride and swung his jean-clad leg over the gleaming bike. The engine roared to life, echoing in my chest as he rode away.

No way I'd let him out of my sight. The insatiable itch of curiosity wouldn't let me leave it alone, even though a tiny part of my mind screamed to just go home. At the end of the day, those burdened shoulders chained my heart to him, rendering leaving out of the question.

Levi needed me, but didn't ask for help, and for that, I'd wage a war against his pride.

Once he hit the road, I turned the key already inserted in the ignition and peeled out of my parking space. Tailing some ways behind him, I used the bike engine to guide me, rather than relying on proximity to avoid detection.

Grinning, I recalled the time Levi followed me home, then took me to Rex's. Life, huh? Did everyone's life flip-flop, or was it just mine?

Looking back on it now, past-me was such a big baby. Needles weren't as scary as I made them out to be. Letting a pin prick derail me from wearing meaningful art? Pure drama queen mentality right there.

My hip burned, making me dig my fingers into the steering wheel.

In that moment, sanity punctured through this absurdity, and I detached from the situation. The fact that I behaved like the scorned housewife's version of James Bond brought on a wry twist of my lips.

Despite the clarity, giving up wasn't on tonight's menu.

Levi screeched into a parking lot.

A ramshackle neon sign, its blue light flickering erratically, cast the words "Moonlight Motel."

Pushing past my racing pulse, I drove over potholes to reach the visitor's parking. Then I sprinted towards the door Levi disappeared behind, while contending with the stench of mildew.

To hell with his rules. Time to flip the script.

With a spike of determination, I pounded down the grimy door of room six or nine—hard to tell because the number hung slanted.

"Who is it!" Levi's muffled voice demanded from the other side of the door.

"It's me. Open up, bastard!" I called out, not caring if I hurt his feelings.

Levi cussed. The door open, revealing his face twisted in dark fury. He reached out and pulled me inside with a rough tug, jerking my head back. The door slammed shut. Lock turned with a metallic click.

Levi shoved me against the door, my back slamming into the hard wood as he slipped a gun behind his back.

My breath hitched. Was this really about the fallout from the investigation? Had things really gone so sideways that it turned him into a paranoid mess?

Levi's voice grated with agitation. "If you got words for me, I suggest you get on with it because you got two seconds before I kick your ass out."

We were past minding each other's feelings.

"Oh my god, what has your life come to? The investigation is over. You can come out of hiding."

Levi's smile twisted with bitterness. "For you, maybe."

"What do you mean? Stop being cryptic *and talk to me.* Or else, I won't leave you alone."

Levi's expression turned grim, his jaw clenched tight. "Can't dive into it right now. The less you know, the better. So leave—"

"Don't even try it!" I interrupted, taking a deep breath to steady myself. Narrowing my accusatory eyes at him, I said, "To think I got a tattoo for the likes of you."

Levi's entire demeanor shifted, his eyes searched mine. "Say what?"

My heart pounded in my chest as I bunched up the fabric by my legs. Then, I froze, debating the wisdom of showing him. But I had come so far already, and it would be a shame to flake out now. Sucking in a breath, I lifted the hem further up my body, revealing a tattoo of a feminine bird with orange and black feathers etched onto my lower stomach.

Levi gulped audibly and dropped to one knee for a closer look.

Hope lit up my chest. Taking his reaction as an unspoken invitation, I shrugged off the dress completely, discarding it on the floor.

The tremor that wracked Levi's body wasn't anger, but a soul-deep sob that radiated from his core. Then he leaned his head against my stomach, and the dampness of his tears soaked through to my skin.

A million tiny pinpricks stung at my eyes. In spite of it all, relief bloomed in my chest that he had finally let me in. His walls were starting to crumble. Yet, witnessing his breakdown gutted me like a double-edged sword. It ignited my need to protect him.

Levi's ragged voice fractured mid-sentence. "I can't believe you did all this for me. I don't deserve it."

All the anger I had held onto for days evaporated like steam, leaving behind sympathy for the man slumped in my arms, his broad shoulders shaking with silent sobs. I cradled his head, my fingers threading through his hair in a comforting rhythm.

"It was partly for me too," I confessed, my voice thick and small, and for him, to rekindle that spark of life in those blood-shot, haunted eyes.

Levi lifted his head, his eyes red-rimmed, locked with mine. In a fluid motion, he rose to his feet. Without a word, he pulled me into a kiss filled with sheer desperation.

His pain, I could taste it. My protective instinct kicked in, longing to hold him together until the storm died down. But this kiss...

I ripped myself away because I had to. He would've pulled me under tow if I didn't. Lungs working overtime to recoup, I joked, "The tat did it for you? You like it?"

"Love it, baby," Levi said, light finally reaching his eyes as he cupped my face.

His callused touch sent tremors through me.

Questions danced on the tip of my tongue about his absence, but instead of voicing a single one, I buried my face in his black t-shirt, which smelled like it should've been laundered days ago, surrendering to the frustration, anger, and fear. Tears streamed down my cheeks, hot and relentless.

Sniffing, I admitted, "I thought I lost you."

Levi stroked my back and said, "You did."

My head snapped up, and I instinctively shoved him. "What?!"

"Dirty cops are coming after me," he explained, his voice low and strained. "I won't let you get caught in the crossfire."

I scoffed. "So, let me see if I get this right. Running away will keep me safe?" A humorless smile spread across my face. "Or are you trying to make me an easier target by leaving me a sitting duck?"

Levi didn't respond to my jab. Instead, he scrunched his lids shut, his breathing slowed as if he were deliberately settling himself down.

I winced. Maybe I took it a step too far.

After a heart-stopping silence, he opened them, leaned in, and planted a soft kiss on my lips.

"Stay here," he said sincerely, his eyes searching mine. "I want you in my bed when I get back."

He moved me aside and opened the door.

As he stalked out, a flash of white caught my eye—a crisp envelope protruded from his back pocket. But the gun concealed in the waistband of his jeans scraped my brain clean of his previous request.

Stay here?

This man didn't know me at all.

CHAPTER THIRTY THREE

LEVI

THE WINNEBAGO'S graveyard sucker-punched my senses as I traversed it. The chirping innocence of crickets in the weed-choked lot had long forgotten its nightmarish past. *Nature.*

My memory wasn't so forgiving, though. Traumatic events had a way of searing themselves in, refusing to fade. Just like the night my parents died, Uncle Al's lifeless body, loaded into the back of an ambulance, is an image that I won't shake.

Life since then had devolved into a bureaucratic nightmare as I tried to arrange Al's burial next to my parents. Al's premature death prevented the bank from releasing funds because his will wasn't notarized.

Luckily, my old friend Nikolaou, the restaurant owner, stepped in to help.

All of it happened so quickly that I didn't get a chance to plan a proper funeral. In the end, I stood alone while the priest read the final rites.

Sucks, but until the dust settles with the police, Aunt Clara won't receive word of her brother's passing. Safer that way.

The rusty hinges of the door groaned as the door swung open. Was it weird to feel like an intruder on my own property? Never wrapped my head around it being mine.

I stepped inside.

Open drawers spewed contents of clothes and personal effects like a busted piñata, amping up my claustrophobia.

Damn. Was this due to Stone's investigation, or had the buzzards gotten here first? A sinking feeling indicated the latter because Stone was too professional to leave a site in this condition.

A faint clicking rhythm started to pulse from behind the dingy plastic panel housing light switches.

The air inside the bus reeked of mothballs, decaying paper, and an undercurrent of wood smoke that clung to every corner.

Yanking on my t-shirt collar, I fanned much-needed gusts of air onto my damp face, then reached for Al's will in my back pocket.

Reading through the contents, one item tripped me up.

Tightening my fingers around my phone, I navigated the screen to the only woman who might be able to decode it.

"Hello?" Abby's voice snapped on the line, all business.

My chest vice-gripped with guilt. This woman had always been vibrant and challenging.

Now.

After putting her through the wringer with my issues, I can't fault her for resenting me.

"Abs, it's me," I said, my voice loaded with regret.

A scoff, sharp and dismissive, crackled through the other end of the line. "Figured as much when your name showed on my screen, genius. Still peeved at you, by the way. And... there's zero chance of me waiting in your bed, you dolt. Newsflash, that caveman crap doesn't fly with me!"

So much for keeping her safe. A defeated sigh rolled out of me. Sweat trickled down my forehead as I ran a hand through the clammy strands of hair plastered to my scalp.

Guess I deserved that.

"My bad, baby. I know I messed up big time and could've handled things better. Promise, we'll hash it out another time.

Right now, I gotta find this damn notebook. Al mentioned it in his will. You see anything the last time we were here?"

Abby's tone softened, a sheepish note crept in. "Um, no. I don't think I did. The place was packed with so much stuff everywhere. Nothing of import stuck out."

The disaster zone inside the Winnebago bore no trace of the elusive notebook, which had entered the realm of mythology at this point. "I don't know, maybe this notebook is important. He wouldn't have singled it out if it wasn't. Do you have any clue where he might have hidden it?"

"Hmm..." Abs mulled for a moment before responding. "He was in the backyard when we showed up. Maybe he hid something there? Come to think about it, I remember that bizarre joke about tomatoes and gnomes, so I'd start with the tomato plant."

An invisible force yanked my attention beyond the smudged windowpane to the expanse of the night. "Tomatoes and gnomes?" I muttered, gratitude flooding like a broken dam. "Thanks, baby. You're a lifesaver."

"So we're back to baby now?" Abby egged, a playful lilt in her voice. "I'm out of the doghouse?"

My jaw clenched. That hit hard, making me feel shittier than ever. Halting my search, I scrubbed my sweaty neck. God, baby, you never were. I was just keyed up and paranoid you'd get hurt like everyone around me has. Seriously, I can't handle losing another person I love. Hate saying it now, but we'll talk later. I need to find a shovel."

Abs went quiet for a beat, as if my words had struck a nerve. Then she recovered and said, "Check under the sink. He stashed them there the last time we came."

"Good thinking. Appreciate it, baby. I'll go check. Talk later." We ended the call, and I hopped over the junk piles to the kitchen cupboard. It creaked open, and sure enough, the garden tools were sitting in the front where he'd last dumped them.

Mud-caked tool in hand, I navigated the clutter and ventured to the field out back. Using my phone's light to cut a weak swath through the dark, I searched for the best spot to start digging. The beam danced across the uneven ground, then caught on something propped against the side of the Winnebago – a shovel.

Relief overran me like a barreling truck. I could've let out a cackle, but contained it and got to work. Hacking at the earth with rusty gardening claws wasn't the best Plan A. Chucking the hand tools aside, grabbed the real deal, and started scanning for the enemy: tomato plants.

New mission, new focus. I shined the light, squinting at various rows of greenery until I found the identifying red bulbous fruit swinging from its vine. Thank goodness, because I wouldn't have recognized a tomato plant if it bit me.

Fueled by optimism, I hacked at the base of it. Soil scattered as I carved into the dirt. The shovel became an extension of my willpower, ramming against the stubborn earth. Unused to this line of work, the handle became a medieval torturing device, grating my palm raw. Added to that, my forearm and shoulder throbbed, which means, I'll be nursing injuries come morning. Rookie mistake not bringing Al's gardening gloves. But a job needed to get done.

A nagging thought whispered in the back of my mind that I never handled grief well, and I should go back to Abby and get some rest. This task can wait for tomorrow.

Yet, adrenaline surged throughout my veins, rendering it impossible to listen to reason.

Sweat rolled down my forehead as each labored breath ripped through my chest, while tunneling to China.

I stopped. This was going nowhere fast.

Plunging the shovel into the dirt, I withdrew it, stabbing in a few more places until the metal thunked against something.

For the first time in days, a grin cracked my face, and I attacked the soil with renewed vigor. Finally, a metal strongbox emerged from its burial amongst the roots.

My heart raced, and my legs nearly buckled with relief. Just as I reached down to grab my prize, a blast of floodlights doused the entire front yard in a harsh white light.

My blood ran cold. Who the hell...?

CHAPTER THIRTY FOUR

LEVI

TERROR LOCKED my body in place; my heart hammered against my ribs, much like Rex's tattoo gun. Standoffs weren't my jam; stealth was.

Unhanding the box, I steeled myself to fend off the lowlifes encroaching on my inheritance, ready to pick it clean. Panic sent my hand darting to the rod concealed in my back pocket. Six rounds. Barely enough for a last stand.

A raspy, age-worn voice, laced with fear, shattered the silence. "Don't shoot!"

An old lady? What the—

Sense returned as I blinked away the last vestiges of alarm.

"Don't worry, ma'am. I won't," I shouted back, my voice echoing across the deserted field, silencing the crickets. "I'm Levi Cross, Al's nephew."

Disgust curled my lips. This inheritance came with a side of Al's paranoia.

A hunched figure, barely more than a silhouette, shuffled across the field. As she drew closer, she clutched a shawl tighter around her frail form.

"Hello, Levi," she said, a smile in her voice. "I'm Rosie."

For crying out loud, she sounded like she came to offer fresh-baked cookies.

Relief whooshed out, deflating the pent-up air from my chest. Maybe tonight wouldn't be a total washout. Avoiding a showdown unwound my pretzeled insides. I picked up the metal box, clutching it close.

"Hi, Rosie," I said, cheeks heating with mortification. "I don't know how to turn off the lights."

"There should be a switch by the panel inside the streamer," Rosie called out.

The Winnebago door slammed shut, trapping me in its musty confines. My fingers danced frantically across every switch and knob, desperate to end the relentless hum that made my eyes squint.

Click. The front yard plunged back into the tranquil darkness.

Exhausted, I sank onto the bench as the adrenaline drained from my system like a punctured canteen.

Until the memory of my visitor jolted me to my feet.

Flinging the door open, an elderly woman stood there, bathed in the Winnebago's interior light.

"Sorry about that, Rosie," I offered, my voice strained but softer now. "Why don't you come inside?" I extended a hand toward her, in hopes of atonement.

Her round face, etched with a roadmap of wrinkles, bore brown eyes that sparkled with kindness, framed by a crown of soft gray.

"Thank you, dear," Rosie replied with gratitude, as she accepted my help.

I blurted the million-dollar question, "So, how do you know my uncle?"

My guest settled into the seat Abs and I had once occupied on our last visit. "I live a few doors down. Al always lent a hand when I couldn't push the mower anymore. I returned the favor by making sure he ate properly. Kept an eye on each other, we did, like two peas in a pod. That's how close we were."

My eyes bulged out of the sockets so far, I could see the happenings behind my head. A rude reaction, but an entirely unconscious one.

Because, seriously? My crazy uncle had game enough to find a companion? Never in a million years did I think that was possible. His eccentricities were so off-the-wall, he scared people away, like he did with Abby. Rosie must be some kind of saint to handle him.

Wait, did she live here?

"Condolences," I managed, the words thick in my throat.

Rosie squeezed my hand gently, her return grip surprisingly firm. "He was undeniably original – rough around the edges, yes, but a kind soul."

"Did he ever tame his sweet tooth?" I asked.

Rosie's eyes widened. "Tame! You know how long I'd badgered him to take it easy on the sweets for his blood pressure?" She chuckled, a soft, melodic sound that filled the Winnebago. "Nothing could get that stubborn old coot to budge once he's set on something."

A wry smile tugged at my lips. Sounds about right.

"Ah, do you live here?" I raised a brow, 'cause invading her home was totally out of line.

Rosie grinned. "No. We needed our space. I live a few houses down, and would make the walk over, or Al would come to visit me. That arrangement suited the both of us. Besides, it's too cramped in here for two people."

My head spun. Were we talking about the same guy? Knowing how close they were, I wondered if she held it against me that I didn't invite her to his funeral. Shame burned at the back of my neck. Rosie deserved better. Her name needed to be added to the growing list of those I'd wronged.

Hunched in the booth, I reached for my wallet and fished out a pair of paint-peeled bobby pins tucked deep inside the leather pocket.

Rosie eyed me, her gaze carrying unasked questions.

Weirdly, my stomach did a flip-flop now that I had an audience to witness my lock-picking skills.

Shoving the hairpins into the lock like a seasoned pro, a flush crept up my neck. I stole a glance at my guest. She chewed her bottom lip, the bright coral lipstick staining her teeth, as she watched with a mix of curiosity and amusement.

"So," I began, "how long were you seeing Uncle Al?"

Rosie rested her arms on the tabletop, a finger unconsciously tracing circles on the worn Formica. "Oh, since I moved in next door. Feels like ages ago," she replied, a wistful sigh escaping her lips. "Though..."

Her sentence trailed off right before she broke out into laughter, sweet like wind chimes. "Well, I'll be darned! You really are good at that. Al had such a wicked sense of humor, I thought he was pulling my leg. Turns out, he was spot-on about you being a whiz at lock-picking."

I froze, not knowing how to respond to that.

Heat crept from behind my ears to my cheeks.

Awesome. Now she'll think I'm some kind of lock-picking Houdini with a secret talent for bypassing properties.

Well, she wasn't entirely off base with that one. Still, I wanted to bolt and hide in the backfields.

"So, Al spilled, huh?" I asked.

Joy radiated from Rosie, zero judgment, all amusement.

Yeah, I see why Al dug her. Can't blame the guy. She seems pretty cool, accepts you for who you are, no questions asked.

Rare these days. Luckily, lightning struck twice and I found it in Abs.

"We talked about everything under the sun," she replied. Reaching into her pocket with the exuberance of a magician pulling a rabbit from a hat, she produced a small silver key.

Laughter ripped from me, a bitter sound that brought tears stinging to my eyes. No joy, just one that paid homage to my colossal idiocy. All my screw-ups, from walking away from Abby, the best thing ever, to falling headfirst into self-sabotage, made me feel like a world-class imbecile.

Abby's hurt, confused face flashed in my mind.

The way I trampled over her churned my stomach with revulsion.

This needed to end. *Now.*

The world shrunk, making it hard to breathe, strangling my laughter into choked sobs. As I slumped forward, the cool Formica tabletop provided a brief respite for my flushed forehead. Everything at once. Grief. Regret. Shame. I couldn't breathe.

"Oh, darling," Rosie said, her voice laced with sympathy. "I'm so very sorry for your loss."

She had missed the mark on the reason behind my breakdown, but shame shut me up. No need to spell out what an ass I'd been to this good woman.

It took me a few minutes to smother my tears and pull myself together. After using the collar of my shirt to dab away the wetness, I accepted the key, unlocked the box, and lifted the lid. Folded papers lay inside. The rusted metal box rattled when I extracted them.

Headlights beamed through the window pane before I even decipher the first line.

CHAPTER THIRTY FIVE

LEVI

THE BERETTA'S rough grip scratched against my clammy palm as I leveled the barrel at my nameless adversary. With a quick swipe of my forearm, I brushed away the bead of water that threatened to roll down my brow.

Never sweated like this before. Even the adrenaline rush of cracking high-security buildings couldn't produce this much perspiration. Turns out, cat burglary was a cakewalk compared to playing hero.

Rosie's gaze darted to the gun, then back at me. "So much like Al," she muttered, with a disapproving shake of her head.

My jaw clenched. Rosie's keen take struck with full force. In this instance, I channeled Al, taking on his reliance on brute force. Not my style, but we needed protection from trespassers.

Al had the right idea all along.

Shoving that notion aside, I slid the window open a crack and yelled, "Ay! I've got a gun trained on you!"

"So do I, buddy!"

My heart lurched, and I squinted, trying to make out her distant shape. "Abby?"

"Don't shoot me!"

The gun, now an iron rod in my hand, branded me with

shame. Hearing her fear, fear that I caused, battered my chest like a physical blow. Eager to comfort her, I holstered the rod behind my back and said, "Sorry for scaring you, baby. Promise, I never meant to."

Exiting the booth, I reached for the switch, eager to snuff out the harsh light. The night returned, but this time, no clicking sound accompanied the panel's silence. The lights only turned on half the time? I hadn't noticed that when I first arrived, nor during the investigation, come to think of it. Did Stone break it while he was here?

No time for wall-switch contemplation. Abby's peace of mind came first. In a heartbeat, I flung the door open and extended a hand to her.

Abby's delicate fingers slipped into mine. I sent up a silent prayer of gratitude and hauled her into my arms, crushing her close.

"Baby," I said softly, "not that I'm not thankful it's you standing here, but why are you out here alone?"

Our tight embrace, muffled Abby's reply. "I'd love to tell you, but being blinded for life makes conversation a little tricky!"

Grinning at her sass, I buried my face in her fiery hair and breathed in its strawberry shampoo scent, letting it calm my frayed nerves. The fear I'd been living with since they loaded Al into the ambulance dissipated the moment she hugged me back.

The whole point of staying away from Abs was to shield her from the investigation's fallout. I had reason. Look at what they did to my uncle. But that genius plan backfired spectacularly. It only proved I'm a walking disaster without her. It scared the hell out of me when my bloodshot eyes and sunken cheeks stared back in the motel mirror. Not my finest moment.

After pulling back, her baffled, blue-gray gaze drifted across my face, trying to read me.

"How did you get here?" The question tumbled out accusatorially before I could sugarcoat it.

"I flew?" Abby's brows arched, and a hint of a smirk turned up one side of her full lips. Then, she playfully shoved my shoulder. "I drove. Same way I get most places. Besides, you were all 'gotta find Al's notebook,' so here I am."

Shutting my eyes, I massaged the dull ache at my temple where a headache brewed. "Things are still messy. This isn't the safest place for you to be right now. Maybe you should hightail it outta here before—"

"Before what, Levi? Where's the danger?" She demanded, speaking with her hands. "Please tell me, because you're the only one waving that gun around like a maniac!"

My shoulders deflated like a punctured tire. She nailed it. I'd been stewing in paranoia for days, and for what? Not a damn thing.

Abby's stormy expression suddenly cleared as she directed her killer smile at Rosie. "Hi, I'm Abby Martin, Levi's partner-in-crime... well, not exactly crime, but definitely chaos."

Her words were the silver light of hope that uncoiled the knot in my chest because it meant one thing: she still saw me as hers. Tears welled, hot and unexpected, distorting the world as she engaged with Rosie.

The older woman greeted Abs, "Hello, I'm Rosaline, but everyone calls me Rosie. I'm... I was Al's companion."

Abby crouched down to enfold her in an empathic hug. "Nice to meet you, Rosie. Sorry for your loss."

When they parted, Rosie's face lit up as she eyed Abby up and down. "Thank you, darling. Now, that dress you've got on – quite fetching. I appreciate a woman with an eye for fashion. Reminds me of my mother, may her soul rest in peace."

Abby's cheeks grew as rosy as her lipstick. She self-consciously brushed down the front of the dress, a shy smile peeking through. Then she slid into the seat across from Rosie, and I joined her.

"Oh, thanks," she said. "I borrowed my style from grandma's

photo albums, and Mom helped me colorize it – well, you know, metaphorically speaking."

Rosie's smile wavered at the edges, and sadness lurked behind her eyes. "Al made life more colorful. He always appreciated a good laugh, especially when I'd teased him about his terrible taste in decorating."

"You know," she said to me, "for all his suspicion with people, or maybe because of it, your uncle had a real soft spot for animals. Always snuck treats to the strays that wandered around here."

Uncle Al?

Seriously?

The man who spouted conspiracy theories, stockpiled Milk-Bones for strays? Huh. There was more to Al than being a grumpy old coot after all.

Leaning closer for more, I asked, "That right? Never knew that about him."

Rosie always seemed to have a smile on her face, which appeared to be her default expression. "He was terribly proud of you, Levi," she continued. "He saw the potential of you growing into a great man."

Even Stone basically said the same thing, except his spiel was geared towards cop training.

Guess I must've broadcasted my thoughts over Wi-Fi because Abby's hand circled my back to smooth things over.

Rosie's smile dimmed a notch. "Al wasn't a patient man, but he knew there was a time for action and a time for letting the dust settle."

She held my eyes. "You know, he used to check up on your house while you were gone and really admired how you looked after the place. Al believed you had a good head on your shoulders. Said you got your smarts from your ma, 'cause his side of the family never had much sense.

"Things might be a bit topsy-turvy, but remember what your

uncle always said: a little patience goes a long way. Just give it some time, and things will work themselves out. You'll see."

The weight of her words settled on me.

Patience.

That wasn't exactly my forte. Shoot. Let's call a spade a spade and admit it wasn't in the ballpark. But something about her quiet wisdom hit deep.

Since I was a kid, I charged in headfirst, fixing family situations by forcing a solution. Maybe it's time to take a seat. I don't know. Hell, maybe Al and Stone saw something I missed because my recklessness blinded me to it.

Suddenly, the door opened, hinges screeching like a dollar store recorder.

Casey Barnes, all lanky limbs, stepped inside and let the door slam shut behind him. Gone was his uniform. His civilian clothing of jeans and a black sweater seemed out of place. His bloodshot eyes pinned us immediately.

"Tampering with police property?"

CHAPTER THIRTY SIX

ABBY

LEVI LAUNCHED himself from the bench, transforming his body into a barricade between us, and Casey.

Exploiting the window of opportunity created by his body block, I dove into my bag and yanked my phone free.

My quivering thumbs typed out a frantic text: "Als, Winn, help."

With a silent Hail Mary, I tapped the send arrow, and prayed Uncle Wyatt would get my message.

Casey stepped fully inside. His towering height forced him to stoop, stealing our air and transforming this already cramped space into a claustrophobic cage. His honeyed words, "Easy there, Cross," held the audacity to paint Levi as the aggressor.

"Just need a word or two," he continued, "A friendly chat among ex-colleagues, you know, like the good old days."

Levi's backbone lengthened beneath his graying, black T-shirt, as though Casey's phony calm didn't fool him either.

I scoffed. A friendly chat? Yeah, right. Sell that to someone more gullible. Casey had only ever been somewhat pleasant on their obligatory "buddy nights." But, given that it originated from Uncle Wyatt's directives, did it really count? Not in my book. He never developed his decency muscle. Found that out during our junior high days, and he's done nothing to change my mind since.

Levi said, "Breaking news, Barns. This property belongs to me now. Get over it." A beat. "And cops, especially crooked ones, ain't exactly on my welcome list."

"You know the drill, Cross. Everything's fair game." Casey's voice dripped with a honeyed condescension that made me want to scrub my skin raw.

He continued, "Especially when it involves stolen property and a boatload of unanswered questions."

My brows knitted together at the word "stolen." Casey masterminded those break-ins. Was he trying to shift blame onto Levi, or was I way off track, and he was insinuating this RV was also hot?

Ugh! This man's convoluted logic was going to make my head explode.

"Let's just cooperate to get this over with," I said, and laid my palm on Levi's back, trying to calm him.

He flinched away.

I didn't hold it against him. This situation required his focus. With a sigh, I removed my hand as worry gnawed at my guts like a feral dog.

Poor Rosie, huddled in the corner of the booth. Her small frame shrank smaller with fear as she clutched her shawl tight, stretching the cream yarn to its breaking point.

My heart went out to her. I wanted to wrap my arms around her frail shoulders to offer some kind of reassurance against our obnoxious intruder. But something told me to sit still and don't move.

"Why are you here?" Levi snarled, ignoring my plea, essentially locking horns with Casey. "Stone himself showed you and your crew the door, didn't he? You ain't in any position to spout laws since you're off the force."

Casey's smile—if you want to call it that—revealed an

expanse of white teeth. His usual spark of assholery hardened into something cold and calculating. Real Casey on show.

Panic constricted my chest, speeding up my breathing. My fingers dug into the tabletop, bleaching my knuckles.

Rosie averted her gaze outside, disassociating from the situation, willing herself invisible.

Gone was the smug jerk I knew. In his place stood someone with a vibe that promised violence. It was as if someone had ripped the sheet off a friendly ghost to reveal the dead eyes and razor teeth of his true face. The sudden switch disoriented me. Like seriously, what the actual hell just happened?

"Badge or no badge," Casey drawled, "this little visit could open a whole new can of worms for you. We might just need to take a closer look at your dusty closet of skeletons. And who knows, maybe your buddy facing trial might be more cooperative if we give him a little nudge."

Levi let loose a dismissive scoff. Whether Casey's taunt struck a nerve, I couldn't tell. He remained unfazed. "Knock yourself out. Ain't got nothing to hide. What I did, I did to survive. No apologies for that. Besides," he kept on, lacing his tone with mockery, "you don't think Stone already ran a background check before he allowed me to work at the station?"

Whoa. Levi had some sort of Jedi power to see through Casey's BS and fling it right back. I would've been stuck explaining forever, falling for it all. But not Levi. He sliced through it like a champ.

The smirk on Casey's face flickered for a fleeting second before he regrouped with a sneer and changed tack. "You could have joined us, Cross. Instead, you went Boy Scout. Stone gave you a merit badge for that one? Maybe 'Basic Bravery'? Seems like you missed a few lessons in the concrete jungle about being prepared."

So, this so-called "friendly chat" was just some pitiful attempt to shame Levi for not joining their ring? Unbelievable.

Levi didn't so much as flinch. Kudos to him for keeping his

cool because I was about ready to give this fool a piece of my mind.

I scanned the distance of inky blackness outside for signs of flashing lights of law enforcement. Nothing. Not even distant sirens. Only crickets.

If backup arrived, would it ignite a standoff? Premonition clocked me in the gut. I'm going to die tonight. This snake will end me. End all of us.

A bead of sweat traced a cold path down my neck, soaking the dress strap. All I could do now was breathe until I couldn't anymore.

The razor's edge in Levi's delivery cut through my thoughts. "Better to be a wolf with bite than a jackal in borrowed fur. Ain't that right?"

I furrowed my brows, questioning the wisdom of his defiance. Did all that swagger amount to a plan, or did it come from the gun strapped to his back?

Casey's hand dove into the pocket of his baggy jeans.

Levi reached behind and yanked the gun from his waistband.

Casey aimed his gun straight at my forehead.

A choked sound, half gasp, half whimper, came from Rosie, but I couldn't take my eyes off the singular point. The barrel that will end my life.

My stomach dropped, and my body convulsed in full-on earthquake mode. Squeezing my eyes shut, I repeated, "please, please, please don't let it hurt."

Levi's gun, aimed directly at Casey, seemed to hold no sway over him. He stood rooted, crazy eyes fixed on me as his target.

His voice rasped, a cold edge slicing through his words. "Two options, lover boy. Easy or not. Your call."

Tears burned my nose and eyes, but didn't fall. Among the possibilities my librarian's life could've ended, I hadn't considered being shot by a cop as one of them.

"Fine," Levi spat. "Take the damn box and go!"

Levi's wrist reached behind him, palms up, a silent demand for the case.

I placed it into his sweaty grasp.

Levi then extended it to Casey.

"Open it," Casey ordered.

"No," Levi countered. "You want it, you do it."

Silence stretched on, punctuated only by frantic breathing from all sides. Casey finally snorted. He didn't argue back, but his gaze snapped onto mine and commanded, "Abby, open it."

Levi's hand brushed against mine as he passed me the case in what would likely be our last contact.

My fingers jittered as I flipped open the squeaky lid. Swallowing back the rancid taste of betrayal, I surrendered the documents and a worn leather notebook to Levi's awaiting palm.

Casey snatched the documents from Levi's hand with a predatory swiftness, a snarl twisting his lips. "Sneaky old bastard. Cracked my code."

My brows pulled together. Was that why he killed Al? He thought Al cracked the code?

Because he hadn't.

I did.

Well, not precisely. I'd nudged Levi and Uncle Wyatt down the right track by suggesting the Playfair cipher. That track led to Al's demise.

My heart ached for the poor guy. He was just trying to be a good uncle. But self-preservation sealed my yap, preventing me from clearing up Casey's misconception. Staying alive ranked considerably higher on my priority list right now.

Sorrow turned down the corners of my mouth, and my vision swam.

Casey anchored his stolen loot under his arm. Then, he reached into his pocket and pulled out a small metallic object. A sharp snap filled the air, followed by fire.

Levi shouted, "Son of a—"

Casey lit the corner of the document, orange flames

devouring it with terrifying speed. He dropped some onto the floor, creating a chasm between us, and lobbed the rest at our table before exiting the streamer.

Levi's gunfire shot through the frame, drowning out the screams tearing from me and Rosie.

My hands thrashed frantically, desperate to smother the flames, but it only fanned them. Al's hoarding provided the perfect accelerant, causing the fire to spread in mere seconds, with cracks and pops in its wake.

"Come on! Let's go!" Levi's voice barely rose over the inferno's roar. His hand clamped around our forearms.

Rosie and I shuffled out of our seats, propelled by his urgency. Smoke billowed around, thick and suffocating. The older woman erupted in a coughing fit, her frail body wracked with each spasm. My hand instinctively flew to my face in a desperate attempt to filter the acrid air.

Through the haze, Rosie pointed a shaky finger and rasped, "Extinguisher."

Levi spun away, scanning the vicinity of the stove. He lunged for the fire extinguisher and snatched it from the counter. Meanwhile, Rosie and I huddled toward the back of the vehicle because a firewall blocked our escape route.

Smoke stung my eyes, and I blinked furiously, trying to ease the burn.

"Get back!" Levi shouted, then aimed the nozzle and blasted the flames with foam, momentarily pushing them back. He shot another stream, maneuvering the hose around until he doused the fire completely, but the smoke still lingered, inducing another round of coughing spasms.

Levi darted past the extinguished flames toward the door. "Open up!" He barked, pushing and pulling the doorknob to no avail. The metal groaned in response but wouldn't budge.

"Damn it," he spat. "Door's stuck! The heat must've warped the frame."

Rosie clung to me, trembling like a frightened sparrow. Every hacking cough that tore from her tiny lungs sent a fresh jolt of terror through me. I patted a jerky rhythm on her back, offering the only comfort I could in this smoky sardine can.

Levi redoubled his efforts, using his body weight to pry open the way to freedom. "Damn thing's locked tighter than a bank vault!" His series of kicks echoed with a dull thud, each one a vent of frustration against the unyielding metal.

"Window," Rosie mumbled, her voice thick with phlegm from coughing.

I yelled louder, "Window!" My outburst caused another round of hacking, but I couldn't care less if it meant we were one step closer to escape. Every breath scorched my throat, while my slick fingers fumbled with the latch, finally managing to slide the rusted window open.

A gust of crisp night air swept across my sweat-soaked skin. My oxygen-starved lungs gulped in air, purifying themselves of the hellfire they had endured.

"Abby!" Levi shouted from behind.

I snapped my attention in his direction, tears running from my smoke-filled eyes.

Levi said, "Climb out first. I'll lift Rosie down. Catch her at the bottom, and I'll follow after."

With a grunt, I positioned a nearby drawer beneath the window, creating a makeshift stool. Hauling myself onto the rickety perch, I kicked off my heels and flung them outside. With my feet dangling out, I took a deep breath and released my grip on the ledge, dropping to the ground below with a jarring thump. Pain exploded up my ankles and calves. A quick wiggle confirmed no broken bones.

"Lift her out now!" I called out.

Rosie stuck her two feet out the window. I wrapped weakened arms around her waist. Every ounce of my being focused on controlling the descent of her hundred-some-odd pounds to the ground.

Fatigue took its toll. My arms just couldn't hold on anymore, and we both tumbled down together. The blow stole the breath from my lungs, and for a moment, Rosie's petite frame pinned me to the knoll.

"Abby!" Levi's voice, sharp with alarm, cut through the haze.

I rolled the older woman off with so much effort, my muscles wailed in pain. "She's down," I gasped, my voice ragged. "Your turn."

One moment bled into another, and he didn't respond.

I pounded on the aluminum frame. "Levi, come on! Your turn!"

Nothing.

My heart bottomed out. Everything inside me froze over.

Raising trembling arms, I banged on the metal sill. "Levi! Get your sexy keister out here now!"

Levi white-knuckled the frame as if it were his last lifeline.

Relief and terror hit at once, speeding up my pulse.

"That's it, handsome," I coaxed. "Swing your body out, and I'll catch you."

He positioned his body, reaching out to me. Fighting fatigue, I took hold of his arms and used my body weight to heave him out of the Winnebago. Momentum, being the cruel bastard it was, conspired against us, and this grown man collided headfirst on top of me. Stars exploded behind my closed lids, and the world went dark.

CHAPTER THIRTY SEVEN

ABBY

THE UNEVEN TERRAIN hammered at my bare feet with every step away from the Winnebago, jarring my already throbbing ankles. Levi and I muscled Rosie across the lot, running on the fumes we had left. I seriously wanted to upheave.

The wail of emerging sirens intensified my headache, making me squint. They ripped through the darkness, just like the night we'd lost Al. This whole situation felt surreal, like a record stuck on repeat. Fortunately, the stars swung in our favor, and we dodged his fate.

Memories of our first visit resurfaced. All those fears and doubts—were they premonitions?

"We're gonna be okay, Abs," Levi grunted, his voice strained by our shared burden.

I pressed onward, unable to reply. The luxury of illness wasn't an option. Every aching muscle protested, punishing me for the night's hardship. But I kept moving in the too-large lot, fueled by the need to gain distance from this hellhole.

Via a megaphone, Uncle Wyatt's voice echoed, "Keep marching. You're alright."

Alright? We were a wreck. Rosie was a dead weight in my arms, her small breaths hitching against the harsh rasp of her cough. This situation was miles from okay! And why weren't they coming to assist? With every step across the seemingly endless field, my legs felt like they were slogging through mud.

The universe finally cut us a break. Like they read my agitated thoughts, the first responders surged up to us and clamped oxygen masks on our faces. Pristine air, cleaner than anything I'd ever breathed, filtered into my lungs, easing the heat in my throat like a magical antidote.

In an efficient, rehearsed ballet, they lifted Rosie onto a gurney and wheeled her away into the belly of an awaiting ambulance. Her owlish, blinking eyes, still filled with fear, will be forever burned in my memory.

Uncle Wyatt approached, his worn face etched with concern. "You two holding up alright?"

My sandpaper-throat rendered my voice useless, so I mustered a shaky nod.

He continued. "Barns is in custody. Attempted murder tacked on to the laundry list of charges against him. We got all of 'em involved, so you don't have to lose sleep that they're roaming the streets."

Levi ripped off his mask from his face. "'Bout damn time. Took you long enough!"

A frigid realization seeped through my veins faster than I could fully grasp its meaning. "Wait a minute," I said, studying the man sitting next to me. The plastic mask muffled my words, but not the accusation burning in my eyes. "You knew about Casey all this time? All this time, and you let him nearly kill us?!"

"About the roundup? Yeah. Stone tipped me off right before we found out about Al. About what happened here tonight? No, Abs. If I knew Barns had that in him, I would've shot him on sight. Even with everything that went down between us, no matter what, your safety is the only thing that matters to me."

I blinked as his words hung in the air, searing away my lingering doubts. Levi's love for me meant he'd never jeopardize me for a case. This was the man I loved, not some cold-hearted monster.

Yet, my suspicion wouldn't let up. As crummy as it sounded, I wouldn't put it past Uncle Wyatt to use us as bait for Casey. Such was his commitment to duty.

"Did you know?" I prompted, my voice barely a rasp, each word a struggle against the mask. "About Barns and the fire, I mean?"

"No, Mops," Uncle Wyatt furrowed his wiry brows. "I never suspected Casey was capable of this. My gut feeling is he snapped when he caught wind of the internal investigation. When Levi found the painting, he figured we were setting him up."

Levi squeezed my uncle's shoulder. "That's rough. But this whole thing with Barns, that was a setup, right?"

Uncle Wyatt's weathered face looked rundown, and beyond that, hurt. He stared at the ground, his shoulders slumped. After a moment, he spoke. "Never saw it coming. After all these years, side by side... I thought I knew Casey Barns better than anyone."

Suddenly, I understood what he might be feeling. Betrayal. Disillusionment. All of it. Decades spent adhering to a strict moral code, only to be crushed by one of his own.

An ache settled in my chest, piled on top of the guilt I was already feeling for my previous blow-up at his house.

The blessed mask dropped like a kettlebell in my hand as I tossed it aside. With renewed energy, I launched myself from the ambulance towards my uncle. Snaking my arms around his waist, I held him as tears ran down my cheeks. Fear transformed me into a destructive force, doubting those closest to me, turning me into a one-woman wrecking crew.

"I'm sorry, Uncle Wyatt. Nobody knew Casey had that in him. Don't blame yourself," I said past the taste of ashes in my mouth. "And for what it's worth, I take back every single vile thing I said to you and Aunt Peg. I owe you two a truckload of apologies and I'll do everything in my power to make it up to you both if it kills me."

Uncle Wyatt enfolded me in his embrace and rested his cheek atop my head. "It's alright, Mops. You were hurting," he rumbled. "This badge comes with the heavy price. It's gotta mean something. That's what keeps us on the straight and narrow, even when it cuts deep. Barns and the rest didn't understand that, and they strayed off course."

Grief pressed down like a tangible thing. I wished I had the right words to say to comfort my uncle, but my brain wasn't exactly firing on all cylinders to craft heartfelt pronouncements. Where words failed, my hug didn't. So I did just that...for a long while.

Levi's voice sounded from behind. "Rosie, how are you doing?"

Rosie rasped, "Oh, I'll be fine. It'll take more than a fire to keep this old gal down."

Straightening, I felt a mix of shock and relief. Then, I swung around to verify it was really her, and I hadn't gone all loopy from smoke inhalation.

Her startled eyes were replaced by her former spirit, or what I knew of it from the glimpse I'd seen.

"Al," she held her throat, "told me to hide the notebook at my place. The real one. The decoy got torched. Al didn't believe in taking chances."

The notebook again. What did this thing contain, the location for the Holy Grail? I couldn't help but ask, "What's so special about this notebook?"

"His medical concoctions," Rosie explained, "He wanted to pass them down, I suppose."

Levi raised a skeptical brow, and his voice held an irritated edge. "Seriously? We damn near died over drugstore alternatives? If that's all it was, why did he carry on with the secrecy and paranoia? Seems like a hell of an overreaction."

Rosie's jaw became a hard line, and she looked ready to spit fire. "That book meant the world to Al. He poured every ounce of his knowledge into those pages, Levi. That man dedicated his life to healing people, in his own way. Deserves some respect, don't you think?"

The harsh lines in Levi's stance melted like hot butter, his irritation giving way to remorse. "Absolutely. I apologize. And for everything you've been through tonight."

Uncle Wyatt's chest rumbled. "See what I mean, son? Work, of any kind, has gotta mean something. It'll steer you right. You'll make a damn fine Sheriff some day."

Levi bridged the gap between us and cocooned me in his arms. He leaned down, his face hovering close enough to make my heartbeat quicken.

A sigh blew from my lips, bringing with it the tension I'd been holding. I sank into him and let go of the need to be strong. The case, the fire, the fear—all of it faded into the background.

Levi's hand drifted to the back of my head, holding me in place. "It's some ways down the road, but if I take on the sheriff's badge," he murmured, his breath on my lips, "will you stand by my side? 'Cause then this job will mean everything."

This man, who drove me up a wall one minute and made me swoon the next, how could I not? I was born to stand by his side. Maybe it's crazy, but deep in my soul, I knew he'd protect me with his last breath.

My answer came without hesitation. "Forever," I choked out, "Always where you're involved."

Levi's lips crushed mine, and the world faded away.

EPILOGUE

ABBY

CARRYING a tray of ice-cold sweet tea and a Disney Princess tumbler, I stepped out onto the front patio. The summer heat blasted me in the face, already baking my skin. How they could stand it, I didn't know. Give me air conditioning any day.

"Thirst quenchers served! Come and get it!"

Levi, waist-deep in our rosebushes, rescuing a rogue pink ball that had become entangled, lifted his head. The relieved smile accentuated his sharp jawline and the crinkles by his warm brown eyes. After all these years of being married, it never grew old, no matter how many times I entered the room. He made me feel like it was the first time.

He hustled to relieve me of my hostess burden, depositing the tray onto a small table beside our weather-beaten picnic bench.

Our five-year-old, Rosaline, wearing a sunflower-printed dress with her blonde hair intricately woven in a French braid, ditched her ball and streaked toward us. This two-legged tornado we called "Roadrunner" because she bypassed walking and went straight to speed demon. So, we installed a white picket fence as a protective measure to safeguard her when she played outside.

Levi extended a bright blue cup splashed with Elsa's face. He held it just slightly above her head and dipped his cheek toward her, inviting a kiss.

Rose gave him a quick kiss, then eagerly took the cup. "Thanks, Daddy," she chirped, taking a tentative sip before dashing off again to her forgotten ball.

"Thanks, Foxy," Levi said, still calling me that after all these years. He relaxed on the bench on a rare day off, since he'd made the force as a deputy.

I eased myself down beside him, the aged wood creaking. Hubby's arm moved along the well-worn path, settling comfortably around my shoulder. We fell silent, mesmerized by our daughter's determined dribbling of her pink ball.

My vintage get-up was officially on maternity leave. It turns out that polka dots and a bun in the oven mixed like oil and a clown costume. Neither did stilettos, which were a definite no-go when sporting a baby bump. Learned that the hard way the first time around, while pregnant with RoRo, when I crammed my swollen feet into size sevens. Seventh circle of hell.

But hey, at least my victory rolls were still on point! Gotta maintain some semblance of style.

Levi sipped from his glass while eyeing our little peanut. He then placed his drink down with a soft clink, the condensation leaving a ring on the weathered table. His hand, cool from the drink, found its way to my belly, resting gently just below my stretched T-shirt.

Sadness flickered across his face, pulling down the corners of his lips into a frown. "Days like today," he murmured, "reminds me of the time you offered me a chance at the sheriff's station. Crazy how I turned you down."

"Dodged a bullet there, buddy. Can you picture yourself imprisoned in a cubicle, drowning in spreadsheets?"

Over the years, Levi's face would cloud whenever the door slamming debacle came up. The memory became a self-inflicted torment that twisted him into a knot.

In an attempt to lessen his regret, I lighten the mood with some friendly joshing.

The end result was all that mattered. For us to come to this point, everything needed to play out exactly as it did. And I wouldn't trade this for anything in the world. Swear it, I'd run through a hundred burning Winnebagos.

Levi feigned horror, his brown eyes widening comically. "Don't even joke," he shuddered. I grinned. "You saved me from that soul-crushing fate for something a million times better."

Warmth circulated, making its way up to my cheeks in a flush. I cozied up to my husband, leaning my head on his shoulder, and letting out a dreamy sigh. "Likewise," I murmured, the words barely audible, but carrying the weight of everything they meant. "More than you know."

Levi brushed a kiss to my temple, the gesture intimate and filled with profound love. My gaze drifted back to Rose, bouncing the ball with surprising accuracy for a little one. Future hoops champion, perhaps?

The End

RECKLESS DISCOVERY SNEAK PEAK!

CHAPTER 3: ASHLEY

LET me tell you something about Millbrook. Even in this paved parking lot, floating dandelion seeds—or whatever you called those clouds of fluff—were giving my sinuses the evil eye. One good whiff was all they needed to set off my hay fever, the last thing you needed when meeting your new employees. Urban life didn't offer much nature. Pigeons with lousy aim? Yeah, a dime a dozen. So, blame my upbringing for my lack of country preparedness. A drugstore trip was in the near future to stock up on sniffle stash.

With my head held high and stilettos clicking to 'Single Ladies,' I strutted my stuff across the parking lot towards the mechanic shop. Nerves? Heck yeah! But "fake it till you make it" was my anthem.

Still trying to process this joint as mine. Never owned a gold-fish, animal, nor cracker. Now, I own a business and a house. Life, huh?

The faded red paint on the beat-up sign announcing "Thompson's Garage - Est. 1973," sent my blood pumping. Like that giddy rush you get when you spot your name on TV. Or at least, I do.

Slamming the brakes, I whipped out my phone and snapped

a pic to commemorate. A couple of taps later, and off it went to Ma. Knowing her, she'll flash it amongst her regulars at the beauty shop.

The reflection in the glass showed my blonde waves, usually neat, now looked like a squirrel's time-share. What's with the out-of-control humidity this year? Using my fingers as a comb, I tamed the frizz, then hiked up the sleeves of my hot pink jacket, ready for showtime.

Okay, Ash, you got this.

After a few more breaths to psych myself up, I pulled on the cool metal handle and opened the shop door. The bell barely made a peep. How they even heard it over the radio blasting Hip-Hop in the back is beyond me.

The shop carried no signs advertising their services. Just a simple, no-frills sign that read, "McGregor's Custom Cabinetry" in faded black paint, followed by digits to call.

Alright, am I missing something here? Did I punch in the wrong address on the GPS? Anchoring my knock-off Ray-Bans to the top of my head, I squinted at the distant street sign outside. Fat chance of reading it from way over here.

Unzipping my bag, I shuffled through the junk—crumpled lottery tickets, a dead MetroCard, a prehistoric Dunkin's tissue, and my wallet—until Lyle's tri-folded will surfaced at the bottom.

"Need a hand, dollface?"

This cat, who slicked down his black hair with industrial-strength goop, fixed me with a judgy look. Hot pink shorts and a matching blazer probably didn't come around too often, I take it.

Whatevs. Can't get too worked up about it now.

Was he flexing his biceps under those blue overalls, or was I tripping?

"Hold up, you guys do custom cabinetry? The sign outside advertises this place as a garage."

The mechanic blinked, then a slow smirk spread across his face, as if he'd just remembered his sales spiel. "Sure is, sweetheart. We do both. We're a jack-of-all-trades kind of shop here. Boss does the finest woodwork in Millbrook."

Huh?

Maybe they weren't strictly a mechanic shop. Back where I'm from, shops advertise other businesses. We often carried flyers on the table for the bakery next door, and they returned the favor. "Scratch my back, and I'll scratch yours" type of deal.

Dialin' back my attitude a notch, I asked, "Custom cabinets and car repair? What's this, Bizarro World?"

"Yeah, we wear a lot of hats. But hey, you gotta diversify your hustle to keep the lights on, right?" the man said.

I planted an arm on the counter and flicked my fresh pink acrylics while taking in the surroundings. Nodding, I said, "So, youse are the Renaissance men of Millbrook, I take it?"

Suddenly, a booming voice interrupted my train of thought, snapping my eyes wide. "Tone! You put in that order for the carburetor bolt yet?!"

Tone? As in Tony?

The writing ran squiggly on his dark blue overalls. It could've said "Tony." All those years hunched over, painting designs on nails, didn't do my sight any favors. A trip to the eye doctor moved up the ranks of the to-do list.

Tony/Tone winced, and then hollered over his shoulder. "Not yet, boss! Talking to this lady, trying to figure out what she needs."

This dude, the size of a refrigerator, showed up from the back. His shoulders nearly took up the whole doorway. Jaw so chiseled, he could bust walnuts with them. Black hair, long enough to tie in the back. But most of all, those eyes. Arresting sea glass blue.

Forget big, forget scary – this guy? Illegally good-looking. I mean, how is that even fair? He can't be walking around looking like an Adonis, giving people palpitations. And by people, I meant me, because I forgot how to breathe.

The boss's scowl morphed into an eyebrow raise as he gave me the once-over.

Great. Just freakin' fantastic. Goosebumps broke out all over my skin. And thanks to my pink shorts, he probably noticed.

Shorts are a tomboy's answer to the mini-skirt. Perfect for July's inferno, except now when it exposed my secrets.

Mr. Big Stuff dabbed his hands on a grease rag and stuck it in his back pocket. "Morning, ma'am. Car troubles?"

Smokes! Even his voice was Nutella-smooth. This guy's CGI, right? If he walked into Ma's shop, my cousin Bianca would be all over him.

That random thought punched me in the gut, and I wasn't having it.

"Ma'am?" the guy prompted, snapping me out of my daydream about the weave-pulling throwdown with my cousin.

Shaking loose the cobwebs, I answered, "It could use a tune-up after that drive from the city."

The guy eyed my car through the window. "Sure," he said. "I'll take a look at it for you."

This shop hasn't seen a mop or Brillo pad since the disco era. And those colored chairs! No way was I parking my behind on those petri dishes. But it was the bare, grime-caked walls that struck me as sus. Not a single sign displayed their rates or even a measly "no smoking" warning. Seriously, how did Lyle keep the doors open? Back home, there's a huge poster hanging in the salon that shows our pricing and services.

Sweeping at the bare expanse, I suggested, "You should really look into displaying your packages to give people an idea of what they're getting into."

Good-looking and Tony exchanged locker-room looks, doubled over, shoulders shaking like I was killing it during my stand-up act. Clearing his tears, Good-looking said, "Lady, whatever you had in mind, this ain't that kind of shop."

Man, I burned hotter than a fresh slice out of Ma's oven. Anyone got a teleportation device? Asking for a friend.

"Damn. Sorry! I—ah—didn't mean it that way!" My voice went all squeaky from mortification.

Good-looking's lips twitched like he enjoyed himself, and his strong chin raised in a dare. "Really? How did you mean it?"

Seriously, this guy had no clue how hard I worked to suppress my goofy grin. My cheeks were cramping, like I partook in some kind of cheek muscle boot camp. It took straight-up Herculean effort not to show I was feeling any type of way.

"I, uh…" I stammered, working my scrambled eggs of a brain to dredge up long-buried legalese.

Fanning out my nails, I gestured around and said, "Hold on a sec… I got questions 'cause this joint is shadier than the back alley behind a social club."

Good-looking's full lips quirked up in a half-smile that set my heart racing a mile a minute. He crossed his arms and said, "Alright, detective. Hit me. Though, for the record, I'd say it's shadier than discounted parts off a truck. Back alley might be pushing it."

Every hair on my arms stood straight up, and my inner daredevil was dying to jump the counter dividing us to get all up in his face—in a good way.

I cleared my throat and cold-shouldered the butterflies. Trying to keep my cool, I said, "Well, that 'custom cabinetry' sign is kind of… unexpected."

His lips went pastrami-thin, and one heavy brow arched. Tilting his head a smidge, he challenged, "Unexpected how?"

"Oy vey!" I rolled my eyes. Wasn't it obvious? "It's just, you know, not exactly your typical mechanic shop offering."

My brain went on strike, leaving me to rely on two-dollar words for million-dollar questions. I needed to pull my act together because I'd suddenly forgotten how to talk.

"Well, let's just put it this way," he drawled deep and smooth, "this ain't your typical body shop. We tinker outside the box. So, what exactly sparked your curiosity, Miss…?" He left the question hanging and leaned forward, all ears.

"Thompson," I filled in. "Ashley Thompson."

Good-looking's openness and faint smile fizzled like a dying light show, and his face became hard lines, his cold blues hurling accusations that hurt my feelings even though he didn't voice them.

"Ashley Thompson," he repeated, all slow. "You finally decided to show up, huh? So, Ashley, what's got you second-guessing our setup here?"

Self-doubt and guilt steamrolled me, and shame prevented eye contact. The bubblegum pink shorts and blazer combo paired with a black crop top seemed like a cute idea this morning. Now, they made me feel like some kind of bimbo. Normally, I couldn't care less what people thought about my clothes. But when those people are my employees and I sported Barbie's Malibu outfit, it hits different.

"Look," I leveled with him. "I just found out that Lyle died and raced over the second Ma convinced Bianca to cover for me at the salon."

The guy's heavy brows pulled together, and you could practically smell his judginess. "In all that time Lyle was laid up, you never thought to contact him? To check up and see if he needed a hand?"

His roast hit like a backhand, and I sized him up, ready to remove my hoops. Any attraction I felt caught the express out of the station.

This bozo didn't know what he was talking about. Ma ran away from Lyle due to his alcoholism. Nona, may she rest in peace, was as devout as they come. Divorce was a cardinal sin in her book. So when Ma showed up on her doorstep with baby me in tow, begging for a place to stay, Nona slammed the door in her face. We ended up in a homeless shelter. First memories? A lumpy cot reeking of bleach.

All 'cause of that loser.

So yeah, my attitude returned tenfold, and I shot him a glare that could turn Hell into an icebox.

My clenched fist rocketed to my hip, manicure digging into my palm, but I couldn't give a damn. "Excuse me?!" I said, dipping my chin. "Who the hell are you to get up on your high horse about my relationship with my alcoholic, deadbeat old man?!"

"Blake McGregor. The manager here and your father's right-hand man," he added, his voice dripping with respect. "Lyle was solid. Decent. Always willing to lend a hand, especially to my dad."

I rolled my eyes. His bigness didn't scare me. City life toughened me up to not care.

"Right," I shot back, the bitterness drifted up my throat like smoke. "Newsflash, pal. That kindness? Never saw it. Never even laid eyes on my old man. Couldn't pick him out of a lineup."

Inheriting all his junk felt like a cruel joke. This stranger acknowledged me after he died. He couldn't reach out to me while I was growing up and needed my father.

Apologies for ranting. That inheritance rehashed the garbage I kept buried. Hand to God, I don't walk around with a chip on my shoulder about that bum. As much as it affected my life, legions of people were in the same boat. So why dwell?

This Blake guy couldn't peel his eyes off me. Maybe he was trying to find a resemblance, who knows? No one on Ma's side rocked blue eyes or naturally blonde hair, so—

Finally, he spoke, in a rumble that goosed along my arms. "In that case, why don't you come back to the office and see what's going on?"

The office? What's up with the office?

Game face on, I tailed Blake deeper into the place, the place smelled like a combo of deep-fried engine and that cherry-almond air freshener they use in repair shops.

My stilettos clacked uncertain rhythms on the grease-stained concrete floor as I crossed the garage towards the office.

Tony/Tone and some other dude in the back glanced up from their cars, eyeballing me as I passed by. Although tempted to smile, I didn't, because figuring out this office mystery took priority.

Blake flung the door wide open, then glanced back, his smirk rubbing me the wrong way. My nerves were already on edge, and his high-and-mighty attitude didn't make it any better.

Inside? A straight-up war zone. Mountains of unopened envelopes avalanched off the desk. Damn. Even a seasoned sherpa couldn't navigate this mess.

My jaw hit the floor, and a primal "Oh, hell no! I'm going back home," nearly slipped out.

"Surprised, Princess?" Blake's deep voice rumbled from behind, jolting me out of my skin.

I whipped around and came face-to-chest with him. If he wanted, he could touch the top of the doorframe, no problem. His sea glass blue eyes roved over me, taking inventory of my faulty wiring and stealing my breath.

My fingers were dying to trace the tempting curve of his lips and jaw, just to prove he was no *fugazi*, but common sense prevented me from acting on it. Who needed a harassment suit?

I wet my dry throat and scooted back, desperate for some breathing room.

"Been waiting a long time for you to show and clean up Lyle's mess," Blake rumbled. "The lawyer never mentioned the paperwork Lyle left behind, did he?" A hint of amusement – or maybe a wiseass grin? – played at the corner of his pink lips.

Right, I gotta chill. These feelings were one-sided, and it wasn't cool to lay that on him. So, I squared my shoulders and set him straight. "Look, pal, if you think I'm some kind of Cinderella, you got it twisted. I ain't afraid of getting grease under my nails to handle business."

Just then, a lady's voice called out from behind him. "Blake?"

Blake's smirk disappeared as he turned to deal with her.

Tall and skinny, a twenty-something-year-old with cascading brown ombre hair stood there, narrowed eyes bouncing from Blake to me, about ready to cuss us out.

I knew that look. Seen it a million times on girls in my hood, right before they commenced hair-pulling. Never been on the receiving end 'cause I've been rocking the single-for-life status forever.

"Now I see why you're suddenly 'too busy' to go on vacation!" she mocked. "Who's this? And what's she doing in *my* garage?!"

Ready for the next book?
Two lives, one huge secret,
and a love that might not survive the truth.

Go here to see entire series catalog

ABOUT THE AUTHOR

Willa Brooks grew up in Queens, New York sneaking her mom's historical romance novels. She also watched a ton of soap operas and fell in love with crazy storylines.

She studied creative writing in college. After taking a long hiatus from writing to raise her son with her graphic artist husband, she decided to go the indie publishing route.

She loves anything retro, and watches a ton of sitcoms from the '70s and '80s.

For more books and updates:
http://www.willabrooks.com